The Cat Tender

Other novels by Martin Drapkin:

Now and at the Hour

Ten Nobodies (and their somebodies)

Poor Tom

The Cat Tender

Martin Drapkin

Three Towers Press
Milwaukee, Wisconsin

Published by
Three Towers Press
An imprint of HenschelHAUS Publishing, Inc.
Milwaukee, Wisconsin
www.henschelHAUSbooks.com

ISBN: 978159598-963-5
E-ISBN: 978159598-964-2
LCCN: 2023939172

For Jennifer

I've Got My Love to Keep Me Warm

I'VE BEEN dreading this day. Mindy asked me this morning to be her maid of honor in August. I was pretty sure she was going to, but now it's official. Damn! I wish I could have said no. I wish I could have told her I'm not interested. "Listen," I wish I could have said, "you're my sister and I suppose I love you and I'll come to your wedding. I'll be glad to come to your silly wedding—glad enough, anyway. But please don't ask me to do this. *Please!* Just let me come and sit anonymously in those wooden pews at St. Bernard with everyone else and watch you and Richard do your thing, and then let me go to the reception and eat the chicken and mashed potatoes or whatever, and a few buttered rolls and some wedding cake, and have a few drinks. Many drinks."

As to my drinking, I wonder sometimes if Lucy disapproves. Almost every time I raise my glass of chardonnay to my lips, she raises her brown head from her usual place on the closed lid of the toilet seat and looks at me with those glassy green eyes. She stares but is otherwise perfectly still, except for mild tail twitching. If she's judgmental about my drinking, it's the only such issue in our relationship—at least that I know about. She stares, too, when I shave my legs in the tub, but I doubt she disapproves of that. Nor does she seem too bothered when I sometimes light up a joint.

No. Our nightly bathtime routine, like now, is the best time of our day and my cat and I are happy to be together again, alone together again, just we two. It's my time to be with my green-eyed girl and think about things—what's behind me, what's ahead. It's my time to relax. *Our* time to relax together, my baby and me.

Each evening, I set up a thick, folded turquoise bath towel for Lucy on the toilet seat lid and she jumps right up and settles in, usually kneading the soft fabric with her forepaws. I shed my robe and put on a CD and ease my bulk into the steamy water in my oversized claw-foot bathtub. Lucy and I mostly like to listen to Ol' Blue Eyes, and occasionally Dean Martin or Sammy Davis, Jr. Lucy's favorite Sinatra song is "Strangers in the Night," with that "dooby, dooby, doo" at the end, but I think she likes Sammy's

"Candy Man" best of all. I believe she finds it uplifting, those comforting lyrics about making everything satisfying and delicious and separating all the sorrow and collecting all the cream.

Maybe Lucy's jealous about all the time I spend with other cats, though. Maybe she's judgmental about that. Perhaps she wonders where I am when I'm not home with her. But I won't hide anything from Lucy. I've always been honest and upfront with her about my dealings with other felines. I think she can take it. If she's upset, she hasn't let on. I try to get her to understand that it's my job—that I'm seeing other cats to make us a living, not because I prefer them to her. I hope she understands.

I don't tell her about every cat that I tend. She just gets selected highlights. Today I took care of Jake at the Morrisons' house, and he and I had an okay time hanging out and watching TV. "So, Lucy," I say, "you remember I've told you about Jake, right? A silver-colored domestic shorthair? Ten years old? Very nice guy. You'd like him."

As I do with all my cats, I started by telling Jake my plan for our time together. "Okay, Jake. Aunt Maggie's here. So here's our plan. I'll feed you and scoop out your litter box and give you fresh water and then water the plants upstairs and downstairs, and bring in the mail and the newspaper and sort the mail by size, and then we'll chill and watch a little TV. What do you think?" He stared at me but didn't seem to object, so I took his silence as consent.

After my chores, I sat on the sofa in the living room and Jake and I watched an episode of *A Baby Story*. "Oh look, Jake," I said, "the baby's coming out. Have you ever seen anything like that?" There came the head, with dark hair, emerging from between those widespread white thighs, viewed, of course, from behind the mother's head. That red, scrunched-up little face. Then came the shoulders. "One more push, now," the mustachioed doctor said. "Just one more good one. *C'mon!*" Then—*whoosh!*—the kid was out and one of the nurses squealed, "Well, how about a *daughter*?" The husband, eyes big and lower lip trembling, leaned down to kiss his exhausted little wifey.

I don't remember the names of the happy parents—let's say *Lisa* and *Randy*. The nurse plopped the baby on Lisa's chest and she held her squalling infant, still covered in blood and amniotic fluid and that cheesy white stuff, and stared at the kid adoringly, eyes wet. "Oh, I love her so much already," she murmured. "I just *love* her." A lot of them on that show say that. Then, in a little while, Randy bounded out to the waiting room and, beaming, announced to the crowd of about a dozen people that it was a girl, seven pounds and three ounces, healthy, all fingers and toes present. Of course there were smiles and cheers and tears all around, and applause and hands clapped to mouths and high-fives, and eyes rolled heavenward.

Then, after a commercial for Pampers, a little sign on the screen announced "Six Weeks Later," and after a brief exterior shot of the couple's nice red-brick suburban house, with well-trimmed shrubbery out front, we were in their living room. The proud parents were sitting in the middle of a long beige sectional sofa and the camera zoomed to a close-up of Lisa holding the sleeping baby—Rebecca Ann, I believe—dressed in a cute pink sleeper with a white bunny on the chest. Their dog, a beady-eyed brown terrier with a dark-green collar, sat calmly next to Randy. The mutt stared, stupidly, directly into the camera. "I didn't think I could ever love anyone so much," Lisa practically whispered, her dark eyes all soft and liquidy, staring at her unconscious progeny. "Life feels perfect. I couldn't ask for more." Smiling Randy nodded in agreement. "Our hopes for Rebecca Ann?" he said. "We hope that she'll be happy and pursue all of her dreams in life." All this while nice soothing guitar and piano music played in the background. Oh, it was all so warm and family-cozy.

I wonder what I'd say if I ever squeezed out a kid and was on a show like that and someone off-camera asked me what they'd asked Lisa and Randy. "What are your hopes and dreams for little Corinna, Maggie?" None of the parents ever says, "Well, golly, we sure hope our precious Noah doesn't grow up to be a mass murderer or a serial rapist." Or, "Gracious, we certainly hope that little Madison doesn't get run over by a bus or blown away by a hurricane or that a loose brick doesn't fall on her sweet little head." Those are the kinds of things I think I might say if that question ever comes up for me. I doubt it will.

The Morrisons' TV is on one of those wooden swivel stands that lets you watch from different angles. They have a nice house, with three bedrooms upstairs and a big living room downstairs that has a dark-brown sofa and a brown leather recliner angled at one end of the sofa, and a low wooden coffee table with three *TIME* magazines and a copy of *The Atlantic* and a paperback novel, *The Human Stain*, on it. I wonder if either of the Morrisons has actually read the book or if it's just for show, with that intriguing title.

They have a huge kitchen with a breakfast nook and a granite-covered island and a stainless steel Viking stove with six sealed burners and a huge convection oven. Their refrigerator door's covered with a weekly schedule of activities for everyone, including various sports schedules; four-by-six color photos, with white borders, of the kids; and six refrigerator magnets, three of them featuring their children's smiling little faces.

While checking out all of their kitchen cabinets the first day I was there to take care of Jake, I noticed that there were seven boxes of Girl Scout cookies on the upper shelf in the far-right cabinet. There were three boxes of Thin Mints, two Shortbreads, a Lemonade, and a Caramel deLites. Thin Mints are my absolute favorite, though I also like Lemonades. A shortbread cookie with lemon icing is quite a lovely thing. I remember that I thought of eating one or two of their cookies, but worried that I wouldn't be able to stop at just that. I don't have that kind of self-control. I could maybe stop at eight cookies, but that's probably it. So I wouldn't want the Morrisons to come home and check their cookie supply and get all weirded out. "What the *hell!*" Mr. M. might say. "Did that fat cat tender wipe out our supply of Thin Mints?"

Mindy was a Girl Scout for a while. I think she was the top cookie-seller in her troop one year. I remember her blathering proudly to Dad about all the wonderful benefits that she and the other little twits would get out of selling cookies—money management, setting goals, people skills, business ethics, and whatever. I was never a Girl Scout. I'm not a joiner of anything. But I remember thinking that if I *were* a Girl Scout, the best thing about selling cookies would be to make enough money to have a big pizza party for the troop. The hell with the goal-setting and business ethics; let's call Papa John's and order a few giganto pies. I even thought that it might be good, when the pizzas arrived, to crumble up some Caramel deLites over each one to get a bit of that toasted coconut to mix with the cheese and tomato sauce. *Yum!*

So I admire these people, Mr. and Mrs. M., for their taste in treats. I myself have eleven boxes of Girl Scouts cookies here in my apartment, mostly Thin Mints. I bought them from a cutie named Sydney who, along with a couple of other girls, set up a little stand outside of Metcalfe's Sentry in Hilldale Mall. Sydney's mother was usually there with her, sitting on a card chair and looking on proudly as her capable daughter counted out change and used her people skills.

Aside from the kitchen, the Morrisons' house is filled with *stuff*: expensive-looking, well-upholstered furniture everywhere; oak bookcases with hard-covered books—Patricia Cornwell, Mary Higgins Clark, John

Grisham, and the like—with the dust jackets on and the books flush to the edge of each shelf; big plastic baskets with red handles filled with toys for the kids; and computers and other gadgets. They have a basement rec room with an obscenely huge entertainment center and a big semi-circular black leather couch that looks like it can accommodate a dozen people—or fewer, if they're my size.

When I go there to take care of Jake when the Morrisons are on vacation, I usually sit on the right side of the living room sofa while I watch TV and try to get Jake to play a little bit. He's reluctant and standoffish at first, but sometimes consents to a little toy time. Mostly, his habit is to sit on his haunches on the floor and stare silently at me with big eyes as I sit cross-legged on the sofa. *What's this guy thinking?* I often wonder. *What's going on in that little feline brain?* Maybe he's wondering who the hell I am, coming into his house when his people are gone. Perhaps he's hoping that I'll change the channel to *Animal Planet* so he can watch *Cats 101* instead of all this baby nonsense. Maybe he's trying to tell me that he'd adore something very special to eat—tuna, maybe, or salmon. Maybe he's hoping that I'll get the catnip out of the far-left kitchen cabinet and rub it between my fingers for a few seconds and put it on a little plate for him so he can get high. Maybe he's thinking that this chick could stand to lose a few pounds, that she's going to put a dent in his owners' nice couch. Maybe he just wants me to open the front door so he can check out the big world out there, maybe catch a little birdie or a field mouse.

"Forget about outside, Jake," would be my advice, if he sought my opinion. "This house is enough. The world outside isn't all it's cracked up to be, Jake, believe me. Just stay inside. It's warm there and safe. You have food, water, two nice scratching posts, a clean litter box, and various soft places to sleep. Out there are dangers: cars, buses, hawks and owls, mean dogs, and nasty people who'd as soon kick you as not."

The Morrisons have a wall of family pictures in their downstairs den. I like to look at them when I'm there, after watching *A Baby Story* or sometimes after *I Didn't Know I Was Pregnant* or my other shows when they're on, and after I've fed Jake and played with him for a while, when he's in the mood, with the multi-colored yarn toy with a plastic handle or my mouse-on-a-wire toy or the long brown shoelace that I bring to every house. I believe he prefers the shoelace. Maybe sometime I'll see if he likes to chase my red laser pointer beam.

At the far left of their family picture wall are three photos from their wedding day: a younger Mrs. Morrison in her full-length lacy white gown, facing sideways and holding her bouquet against her tummy, head turned to the right and looking directly into the camera, smiling sweetly and showing nice white teeth; the two of them standing by the altar, angled in toward each other, his hands cupped over hers, the groom taller by a head, both smiling nicely; and a group family portrait with maybe twenty well-dressed people standing straight and looking into the camera and the newly married couple in the front middle, looking happy and proud—the center of attention for that day, surrounded by their extended family, their new lives together ahead. Then, left to right, are maybe two-dozen black-framed family photos that show the expansion of their little family group over the years. There they are in the back yard with their first kid, a little boy in short pants, the three of them sitting on the wooden edge of a sandbox and looking directly into the camera. There they are a few years later, the boy maybe four or five now, and Mrs. M. preggo, belly huge, sitting on the brown sofa. The boy's leaning his head on her round tummy. And on and on, with several photos of the two kids, the second one a girl, playing in the sandbox or on swings, and others of the kids with both sets of grandparents at some family event.

At the far right is a formal posed family portrait, in muted colors, under studio lighting, of the four of them dressed nicely in various pastel shades with Mr. and Mrs. M. kneeling and the two brats standing between them, contented little smiles all around. I guess I shouldn't say *brats*. Maybe that's what they are, but I don't know them so I shouldn't be harsh. Some kids you see, that's just what they are—go into a Walmart on a Saturday afternoon—but probably not these.

I always have mixed feelings when I see all the happy little family photos in these houses. On the one hand, I'm glad for them. It's nice, I guess. On the other hand, I'm maybe a little jealous. I only have one family picture on the wall in my little apartment, and looking at it doesn't quite bring happy tears to my eyes.

Then again, how do I know if these people, or others at the houses I go to, *are* really happy? They may *appear* to be but, really, all I see is the surface. I only met the Morrisons once, when they hired me and gave me a key. The pictures on the wall may be nice, and Mr. and Mrs. M. seemed perfectly fine in my limited contact with them, but who knows? Maybe they're actually deliriously happy and just can't wait to see each other at the end of their workdays and their little hearts still throb at the sight of the other, and both of them hug and kiss their kids numerous times a day and say, "Oh, I just love you!" and do what they can to foster self-esteem in their precious little offspring. Maybe their sex life is still amazing and they do it three or four times a week, with great enthusiasm, and now and again even have simultaneous orgasms. Or they take turns. Perhaps they still call each other by terms of endearment—honey, baby, snookums, darling.

More likely, after years together, they're utterly bored with each other. Maybe he cringes at the sight of her and finds the sound of her voice grating. He likely didn't feel that way for their first years, but does now. Maybe he talks to her rudely and disrespectfully, like my father, barely hiding his contempt. Perhaps she rakes him over the coals for not making enough money and calls him a lazy asshole and rags him about stuff he said he'd do but then forgot to do. "I told you to pick up water softener pellets," she might say shrilly. "I can't believe you forgot *again*!"

Maybe at night, before sleep, she fantasizes about being with a man who'd look at her with affection and passion, the way Mr. M. used to when they started out, and make her feel desired. Late at night, perhaps, he sits in the dark in the living room and drinks scotch and whispers to the cat. "I've had it with that woman, Jake. And these damned kids are driving me crazy, too—need this, need that. They keep growing out of their shoes, for Chrissake. What the *hell* did I get myself into? For two cents I'd pack a bag and get in the car and drive and drive. You could come with me. Maybe we could sail to the Galapagos, Jake, and study those huge turtles or something."

It's strange, what I do. I go into people's houses when they're not there and spend time alone in their homes, taking care of their cats and doing assorted other chores, and I can look around and see what they have in their houses and look at their pictures on the walls, but I usually know almost nothing about them. It's always interesting to see what clients' houses are like. I wish I *could* learn about these people—their inner lives, their thoughts, their fantasies, their disappointments. Not everyone, but most. Sometimes I wish I could interview them, as part of our business arrangement. At our initial meeting, right after we got done with the small talk and any questions to me about my background and experiences taking care of cats and my ideas about cat tending, and after they'd shown me where the food and litter boxes are, and the fuse box or circuit breakers, and told me about the habits and needs and eccentricities of their cats, and after I gave them my "Vet Agreement" form for them to fill out, I'd say, "And now I'd like to ask you a few things, just so we can get to know each other better. How did you meet? How did you get together? Let's start with that."

They'd tell me their lame story, which I don't imagine I'd find all that fascinating, but it would be an icebreaker. Maybe she'd tell me they met on a blind date set up by her cousin, and she had low expectations but found him to be funny and even initially charming. "Okay," I'd say. "That's a lovely story. Oh my God, so romantic! But tell me, what did you see in each other after a while, after the bloom wore off? What was the attraction? And how did you decide to get hitched?" She'd perhaps tell me about how handsome he was and what fun they had, and maybe even what a good lover he was, and about his romantic proposal—maybe how, on her birthday or Valentine's Day, he took her out for a very special seafood dinner downtown at The Blue Marlin and he hid a beautiful diamond engagement ring in the raspberry crème brûlée dessert, and she acted all surprised and teary when she saw it, even though she was pretty much expecting him to propose.

Then we'd get to their tedious wedding story. *Yawn.*

Then, if I can get them to keep talking, maybe they'd tell me how things are now. "I see," I'd say. "Well, tell me, what about these days? How about the sex? Do you still have the hots for each other at all, or is it now just dull, tedious routine—maybe once a week on Saturday night after the kids are asleep? Are you totally *bored* with each other yet? Don't you ever fantasize about something different, something better? Do you wish maybe you could be with someone else, even if just for a while? Do you wish you didn't have to work so hard to pay for this oversized house and all the crap you have? Don't you sometimes regret having these obnoxious kids?"

Maybe we could all have a few drinks or smoke some weed, or both, to loosen their tongues.

Or maybe I could go through their drawers or closets to see if I could find their journals. Or go through their computer files. I don't imagine that'd be okay, but it's what I'd *like* to do. I probably won't, but there's a part of me that wants to.

"What do you think, Jake?" I'll maybe ask him when I go there tomorrow. "Do you like living here with these folks? Do they treat you okay? Do you wish there were other animals—another cat or two, a dog perhaps, maybe even a bird or a gerbil? Is it lonely? Are you okay with these two kids being around or would you just as soon they'd disappear? Do you get enough attention what with these noisy, needy little ragamuffins running around? Do they maybe torture you by pulling your tail or ears? Or would you prefer being with someone like me—living quietly in a small one-bedroom apartment, just the two of us and Lucy, and no nasty kids throwing toys at you or dripping grape jelly on your precious fur and soaking up all the attention from the adults?" He wouldn't have this big house to run around in or all the company, but maybe there'd be other benefits to compensate.

But Jake probably won't reveal his thoughts. He'll sit on his haunches and stare and occasionally scratch the side of his head with his left rear paw. He's not one to emote.

Well, I don't know if Lucy would be okay with another cat. "*Would* you, Lucy-Goosey?" She just looks at me with one eye closed.

Maybe I shouldn't be cynical. The Morrisons seem nice enough and they're probably perfectly happy together and thrilled to be parents, good with being a nice little nuclear family like so many of them—most of them—on *A Baby Story*. I liked Mrs. M. when I met her during our initial meeting. She has pretty blue eyes and one of those puckish little smiles, like Renée Zellweger's, and she's a low talker. I had to lean in a bit to hear her when she told me about Jake's habits. It was cute that she kept rubbing a strand of her hair with her right hand as we talked.

And they probably like each other just fine, or at least have learned to tolerate each other, and like their house and all their junk and are happy as clams with their jobs and their oh-so-busy lives. They're likely okay with the frantic daily business of being a family. Probably they have nice extended families, too, with lots of relatives—parents, brothers and sisters, grandparents, uncles and aunts, cousins—and they all like to get together and have jolly family times. They likely have big get-togethers on Thanksgiving and Christmas and Easter and Labor Day and Super Bowl Sunday, and fill their bellies, first with nice snacks—Lay's Cheddar and Sour Cream Potato Chips, salami and cheese, Hostess Twinkies, deviled eggs, Oreos, and those amazing salted-in-the-shell Australian peanuts—and later a magnificent roast beef dinner with lovely brown gravy and little boiled potatoes and green beans with almond slivers mixed in. The kids would eat at card tables. Maybe they'd have healthy adult discussions about issues and events—why the Republicans are so nasty to Obama, whether Bush should have invaded Iraq, whether climate change is real or a hoax, why the divorce rate in America is so high, whether Pete Rose should be in the Hall of Fame, their thoughts on Kim Kardashian's butt, why Donald Trump's hair is so weird. Maybe they'd actually listen to each other respectfully. Who knows? And most likely they can't wait to see each other again when the next holiday or big event rolls around.

When the Morrison brats were born, probably the waiting room at the hospital was lousy with relatives both times—probably some of those people in that wedding group picture—and Mr. M. gleefully announced each new addition to them, like Randy did on the show this morning.

And if someone in the family gets sick or dies, they're there for each other. All those people. I imagine that would be comforting.

"What do you think's ahead for Lisa and Randy from the *Baby Story* episode, Lucy? Any thoughts on that?"

They just had their first kid and all is good. They're so thrilled, and, of course, have high hopes for their child. But I wish the TV people would check back in with them at five-or-ten-year intervals so we could see what's happened. Hopefully, good things. Maybe little Rebecca Ann will have become a piano prodigy with a promising Carnegie Hall future ahead. Maybe they'll have had two more kids, and they'll all be on swimming and soccer teams and have decent manners and respect their elders and be active in the church religious education program.

Or maybe sweet Rebecca Ann, in time, will have turned into a sad and hopeless heroin addict, renting out her precious little body to get money for her next fix. Maybe Lisa will have decided she prefers women and will have taken up with a short-haired bull dyke who's good at carpentry. "Hey, Lisa," her new partner would yell from her perch on the ladder leaning against the west side of the house. "Bring me that damned hammer. No, not the ball peen, for Chrissake, the *claw* hammer." Maybe Randy will have tired of Lisa and started going out with some cute little thing with a pageboy haircut and a tight butt and a tattoo of some inscrutable Chinese symbol or character on her lower back. She'd likely be willing to do things in bed that Lisa never would.

Maybe Lisa will sit in her living room at night with the lights out and a drink in her hand, like my mother, ruminating.

I had to use the bathroom before I left. The Morrisons' downstairs bathroom has obnoxious wallpaper, with a paisley pattern of abstract curved shapes, mostly swirls, against a lavender background. I had the thought that if I were drunk and sitting on their toilet for any length of time and had to stare at that wallpaper, it wouldn't be good. I'd maybe start hallucinating.

But at least they have good toilet paper. I always like going potty in houses that have toilet paper that's higher-quality than what I buy. Well, that's most houses, since I tend to buy the cheapest, ugliest, one-ply paper I can get. It's usually fairly coarse—just a step above newsprint-grade. But the Morrisons have quilted, scented, probably four-plied toilet paper, very plush, with delicate flower patterns. It's lavender, to match the background of the wallpaper. They probably special-order it from Italy. It's a luxury for me to be able to use such hoity-toity toilet paper—*bathroom tissue*—during my cat-tending rounds.

At least they hang their toilet paper with the over-the-roll orientation. That's clearly best. I don't understand why anyone would use the under-the-roll method. Aunt Grace, Dad's haughty sister, does, but I don't know why.

Jake likes jokes. Many of my cats do. I think they do. They don't guffaw or even titter, but at least they pay attention and seem okay with it. "Hey, Jake," I asked him as I was getting ready to leave. "Why did they have to stop the leper poker game?" He looked at me, waiting. "Everybody threw in their hands. Get it?"

It was sad to leave Jake this morning. It always saddens me to leave my only-child cats because they're going to be alone until I come back the next day, or, in some cases, later that same day. It's not as hard when there're two or more cats, because then they have each other. Jake knows when it's time for me to leave. He either has a clock inside his head that tells him that my forty-five minutes or so have passed or he has some kind of extra-sensory perception. Even before I start gathering my things to get ready to go, Jake knows. First, he looks sad, sitting perfectly still on his haunches and staring into the distance, and then he looks up at me for a moment, almost accusingly, and then slinks away, tail down. "Sorry, Jake," I said softly. "See you soon, kid."

The last thing I did was to turn on the downstairs radio for him, to the FM classical music channel. I do that with all my cats if I can. The nice music calms them, I think, and makes them feel less lonely. I hope so, anyway. If I could, I'd put on harp music for them. I read that that's the most calming. Whenever I'm gone from my apartment, I put on harp CDs for my Lucy. Her favorite is a two-CD set, *The Most Relaxing Harp Album in the World—Ever!*, with various artists. You have to admire an album that has a good word to say for itself. "You like that one, don't you, Goose?"

It's a cold early-January night here in Madison. It's snowing out—big, fat flakes. Tomorrow, I'll have to shovel out my car before I go on my cat-tending run. I'll worry about that then. Tonight, I'm here in my steamy bathroom, warm and comfy in my big tub, with my little furry companion nearby, listening to Frank, and the world is good. I need to rub some lotion on my boobs, though, when I get out of the tub and dry off. They've been itching lately.

After my bath, I'll get in my red flannel nightgown and snuggle under my comforter and Lucy will curl up beside me and we'll watch TV for a while, and maybe I'll read a chapter or two of *Pride and Prejudice*. Maybe I'll read a passage to Lucy. She and I love Jane Austen—all that obsession with engagements and marriage and finding someone with a fat wallet. All those walk-and-talks through the green English countryside, the women's long dresses swishing in the grass.

Lucy likes it when I sing to her, along with Sinatra. We like the song that's playing now:

The snow is snowing and the wind is blowing,
But I will weather the storm!
What do I care how much it may storm?
I've got my love to keep me warm.

I can't remember a worse December
Just watch those icicles form.
What do I care if icicles form?
I've got my love to keep me warm.

Well, as warm and comfy as I am now, I'm thinking that this whole maid of honor thing is going to be majorly aggravating. The thought of it makes me want to double my bathtime chardonnay intake. Maybe Mindy and Richard will change their minds and decide to just get married over their lunch hours by some sallow-faced municipal judge who charges twenty-five dollars a pop and who'll manage a well-practiced little smile after they've signed the marriage certificate. "Good luck, you two," he'll mumble, trying to stifle his boredom. "You're all nice and official now in the eyes of the great state of Wisconsin. Isn't that just peachy? Wisconsin certainly wishes you nothing but the *best*. Have a nice life."

Well, one can only hope.

My Funny Valentine

THIS MORNING I watched *I Didn't Know I Was Pregnant* at the Barretts' house with Maria sitting beside me on the sofa, purring, while I stroked the silky top of her head and then her neck and back. I like seeing Maria. I like hearing her purr. "Happy Valentine's Day, kid," I told her when I arrived.

When I'm done with my chores and Maria and I are chilling, she now and again closes her eyes and catnaps. Then she'll wake up and look up at me for just a moment, and will usually yawn, and then close her eyes again. Maybe I bore her. I wouldn't be surprised; I'm not exactly Miss Excitement.

It was good to relax with Maria, since I felt like crap. I have my usual PMS, and feel irritable and tense. Stroking a cat is the best thing I know for that. I even gave Maria a little back-and-tummy massage, which she loves. At least I remembered to bring two bags of Brach's Circus Peanuts. It's weird, but those sugar-loaded peanut-shaped marshmallow candies are always what I crave before I have my period. It's been that way since middle school. I like to lick each orangish piece lengthwise along the rippled top side before eating it—usually in one bite. Yum! And then when I get my period, I usually want Froot Loops and mint-chocolate-chip ice cream with either chocolate or butterscotch sauce, or sometimes both. I'm sure it would be healthier if I craved celery sticks.

The episode Maria and I watched was about yet another young woman who didn't know she was pregso and, in a televised re-enactment, she started feeling horrible in her tummy and thought she was constipated and sat on the toilet and strained and grunted and bent forward, elbows on her knees and holding her face in her hands, panties bunched around her ankles, sweating, not getting relief...until with a mighty push and a groan she finally felt better and sighed and peeped into the toilet to check out her results and, OMIGOD!, what did she see in the bowl, in the water, but a baby instead of a bowel movement.

Naturally, she was startled and freaked out and screamed for her boyfriend who, wide-eyed and bewildered, called 911—"I think my girlfriend just had a baby…Yeah, it's in the toilet…Yes, the *toilet*!"—and the operator told the idiot to take the baby out and dry it off and keep it warm, and pretty quickly the paramedics were there and hauled the woman and her kid to the hospital. The new mommy was, understandably, all worried and upset—being born into a dirty toilet can't be good—but everything turned out okay. The baby girl was just fine, and her watery beginning didn't seem to have harmed her.

Then they showed the woman's face in close-up—the real mother, not the re-enactor—and she said the same thing that a lot of them on this show say: "If I'd'a known I was pregnant I woulda ate better and not drank so much and, ya know, took vitamins and stuff." Once in a while, I half-expect one of them to say she probably shouldn't have smoked weed. But they don't. Maybe the producers edit that out. Usually, the mothers' regrets are limited to eating junk food, drinking alcohol, smoking cigarettes, and no prenatal doctor's visits.

The episode ended, as it seems they all do, with the big question: *How could a woman not know she was pregnant?* This particular chick said that she had no morning sickness, didn't show, didn't have unusual food cravings, and still had her periods. Big mystery! Yeah, she gained some weight but she thought it was because, she said, she stopped going to the gym much when she sprained her ankle. As to the periods, the usual explanation, delivered by a talking-head doctor or nurse, is that a pregnant woman has normal spotting or light bleeding and mistakes that for her period. As for not showing, the reason was that she probably carried the kid "high," so that there wasn't the usual big belly.

And, finally, the episode ended with an epilogue, the way most of them do. No, she hadn't known she was preggers, and no, she hadn't been ready for a baby, but now it's some months later, and, lo and behold, she just *loves* her surprise baby and is oh-so-happy to have the kid, who is a miracle and the *light* of her life, and she and her boyfriend are thrilled, and have even had discussions about getting married down the road, and the three of them will certainly be the loveliest little forever family imaginable. They'll live happily ever after, we hope, yet another perfect little nuclear family, and will probably have more kids. The next time, she'll hopefully know she's preggo, so she can take vitamins and stuff.

In some shows the women who don't know they're pregnant find out that they're mommies when, while sitting on the toilet or a bathtub or somewhere else, they reach down and feel a head coming out of them. Or, they discover a strange thing protruding from down there. *What the hell is this? they wonder. Are my insides coming out? Wait, it's...an umbilical cord!* Then they look down and see a wondrous sight—a baby, a tiny human being, attached to the other end of the cord. Surprise, surprise!

Well, hell, I've been constipated as much as the next girl. So now do I have to worry about having a kid instead of just pooping if I'm backed up? Guys don't have that worry. If they're backed up, the options are limited—either they get relief or they don't. They never have to worry about producing a new human being instead of just dropping a loaf. I guess I don't have to worry about getting pregnant now, though, because I'm not doing anything these days that can swell my belly. My vagina is currently unemployed.

"Well, Lucy," I say, "you don't have to worry about that either. You've been fixed, so you'll never have to worry about going into your litter box and, to your great surprise, squeezing out a batch of kittens. Then, when I come to scoop out your box, you'd look up with your eyes wide open as if to say, 'Well, my goodness, Mommy, I didn't even *know* I was pregnant.'" She just glances at me from her position on the toilet seat lid and then closes her eyes again. The subject doesn't interest her.

Maria used to have a friend, Carlos. He was an orange tabby who got an aggressive cancer and went fairly quickly. The Barretts had him cremated and his ashes reside in a little square flower-patterned tin can in their bedroom, resting for eternity on a wooden ledge just above their king-sized bed. I knew Carlos just a little, having taken care of him once, over a three-day weekend, before he got sick and tipped over. Nice guy. Very mellow. He liked to jump on the dining room table and eat flowers that were in a vase. He and Maria mostly went their separate ways, but every now and again they'd chase each other around the house, and Mrs. B. once told me that the two of them sometimes slept curled up together at the foot of the king-sized bed on particularly cold nights.

"Maria," I asked once, "do you miss Carlos?" I'm sure she must have for a while, but most likely cats live in the present and don't have much time or energy for sentimentality. Others come and go, and we have to get up the next day and keep on going until it's our own turn to expire. When Aunt Helen tipped over last year, I remember that I felt sad for a day or so, but I don't recall that I ever cried. My ridiculous sister, on the other hand, didn't stop bawling for two days. She does this ugly thing where her lower lip starts quivering and then her eyes get all red and misty and turn a lighter shade of blue-gray than usual, and her face gets kind of pink and splotchy, and then the stupid waterworks commence, and the sniffling and gulping, and then, between sobs, she starts blubbering about how much she *loved* dear Aunt Helen and how much she's going to miss her and, oh, she just can't believe she'll never see her again. And on and on.

I know what's coming when I see the first signs, the moistening eyes and the chin trembling, and want to say, "Oh, for God's sake, Mindy. *Cool* it! Yeah, it's too bad she's dead, but enough already. Life goes on."

We didn't even know Helen all that well. She lived in California and we only saw her every few years, for holidays and the like. She used to call us on our birthdays when we were little, but that stopped a long time ago. I'm sorry she's gone, but, really, it doesn't change my life much. That said, I won't miss her telling me that I "have such a pretty face for a big girl." Hah! I don't have a pretty face, for a big girl or any size girl. It's *okay*, at best.

Then again, maybe Mindy's right. Maybe her way's best—to get all hyper-emotional about other people and blubber like a fool when some obscure relative tips over. Maybe that's the more human way to be. I don't know. I did cry a little when Grandma Violet died four years ago. Even though I didn't know her that well—she lived in Ohio and had been disabled for a long time—I felt bad for my mom for losing her own mother. So there's that. Mom was an only child, so I'm sure she was close to her mother.

Well, how would I feel if Mindy died suddenly—car accident, heart attack, brain hemorrhage, bridge collapse while driving, catastrophic mudslide, terrorist bombing? Whatever. I'm sure I'd feel terrible. She's the only sister I have. My only sibling. I'd probably get all misty for a while, but eventually I'd get over it. She's a major pain in the ass, but I suppose I'd miss her. I don't think I'm that cold.

But if Mindy's destined to kick the bucket—as sad as I suppose that would be—I'd be okay if she did it before her damned wedding. I'm just dreading everything about it—all the duties of being maid of honor: the planning, the bridesmaids' dresses, the wedding shower, the bachelorette party, the rehearsal, and then all the nonsense about the wedding day itself. I get nauseous thinking about walking down the aisle holding my stupid bouquet—everyone eyeballing me and taking pictures with their phones or cameras—and then standing up there for a time with the other bridesmaids during the ceremony and knowing that people are staring at us. Then there's having to walk up the aisle arm-in-arm with the best man; standing in the receiving line and having to smile and shake hands with people and listen to who they are, as though I care, and make small talk; and, of course, the damned photos. And then the reception, where I'll have to give a toast and say good things about Mindy and how close we were growing up and how having a sister is so special, and how I just love her new husband, and what a wonderful couple she and Richard are, and how happy I just know they'll be, and how glad I am that he's part of our family. Hah! And then the dancing, hoping that my boobs don't fall out of the ridiculous strapless gown that Mindy wants her attendants to wear. I'll have to tape the damned things in, I'm sure.

The only thing I'm looking forward to is the open bar at the reception. And, certainly, the next day, Sunday, after the gift-opening, when, thank God, it will all *finally* be over with.

One good thing, wedding-wise, is that Mindy agreed with my idea to go to Gigi's Cupcakes in Hilldale Mall to see about her wedding cake. My friend Sheila worked there for a while, so I knew about it. Sheila used to give me free samples when I'd stop in. *Yum!*

Well, okay. Yes, I would miss my sister if she tipped over. "There, Goose, I admit it. Okay? I admit it. So I'm not a horrible person, right?"

And I know I'll miss my Lucy when she goes. She's young, so hopefully she'll be around for a long time yet. But anything can happen—like poor Carlos, here one day and gone the next. There'd be a big hole in my heart if Lucy died. My little apartment would be lonely. My bed would be very empty. I'd look over at the space on the comforter next to me or at the foot of the bed, and I'd horribly miss seeing her there. I'd miss that whiskered little face, those green eyes, her little blurps and chirps and other sweet sounds, her soft snoring. I can't imagine waking up each morning and Lucy not being there on our bed, ready for her breakfast and then another day stretching lazily ahead of her. I can't imagine coming home and unlocking the door, knowing how excited she is to hear that sound, and seeing her curled up on my dingy sofa, on the white afghan that I put down for her. She always looks up at me, glad I'm home.

I can't think of taking my bath in the evening, like now, and Lucy not sitting quietly on her folded towel on the toilet seat lid. This is our special time together. And I can't imagine reading in bed for a while before sleep, after my bath, usually with the TV on, maybe watching one of our DVDs, and Lucy not being on my lap or curled up beside my left hip, her head on her paws and eyes closed, until eventually I get tired and put my book on the nightstand. Just before turning off the light, I tell her, "Goodnight, Lucy -Goosey. Sleep tight. Don't let the bedbugs bite. If they do, hit 'em with a shoe until they're black and blue." Sometimes if I have to get up in the night to pee, my moving disturbs her and she protests with a little "*grick*."

The Barretts don't have kids. They've been married for two years. I don't know if they want to "start a family," as they say. Maybe they don't want children. Maybe they're fine with just each other for all the years they'll hopefully have together. Maybe they have common interests that are enough for them—growing a vegetable garden, saltwater tropical fish, French cooking, medieval art, collecting rare coins, national politics, kinky sex, or even being in that weird religious sect where people fart around with poisonous snakes and trust that the snakes won't bite them because the sect members have faith. Maybe with their shared interests, the Barretts don't feel the need to reproduce.

Hopefully, neither of them will get bitten by one of the snakes. "Damn," Mr. B. might say to his wife. "I thought this would work out, but I guess I was wrong. See you in heaven, honey."

Maybe they have lots of nieces and nephews they're close to. Mrs. B. —Maureen—never talked to me about any of that, and I've never met her husband. I suppose I could ask her directly. "Tell me, Maureen, do you and Ralph intend to have some brats?" I suspect that wouldn't be polite, though. Grandmothers and aunts and close friends and maybe therapists can ask that question, but probably not the chubby chick you've hired to come into your house to take care of your cat when you're gone.

I don't want kids either. At least I don't think I do. Maybe I'll change my mind later, when I'm older, but now, at twenty-seven, I don't see myself as a mommy. When Mindy sees any baby she gets all gushy and misty-eyed and trembly-chinned and goes "*Aw-w-w!*" and you can tell she just can't wait until she can squeeze out a few of those little things of her very own. Not me. Babies don't do it for me. Sure, they're little and cute and soft and helpless and needy and their heads smell good, and they have all this potential, and they're not nasty or obnoxious yet, and you can cuddle them and dress them however you want. And, if you're a mommy, your baby is your Real Woman merit badge. But I just think, *Okay, fine. Nice-looking kid. Cute. Yeah, yeah, okay. What should I have for dinner?*

Sometimes I wonder what it is about children that I don't get that most people with uteruses seem to.

It's hard to believe that 9/11 was a decade ago. This September will be the ten-year anniversary. How can you bring children into a world where horrors like *that* happen? Besides terrorists, lots of bad things can happen—train derailments, airplane crashes, school shootings, avalanches, tsunamis. I remember that on the night of 9/11 we were watching TV in the living room after dinner. Mindy was watching people tumbling from buildings and doing her blubbery-faced crying as she clapped her hands to her mouth. "Oh my God! Oh my God! Oh my *God!*" she whimpered over and over again. At one point, Mom shook her own head in disbelief and said, "Oh, Warren, how can people do things like that to other people?" Dad glared at her scornfully from his seat in his brown La-Z Boy. "Come on, Lillian," he practically hissed. "Don't be naïve. Grow up, for Christ's sake."

What a jerk, my father.

An interesting thing happened earlier today. This morning when I stopped at the PDQ in Middleton to buy a chocolate cream-filled pastry and a Diet Pepsi, I saw a short, thin, older woman with dyed-red hair filling her car with gas. She wore a red-and-yellow polka-dot dress under her parka and a neon-green headscarf. A sign on her car said "KAT GRAMMY," along with her phone number. I wondered what that's about, what she does. Maybe I should have asked her.

"Happy Valentine's Day, Lucy-Goosey," I tell her as I'm drying off. "You're my funny Valentine, my sweet comic Valentine, today and tomorrow and forever. You make me smile with my heart. And I hope I'm yours. Am I?" She looks up at me with those green eyes opened wide as though to say, "Yes, Mommy, you're my special Valentine too, and I love you very much. Any chance for some catnip to celebrate the occasion?" We can do that. I'll get her some high-quality catnip—KONG Premium, I think we have—and pour myself another nice stiff Valentine's Day vodka and tonic. Then we'll head into bed to read *Pride and Prejudice* for a little bit and watch a DVD before sleep—maybe one of our revenge movies.

I love my cat, but I wish I had someone besides just her to spend this day with, this night with—to be with on Valentine's Day. I don't know who that would be. If nothing else, I'd be okay if Alex stopped by for a Valentine quickie—as long as he brought some decent chocolates, including a few with almonds or walnuts inside, and left no later than tomorrow morning.

A lovely fantasy, of course, would be good old Frank sitting on the bed beside me, his delicious blue eyes looking directly into mine, holding one of my hands in both of his, singing softly to me:

Is your figure less than Greek?
Is your mouth a little weak?
When you open it to speak,
Are you smart?

But don't change one hair for me.
Not if you care for me.
Stay, little Valentine, stay.
Each day is Valentine's Day.

He'd be wearing one of his expensive suits with a red tie for the occasion, and maybe a fedora with a colorful hatband. His warm eyes would sparkle. After he'd finished the song, he'd reach over and touch my cheek gently with the pads of his fingers, then brush an unruly strand of hair from my forehead. "Has this been a good Valentine's Day, my sweet Miss Maggie?" he'd murmur. "Oh, *yes*, Frank," I'd answer, smiling coyly. "Now that you're here, it's the best." He'd look deeply into my eyes and nod and smile subtly and then lean over to kiss me gently—very gently. "I feel the same," he'd whisper. "I really do."

Am I smart when I open my weak mouth? Probably not. Is my figure less than Greek? Oh, *much* less, Frankie. Do I wish it were more Greek? I don't know. I guess so.

I hope to hell I don't have my yucky period when the damned wedding rolls around. PMS is bad enough, but if that's all I have on Mindy's blessed day I can at least bring my Brach's Circus Peanuts and munch a few during any down times. And, of course, my butterscotch hard candies. I'll have to remember to put a few pads and tampons in a tiny purse, in case my crimson wave—or, as Sheila calls it, "code red"—starts unexpectedly. Feminine hygiene supplies and marshmallow and butterscotch candies should get me through the day—at least until the damned bar opens at the damned reception.

Strangers in the Night

SOMETIMES I wonder if I'll end up as one of those cat ladies, an old woman who lives alone in a house or apartment with just her cat or cats and doesn't talk to many people but probably talks to herself, and certainly talks to her cats. Then one day she tips over, alone, and someone has to deal with her dead body and all her stuff and hopefully find new homes for the cats. You just hope she hasn't been dead too long before they find her—before she's started to ripen and her cats have eaten off half her face. If she has no children or other relatives, the cops or a landlord or one of her few friends will have to take the cats to the shelter, and hopefully it's not one of those shelters where they execute the cats if someone doesn't claim or adopt them within a few days. And if there're no kids or other relatives, the old lady will likely be forgotten in a short while. She'll have lived her pathetic, lonely life with her cats—eating her meals alone, watching television alone—and then that life will be over, probably suddenly, and the world will go on as before. It will be as though she'd never existed.

Maybe someone will kindly write a little obituary for the newspaper:

> She loved her cats and always fed them special treats. She enjoyed watching *A Baby Story*, *I Didn't Know I Was Pregnant*, *16 & Pregnant*, *Teen Mom*, and her other shows. Like also-dead Elvis, she liked peanut-butter-and-banana sandwiches. She imagined dire outcomes. She liked revenge movies. Maybe she never made much of a splash in the world, but at least she wasn't a mean and spiteful bitch, like some.

A childless old lady with just her cat. Yes, that could be me down the road. That's what I'm thinking while soaking in my tub with my Lucy-Goosey blessedly snoring away softly beside me. But so what? What should I do instead? Marry someone who'll bore me to death after a while and have snot-nosed kids with him just so I'll have kin to take care of me when I'm old, and I won't have to die alone with my cat staring at my corpse, ready to chew on my face? No, thanks.

I guess I'm rehearsing for that role now, living alone with Lucy and liking it just fine, thank you. We enjoy each other's company and get along splendidly and never argue and I'm never ever bored with her, like I became with Alex. "Right, Goose?"

The evenings and nights are our best times. After we happily retire to bed I can reach down and stroke the top of Lucy's brown head and her smooth neck and play with her pointy little ears. Sometimes I tell her about what I'm reading and she may even look up at me with her glassy green eyes and feign interest. "Why, how *fascinating*, Mommy," she may seem to be saying. "What an interesting thing! Miss Bennet sounds like a lovely person. Let's hope that she and Mr. Darcy get together, huh? Please tell me more."

I think she likes hearing about the adventures of Laura and Mary and Ma and Pa from the *Little House* series best of all—that happy little pioneer family, facing many adversities and liking being together.

Sometimes I tell her stories of heroic cats throughout history, but in abbreviated form since cats have, I believe, short attention spans. "So, Lucy," I said to her tonight when I started my bath. "There once was a little boy in Ohio who fell down a well and his gray cat, Winston, ran to the house and meowed real loudly until the boy's daddy heard him and ran to the well and saved the boy and gave him chicken noodle soup with saltines. Then he gave Winston a certificate of merit and a very special salmon treat. 'Oh, how proud we all are of Winston, and oh, we just love him so very much!' the boy's mommy said. The end."

And, of course, she gets selected highlights about the felines I've encountered that day. She always seems at least mildly interested, but I'm not sure how she really feels. Maybe she's insanely jealous that I'm spending time with other cats. Or maybe hearing about other cats makes her feel less alone, and perhaps she even imagines being friends with Jake and Maria and Bella and the others. Sometimes I feel bad telling her about houses where there are two or more cats, though, because she might be envious. Lucy doesn't seem unhappy being an only kitty, but who knows? Maybe I should tell her stories about imaginary feline friends of hers, and that would make her feel less lonely. It would give her something to think about when I'm gone on my cat-tending rounds.

I like the *Little House* books. I've read and re-read all of them. I have them in a special place on my bookshelves. When Mindy and I were little, we liked watching reruns of the TV series, with that pleasant Melissa

Gilbert as Laura and Michael Landon as Pa. I suspect the real Pa wasn't as good-looking as Landon. Mindy—no surprise—always cried at the frequent hyper-emotional moments, signified with soaring music.

Dad noticed how much we liked the show and got a set of the books and read them to us before bedtime, the three of us sitting on the couch with our cat, Wolfie, sometimes sitting beside us. That's a nice memory. I remember that I didn't like the part in *Little House on the Prairie* when Dad read to us that their dog, Jack, had to be chained outside all the time because he disliked Indians who came to their little house and Pa was afraid Jack would bite one and cause a ruckus. Mindy hated the part in *On the Banks of Plum Creek* when Pa had to trade their two horses, Pet and Patty, to Mr. Hanson. She sniffled and blinked her eyes, and her lower lip trembled, and then she bawled for almost five minutes. Christ! She was happy, though, when Pa got two replacement horses, Sam and David, as Christmas presents for the family.

I don't have a lot of good memories of my father, but him reading to us is one.

I just got done shaving my legs in the tub and, as always, Lucy opened her green eyes and watched intensely. "What the heck are you *doing*, Mommy?" she might ask if she could talk. Seeing me shaving every few days seems to be one of the highlights of Lucy's life. What a restricted existence she leads. How uneventful. But just how is my life more interesting? Maybe my cat's worldview is narrow, but how wide is mine? Hah! I sit here alone in this little apartment or sit alone in other people's houses while others are out there in the world thinking great thoughts or doing noteworthy things—finding cures for cancer and dementia and post-partum depression, persuading those nutso Arab terrorists to make nice and stop blowing people up, pushing for more no-kill shelters—and enthusiastically propagating so as to ensure continuation of the species.

But that's okay. Lucy and I are okay. We don't need to make much of a splash in the world. We love being here listening to Frank. Maybe it's my imagination, but it seems that Lucy's ears prick up and she smiles a bit when she hears "Strangers in the Night." Like now. She waits quietly and patiently for the end of the song: "Dooby, dooby, doo. Dah, dah, dah, dee, dah..."

It would be nice if Lucy and I could go on together like this for years and years. "Right, Goose?" I hope we will. I like our life together. But, sadly, her allotted life span is way more compressed than mine. Also, bad things can happen to either or both of us before the end of those allotted spans. Like poor Carlos getting cancer. Cats can get all kinds of diseases, kidney stuff and leukemia and nasty infections and whatnot. Or I can. Or a tornado or an earthquake could come along and reduce our building to rubble with us inside. Or there could be a carbon monoxide leak, and we'd expire together in the bathroom, me in the tub and Lucy on the toilet lid, neither of us knowing what hit us. Sinatra would still be crooning away: "Two lonely people, we were strangers in the night…" Or a deranged psychopath might burst into the apartment and scream obscenities and take me hostage and then, when nobody paid the ransom, smash my head with a rock and dump my body in a swamp. Poor Lucy would be all alone and wondering what the heck happened to her mommy. You just never know.

It's good to relax in my tub. I put in just a bit of Rain Bubble Bath and Foaming Bath Gel that I bought for myself at The Soap Opera on State Street as a Christmas present last December. It's a nice little luxury.

Today was a crappy day. Mindy and I and the other three bridesmaids went to Vera's House of Bridals on Big Sky Drive to choose the bridesmaid dresses. It wasn't as though we attendants—Julie and Katie and Diana and I—had much say about the whole deal, though. Mindy pretty much ran the show and did all the deciding. She told the *consultant* we worked with, Amy, a cute though short little thing with fluffy, brown blond-highlighted hair and decent cleavage, that she wanted us to have floor-length strapless gowns. The two of them then had an unbelievably boring discussion about how the gowns should "flatter and enhance" Mindy's already-selected wedding gown, an ivory-colored Allure Couture strapless with symmetrical ruching and a chapel-length train of delustered satin, as she so proudly articulated for the benefit of everyone in the damned store.

Mom and Mindy had worked with Amy to choose that dress some time back. Happily, I'd been excluded from that drudgery. I'd been anticipating a horrible *Say Yes to the Dress* drama in which Mom and us bridesmaids, maybe along with Richard's mother and even Aunt Grace, would all have to sit around while Mindy tried on fifteen or twenty dresses, agonizing over each as all of us exhausted ladies opined on her selections—"No, no, Mindy, I think that dress makes your butt look too big!" Finally, after several long hours, she'd say yes to one of the stupid things. On the day they were heading to pick out the dress, I lied and told Mom and Mindy that I had a rotten cold and couldn't go dress shopping with them.

"That was horrible of me, Lucy, but at least I feel ashamed of myself. At least I have guilt. At least I got *that* from my Catholic education. That's *something*, right?"

Anyway, when all of us were at the shop today, Amy showed us a few bridesmaid dress possibilities, and within forty-five minutes Mindy had decided: Bill Levkoff chiffon and taffeta strapless floor-length gowns with natural waists and, like her own dress, ruching. Ruching! "Mindy!" I should have said. "For God's sake! Gathering of folds like that is NOT flattering to full-figured girls such as myself. It makes us look fatter."

But I didn't. Nor did we have much say on the color. Amy tossed out several options—dusty rose, melon, espresso brown, plum, and Capri blue—and Mindy asked us what we thought. Julie liked the espresso brown and Diana, Richard's sister, liked the plum. So did Katie. I didn't say anything. I couldn't have cared less. I'd be content wearing my gray, stained sweatsuit and my worn blue slippers to the damned wedding. Or one of my denim jumpers. But Mindy chose the Capri blue. "Oh, it just reminds me so much of the Caribbean," she'd chirped.

So the stupid dress is going to set me back $240, which is a lot for me. I had to plunk down half of that today. And that's in *addition* to what I'll have to shell out for the alterations—probably another hundred—and for the shoes, the bra, the accessories, the hairstyling, the bachelorette party expenses, a gift, and I don't know what the hell else.

And, of course, the dress is strapless, which I knew it would be and had been dreading. That's not a good look for us heifers. Hell, I'm not sure it's a good look for *anyone*—visible tan lines, spillover cleavage, those pouches of skin that bunch around the armpits. Strapless gowns are even more horrible if you have either broad shoulders or stick-figure arms. Yikes!

But the worst thing this morning was when they did the fitting and we were told that bridesmaid dresses are always small, and we'd have to get dresses that are two sizes *bigger* than we normally wear. So I normally wear a size sixteen, and now I have to order a size twenty. *Twenty!* Good Christ! "Oh, Maggie," some knucklehead at the wedding will say, maybe in the receiving line. "What a lovely dress. Oh, I *adore* the blue!" I'll stare at her for a moment. "Yeah," I'll reply snidely. "It's a size twenty. *Twenty!* Isn't that just *wonderful*?"

And to top it off, Amy said it'll cost about forty dollars more for a bigger girl, someone who needs a size eighteen or twenty dress—more fabric, special cutting. *Perfect!* Why the hell couldn't my sister and that numbnuts Richard just elope in the middle of the night and spare me all this damned aggravation?

The only good thing was that when we were leaving Vera's and were about to head over to Rocky Rococo for lunch, Diana turned to me and whispered, "What a pain in the ass, huh?" I don't know if she meant Mindy or the whole stupid experience, but either way I think I'm going to like her.

Sometimes at night, like now, I worry that I don't have more ambition. There's Mindy, who's filled with ambition and overflowing with plans: a big Catholic wedding, marriage to Richard, and going to school to be a paralegal. No doubt they'll have a nice house someday with a well-manicured lawn and a new five-piece bedroom set and a big kitchen with an island the size of Oahu and high-end stainless-steel appliances and lots of matching furniture and gadgets. They'll have a lovely bathroom with fashionable fixtures and, no doubt, high-end four-ply toilet paper, like the Morrisons have. Outside will be a fenced-in yard with room for a sandbox and wooden playground equipment for when they have their brats, and a deck and a huge gas grill, big enough to cook six steaks, with long spoons and spatulas hanging off the sides. Yes, they'll certainly want children down the line. That's a given.

Most of her many friends and my few friends have ambition, plans, goals, too. Sheila wants to be a nurse, preferably in an emergency room. She was a nursing assistant and now she's in school to become an RN. Richard's a certified public accountant. Mindy's best friend, Katie, wants to be on television somehow. Probably her dream is to be one of those glossy-lipped, long-haired, bleached-blond chicks on Fox News who wear short dresses and show off their always-crossed legs. Most of those women have good calves and ankles, I'll say that. And you never see one of them with a skinned knee. Their teeth are usually perfect, never crooked, and *very* white. I wonder if their boobs ever itch or sweat, like mine do.

Then there's me, with minimal ambition and few plans. I like taking care of cats, but beyond that I don't know. I can't think of anything I want to do for a career or a job, and I don't want to get married or, after Alex, even live with anyone. And, as of now, I don't want a rugrat. I might be okay with a boyfriend, I guess, for sex and some companionship, as long as we had separate rooms or, better yet, separate residences, and he didn't disgust me or bore me too much or want to spend every damned minute together.

Also, I don't want to live in a big house with lots of junk, like so many of the houses I go to. It's too much of a burden, too much to worry about. I like what I have now and don't long for anything else. Well, maybe a little bigger bathroom. That would be okay. But one thing I *never* want to have to do is share my bathroom with anyone, male or female. Lucy's okay to share it with, but that's it.

One minor ambition I'm thinking about is doing watercolors, like Mom does. She's been doing it for a long time—at least since I was in second grade—and she even belongs to a group, the Madison Watercolor Society. I think it's mostly women. She's not much of a joiner, but she likes that bunch. I'm not a joiner at all, but if I were, that group might be okay. Mom mostly likes doing paintings of quiet ponds and streams. I used to like to watch her sketching in her preliminary drawings with a graphite pencil and then using her brushes—a large inch-and-half-wide flat brush and a round sable brush—to create her images on sensuous linen paper. Her favorite color for her ponds has always been ultramarine blue. I liked watching her using cotton swabs now and again to create more velvety images. I think painting would be a good way to relax after a day of cat tending. And it would be something my mother and I could share.

If I do that, I think I'd like to paint flowers. Flowers are good. Maybe I'll do flower paintings like Georgia O'Keeffe's, that look like female "down there" stuff—vulvas, with the labia and vagina opening and little clitorises and all. My favorite of Georgia's is "Abstraction Seaweed and Water." If *that* isn't a vajayjay, nothing is. But she always denied that her flower paintings were meant to look like cooches. "Oh, my goodness, no," she'd say with a straight face. "Oh, no, not at all. Just turned out that way." Hah! I wonder what the truth is.

Vajayjays are good. They *are* like flowers. They're dormant most of the time, but when the sun shines and the mist of May is in the gloaming, they can get all nice and moist and sort of blossom. Before getting into the tub tonight, I looked at mine with a hand mirror. I can't say it was beautiful, but it's okay—all those interesting folds. I wonder how my hoohah, the way it looks, compares to other women's.

Maybe I could even sell some of my flowers-that-look-like-vaginas paintings. Maybe there's a market for that. I have to think there is. Cooches are, understandably, popular. "And if I make a few bucks on it, Goose, you'll get a cut—maybe some high-quality catnip, perhaps Cosmic brand, or an extra-special mouse toy. I promise."

One job I think I might like would be to go after horrible people who abuse cats. I want to punish them—but not like some candy-assed government official who issues a lame citation and maybe takes the abuser's cats away. No. I mean punish them like hurting them, being an avenger. If I heard about some miserable excuse for a human being who did bad things to a cat—starving, beating, kicking, keeping them in a cage for no reason—I'd learn all I could about that lowlife and stalk him or her and think of the nastiest thing I could do short of death or permanent injury or disfigurement. Maybe break one of their knees, like Mob guys do. As to disfigurement I'd consider tying them up and tattooing "I'M A NASTY ASSHOLE WHO ABUSES CATS" on their face, along with a graphic of a sweet little calico drinking cream from a bowl. My inclination would be to do the tattoo on the doofus's forehead, but then they could cover it with hair. So maybe I'd do it on their cheek—the upper cheek if it's a guy, so the jerk couldn't hide it with whiskers. I'd be an avenger, like Charles Bronson in the *Death Wish* movies, the best revenge flicks ever. Except that I wouldn't shoot people. Oh, that wonderful Charles Bronson!

Children wouldn't be exempt from my justice. There're lots of little budding psychopaths running around who set cats on fire and the like, and they need to be dealt with early and severely. My idea would be to set *them* on fire very briefly, so they'd know what that's like, and then quickly extinguish the fire with a hose. "How did *that* feel, Shorty?" I'd ask. But maybe that's too severe. Maybe it'd work just to threaten them, to put the fear of God into them with the implied threat that future psychopathic behavior will have dire consequences. "Do we *understand* each other, you nasty little moron?" I'd ask.

I wonder how a woman feels if she has a baby and it's all soft and cute and cuddly and she loves it so very much, blah blah, and then in a few years the kid shows signs of being a psychopath: torturing animals, vandalizing property, setting fires, pushing other kids down stairs, lying about everything with a straight face, showing no guilt. She'd have to face the sad truth that her little darling's a monster. That can't be a good feeling.

Well, there's probably not much money in being a cat avenger. A girl should do something in life that makes her at least a little happy and at least somewhat fulfilled and also puts bread on her table. I just don't know what that is for me, besides taking care of cats and maybe, someday, selling my watercolors. Punishing cat abusers is a nice fantasy job, but I'm not sure I'm temperamentally suited for it. I like the *idea* of causing pain to horrible people, but don't think I'm up for the actual doing of it. Also, who'd hire me? Maybe there'd be some rich old lady who loves cats and despises cat abusers and would be happy to pay people to be avengers.

Maybe she'd even hire a bunch of hefty young women with attitude to get revenge and I could be one of them, part of a team. We'd call ourselves the Legion of Overweight Cat Avengers. We'd have weekly meetings to identify our victims and plan strategies and tactics, and we'd serve wonderful snacks: Chicago-style hot dogs, soft pretzels, Doritos, butterscotch pudding topped with Cool Whip, peanut-butter-and-banana sandwiches, chicken wings, Hostess Ho-Ho's, Milky Way and 3 Musketeer bars, mint-chocolate-chip ice cream, whole cashews, Diet Pepsi, and more.

After eating, we'd get down to business. "Hey," one of the fat women would say, "I heard about this guy on Whitney Way who starves his Abyssinian because he doesn't want to pay for cat food. The miserable lowlife spends all his dough on booze and dope. Let's *get* him!" We'd all clap and yell, "Yeah! Let's get the bastard!" Then another porker would offer an idea: "Let's kidnap him and tie him up naked and slather him with honey and set him on top of a huge anthill. I know this vacant lot off of East Washington where they have *tons* of anthills." We'd all nod enthusiastically and applaud again.

And, needless to say, we'd immediately liberate the guy's cat and find it a new home, maybe with one of us. Or maybe the rich old lady would take the abused cats. Maybe she'd have a mansion in Maple Bluff with room for dozens of cats and they'd all be very well taken care of, with daily canned wet food and kibbles and morning, and evening treats, and catnip all around on Saturday nights. There'd be ongoing veterinary care, and maybe an on-site groomer, and, certainly, plenty of litter boxes filled with the highest-quality clumping litter.

Maybe I wouldn't mind being Mindy's maid of honor so much if some of the overweight cat avengers could be the other bridesmaids. When Mindy told me she was engaged and asked me to be her maid of honor, I immediately anticipated that her other attendants would be slender little things with nice round butts—neither too big nor too little—and curvy hips and perky boobs that don't slip to the side when they lie on their backs. They'd all, I thought, have perfect oval faces with clear skin, cute upturned noses, full lips, and magnificent cheekbones—not a hunk-of-blob face like mine. They'd have long delicate eyelashes and perfectly plucked eyebrows. Their eyes would sparkle. I'd look like Moby-Dick standing next to them.

But if we were *all* porkers, it'd be better. I wouldn't stand out. We'd all plomp heavily down the aisle and then stand on the steps of the sanctuary looking like the offensive line of the Green Bay Packers, all of our boobs securely taped in so they didn't spill out of our strapless gowns. We'd all have huge arms and shoulders, not just me. We'd hold our bouquets delicately against our bulging tummies. We'd smile sweetly during the ceremony, our bloated, heavily-made-up faces radiant with the joy of the occasion.

When Mindy and Richard lit the unity candle and exchanged their vows and then did their first married-couple kiss, maybe some of us, for the sake of appearance, could manage to squeeze out a tear or two that would ooze down our fat cheeks and streak our carefully applied makeup.

But all the while, we'd scan the audience for potential cat abusers, people who might be the kind of nasty trash who'd do unspeakable things to felines. We'd make mental notes and collectively debrief our observations about the potential abusers later. Maybe we'd have time to get our heads together to compare notes during the photographs, the formals—any time we weren't being featured and didn't have to stand still and look into the lens and smile like idiots. Like when it was time, say, for the bride pictures or the couple pictures or the groom and groomsmen or the families. Or maybe we'd have time to talk later, during a lag time at the reception—perhaps before or after the tedious slide show with the endless pictures of Mindy and Richard as babies and then children and then teenagers and then a happy little couple, with that usual putrid medley version of "Somewhere Over the Rainbow/What a Wonderful World" by that dead Hawaiian guy as the sound track.

If they'd at least play the Judy Garland version of "Over the Rainbow," it'd maybe be palatable and I wouldn't feel like puking.

Now, of course, I know that two of the other bridesmaids, Katie and Julie, are indeed thin and pretty. Well, Julie's maybe *too* thin. And Diana's not a porker, but she's…well, just a bit solid.

"What a pain in the ass, huh?" Diana'd said. I love it!

All the Way

"HEY, LUCY, guess what? Larry told me this morning that Chester and Festus are brothers. I was surprised he'd never mentioned it before. They don't look at all alike. Chester's a tuxedo cat, black and white, and Festus is a bigger, mostly dark-silver guy with thicker fur than Chester. I think you'd like them. It's cute that they hang out together a lot, but poor Miss Kitty's left out."

Miss Kitty doesn't interact with the brothers much, just spends most of her time sitting on a stuffed chair in the living room. Larry put a thick white pad on the chair, so at least she looks comfortable. But that cat could use some exercise. She's a bit of a heavyweight, an obese ginger-colored girl, and when I come over all she ever does is to lie Buddha-like on her oval pad, front paws folded under, rarely even moving, and now and again opens her yellow eyes to see what the brothers are up to. They mostly ignore her, and play their little game wherein Chester saunters from one room of the condo to another, tail up and swishing, and Festus hides behind corners and furniture and ambushes his sibling. He's a riot! He hunkers down to make himself as small as possible, hugging the floor, and when Chester's just past him Festus wiggles his behind and then leaps out to attack. He jumps on top of Chester for just a moment, often knocking him over, and then immediately retreats. Sometimes Chester chases Festus, but more often he just shakes his head a few times and resumes his sauntering.

Or, the two of them spend time together on their favorite perches in the cat tree that Larry set up by the south window in the living room. There're five perches, each at a different level, but the guys almost always sit in the same ones—Chester on the very top and Festus on the middle perch. Either they have no imagination or, like so many of the cats I take care of, are wedded to their little routines.

I remember once when I thought Festus was being particularly obnoxious to his brother. I tried an experiment. "Festus," I said, "you are a *horrible* cat. You're a nasty bully and you're a miserable excuse for a feline. You have absolutely no redeeming qualities. I do *not* approve of you!" But I said it in a sweet, soothing, complimentary tone of voice. He responded by rubbing against me and flopping down to expose his silver tummy, which meant, I believe, "I like you. I trust you. Tell me more." So maybe cats understand some words, but what they *really* respond to, it seems, is tone. I'm going to have to try that sometime the opposite way: kind words, mean tone.

Larry's condo is small, with one decent-sized bedroom in the back and a cozy living room with a small baby-puke-green couch and two older stuffed chairs grouped around a shiny black coffee table. The only thing on the coffee table is a single blue plastic coaster. When I'm there, I always sit on the couch, with Miss Kitty in her chair to my left.

Everything about his place is modest, including his TV. It's an older thirty-two-inch Sony and sits on top of a battered chest of drawers. Some of the drawer handles are missing. None of my shows were on today, so I left the TV off and just played with the cats. I like it that Larry's place isn't filled to the rafters with crap, like so many of the places I go to.

He has one small bathroom. I was surprised, the first time I went in there, that he has a pink toilet lid cover—one of those soft, furry things that fits snugly around the lid. If that cover had been blue or green or red, I wouldn't have been as surprised. His toilet paper is a simple white, and it seems to be somewhere between high-quality, like the Morrisons' bathroom tissue, and the bargain-basement-quality junk that I usually buy. A funny thing, though, was that there were three magazines on the floor next to the toilet: *Barbers Only*, *Modern Barber*, and *Mademoiselle*.

"Maybe I should get one of those nice furry toilet lid covers for you, Lucy. Would you like that?"

Larry's never been married and lives alone. My kind of guy.

He doesn't have a wall of family pictures in his condo, bless his soul. The only two personal framed photos he has are on the dresser in his bedroom. One is of him and his Madison West High School basketball teammates in their yellow and blue shorts and jerseys. Larry's number thirty-two. One of the shorter guys in the front row is *really* cute and has amazing crinkly blue eyes.

The other personal photo is of him standing in front of some pine trees with his arm around the waist of a skinny long-haired chick who's wearing tight jeans and a light-green tank top. She has an unusually shiny forehead. They're both looking into the camera and grinning. She has long and very white teeth and pretty blue eyes. Larry'd once mentioned that he'd been engaged, but it hadn't worked out, though he didn't say why. So is the babe with the teeth his former fiancé?

My guess is that his fiancé jilted him, rather than the other way around. He seems too nice, or perhaps too timid, to be the jilter. Maybe she just got tired of hearing Larry tell his stories, perhaps about when he played high school basketball and all the wise or witty things the coach said, and how Larry won the big game in the state tournament at the Kohl Center with a midrange jump shot in the last five seconds of double overtime.

Or maybe she was one of those women who secretly wants a mean, nasty guy who'll sneer at her and demean her and order her to cook him a hearty and delicious meal—pot roast and boiled potatoes and gravy, with rhubarb pie for dessert—and then order her to clean up the kitchen immediately after the meal and to put away all the clean pots and dishes and glasses and silverware and wipe the countertop very thoroughly, with disinfectant, so that the kitchen's immaculate. "I want this damned kitchen SPOTLESS," he'd yell. "Do you *hear* me?"

Larry wouldn't have been that kind of guy.

Or maybe Miss Straight White Teeth didn't want to settle for a barber and decided at the last minute, just before they were ready to send out the invitations, that she preferred to hitch her star to a guy with more ambition and a bigger wallet, perhaps holding out for a doctor or a lawyer or some such who could make all her little dreams come true and father the three children she'd always wanted since she was a little girl, and give her a big house with a long driveway and a three-car garage and a huge kitchen with a breakfast nook and top-of-the-line quartz countertops and a Viking stove, and pay for her many pairs of Manolo Blahnik and Jimmy Choo shoes, and take her to Cozumel for long sunny vacations. Of course, he'd be so busy making money that he wouldn't be home much to bore her and waste her time and interfere with her fantasies about the poolboy. She'd be just fine with his being gone long hours—the longer, the better.

But I could maybe see being with a guy like Larry. He once said that he likes being a barber, and his big ambition is to one day own his own shop. He doesn't seem too complicated or neurotic, and when he's not working he likes being home and watching *Andy Griffith* and *Gunsmoke* reruns. He has two framed pictures in his front hallway, one of Andy and Barney from one of their early shows—the black-and-white days—with Andy sitting at the desk in the courthouse and Barney standing beside him, looking flustered or maybe even a bit drunk, his hair messed up. The other picture is of Andy and Aunt Bee and Opie sitting on their front porch. Opie and Aunt Bee are eating ice cream, probably homemade, and listening to Andy play his guitar.

But the funniest thing is that Larry has a big, silver double-picture frame in his living room with two color photos side by side: one of his ginger cat when she was younger and less of a porker and the other of a middle-aged woman with red hair piled on top of her head, held in with pins and combs. She's wearing red lipstick and has a black beauty spot on the right side of her face, just over the cheekbone. She's looking directly into the camera, not smiling, and you have the idea that she's not a woman to be messed with. Below these photos is a propped-up green index card with red block lettering that says "MISS KITTY." I didn't quite get that, and asked Larry about it the time I first came over to meet his cats. He said the woman was Kitty Russell from *Gunsmoke*, known by all as "Miss Kitty," and that she owned a saloon in Dodge City, the Long Branch, and was the marshal's sort-of girlfriend.

So a guy like Larry might do—*if* I were interested in being with anyone. He's simple enough. I'd be fine with a barber. I don't want a doctor or a lawyer or a house with a long driveway or a kitchen with an island, and I could give a rat's ass about going to Cozumel. I wouldn't know Manolo Blahniks from Keds sneakers.

Of course, I'd have to find out if he's okay with an oversized girl like me or if he insists on twiggy anorexics like Miss Teeth. He's one of the few clients that I like talking with, even though we've never talked about anything very deep or about me much, other than my experiences taking care of cats.

We do have one thing in common that we've talked about. Larry and I went to the same Catholic grade school, Edgewood. I knew that because I'd seen one of their mailings on his kitchen table, and asked him about it. We even had the same fourth-grade teacher, Sister Agnella. I told him how she once chastised me for having a little mirror propped up on one corner of my desk. Sister said I was being vain. Vanity is probably one of those venial sins that priests and nuns get worked up about. Anyway, I didn't bother to tell Sister the real reason for the mirror. It was so I could look at Walter, a boy that I had a little crush on, whose desk was three rows behind mine. Larry chuckled at that story.

So we do have something we share. That's good. Maybe if Larry and I become a couple and, after a time, we were sitting across from each other at the dinner table wondering what the hell to talk about, we could dredge up memories about Sister Agnella and some of the other humorless nuns we've encountered.

Larry doesn't seem overly impressed with himself, like some men. Many men. But I'd worry about feeling bored with him after a while, like I did with Alex. I don't want to go through that again.

Then again, maybe Larry has deep dark secrets. Maybe he's more complicated, more sinister, than he seems. Maybe he's a closet sociopath with an anger management problem who fantasizes about slicing off the ears of his customers. "Oh, yeah? 'Just a little more off the top,' you say? Well, how about *these* off?"

Perhaps I'd have to break my general rule about not invading the privacy of my clients and see if he kept a journal or a blog of some kind. Maybe I could figure out how to access the HP desktop computer in his bedroom. I hate to do that, but if a guy's a potential boyfriend then a girl has to take steps to find out about him. Relationships are enough of a crapshoot as it is.

But what if I read his journals and found out that he's a homicidal maniac or a secret porn star who's done it with eight hundred women? Or is even just one of those survivalist guys who thinks the government's out to get him and take away his guns, and he keeps looking at the sky for black helicopters, and aspires to hole up somewhere in the mountains of Idaho in a shack that's stocked with a generator, stacked cases of bottled water, and shelves of canned baked beans and Spam and corned beef hash? What then? I imagine that would damper any prospects for romance.

On the other hand, I already know that he's kind to cats. He told me that he got the brothers and Miss Kitty from the local shelter, and that he'll get any future cats from there as well. So does liking cats and being good to them balance off doing nasty things to human beings or being too much of a weirdo? Hmm.

Spam. *Yuck!* Whoever invented that should be shot.

Of course, I'd have to find out if Larry wants kids. With my crappy luck, he would. Tons of them, probably. "I love you dearly, Maggie," he'd say. "You're the most wonderful woman in the world and I see us having a long, fabulous life together. I want to grow old with you. But before we get there, I fully expect you to squeeze out some progeny—three, maybe four. I think two boys and two girls would be lovely. Don't you?" What then?

The two of us could watch Andy and Barney and Marshal Dillon and his deputies over the years—Chester and then Festus, as Larry explained—and maybe we'd be compatible enough. I'd certainly be happy, too, to sit with him and watch other old westerns that he might like—*Bonanza*, *Bat Masterson*, *Maverick*, whatever. Hopefully, he'd like to watch revenge movies with me now and again, and, also hopefully, the other shows that I like.

With Chester and Festus on the little couch beside us or maybe between us, and Miss Kitty comfortably ensconced on her pad on her chair nearby, and with a big bowl of chocolate-covered peanuts on the black coffee table, we'd watch *Teen Mom 2* and crack wise about the people on it. "Oh, my, God, Larry," I'd say. "Can you believe that stupid Jenelle? She knows how to pick 'em, huh? What in hell did she ever see in that idiot Kieffer? And then that horrible Courtland and now that lowlife Nathan? And her mother, for God's sake. Barbara. What a *bitch!* God, if that woman was my mom I'd, like, totally throw myself off a cliff." Larry would nod and look thoughtful. "Yeah," he'd say. "I know what you mean. She's horrible. They're always fighting. And what about that ugly blimpo Gary in *16 & Pregnant* and in the first season of *Teen Mom* and now? The guy must weigh four hundred pounds! His head's as big as a watermelon. And that pathetic beard! That horrible chunko Amber's screaming at him and whomping on him every two minutes, and while fending off her blows all he can squeal is, 'But I love you, Amber. Oh, I *love* you!' Man, he should have turned and run from that fat-assed, big-mouthed broad as fast as he could've."

But probably Larry wouldn't say that. He's probably too nice to talk smack. Most likely he'd just delicately pop a chocolate-covered peanut into his mouth and smile weakly and give everyone the benefit of the doubt. "Oh," he'd say, "I'm sure Jenelle's a wonderful mommy to little Jace when she's not in a bad mood. And I'm quite certain, Maggie, that Barbara does the best she can. She probably just yells so much because she's understandably stressed out due to their difficult circumstances, what with her having temporary custody of that sweet child and worrying so much about poor Jenelle and all of her unfortunate decisions—using heroin and getting involved with not-so-great guys and so on. After all, it must be tough for Jenelle, being a teen mom. She just wanted to be a normal teenager and hang out with her friends and go to prom. I can certainly understand that. And as for Nathan, I'm fairly confident that he'll straighten up and be a wonderful daddy and an upstanding citizen when he gets out of jail for DUI."

That's probably what he'd say.

"And," he'd add, "Amber and Gary certainly have their problems, but they love their little Leah and they're trying hard to be good parents."

But could I be with someone *that* nice, that tolerant? Maybe for about five minutes. After that I'd have to insist that he cool it with the saccharine and be willing to be as snarky as I am—or at least *almost* as snarky. I guess I'd be okay with a boyfriend who's nice and pleasant and takes the high road as to other people some of the time, maybe even much of the time, but probably not *most* of the time and *definitely* not all the time.

"Lucy, do you think Larry'd go to the wedding with me as my escort, my date?" Most likely the other bridesmaids will have escorts—boyfriends or husbands, whatever—and maybe I should too. Katie's married, I know that. Larry wouldn't have to do much: just spend a little time with me here and there when I wasn't doing maid of honor stuff and dance with me at the reception after I did the obligatory bridal party dance with the stupid best man, Mark, Richard's boring and arguably ugly older brother. He parts his hair horribly down the middle and has a very scruffy goatee.

I wouldn't be able to sit with Larry during the dinner because I'd have to be up at the head table with the happy couple and the other bridesmaids and the groomsmen. Larry'd have to sit at one of the round tables with the other guests, and I'd try to be sure that Mindy put him at a table with people he could talk with a little. Maybe we could find out if there were any other barbers in the crowd, so he'd have something in common with someone. It could be horrible. "And what's your connection?" people at the table would ask him. "Well," he'd say, "I'm here with Maggie. The maid of honor." There'd be an uncomfortable silence. "Oh," someone at the table would say. "I see. Maggie. She's your, uh, girlfriend? *Really?*" More silence, and perhaps some throat clearing. Finally, one of the guests—a short, clean-shaven guy wearing a nice blue suit and a ten-year-old tie with red and yellow stripes—would say, "Hey, I hear you're a barber. Me too. How many chairs do you have in the shop?"

Maybe Larry could tell the group at the table some Barney Fife anecdotes to relieve the tension. He could tell about his favorite *Andy Griffith* episodes. He once told me that his very favorite is the one where Gomer Pyle does a citizen's arrest of Barney. He did a funny imitation of

Gomer: "*Citizen's aray-ust!...Citizen's aray-ust!*" Or he could tell a joke or two.

I don't know if Chester and Festus like jokes, but I believe Miss Kitty does. "Hey, Missy," I said to her before getting ready to leave. "What do you call a one-legged ballerina's costume?" She looked up at me with her yellow eyes, waiting. "A one-one. Get it?" I think that she sort of nodded approvingly, but maybe not.

I wish Miss Kitty liked playing with the shoelace, but she doesn't. When I dangle and twirl the lace in front of her, she just glances at it and then closes her eyes, totally uninterested. The boys, though, like it. Chester leaps and twirls at the shoelace, and Festus lies on his back and bats at it with his right paw. The other thing the brothers like is when I use my laser pointer and shoot a moving red dot across the floor. Festus leaps and twirls to get the dot, his eyes wide, and Chester tries to bat it with his left paw.

Chester and Festus are good guys, but with hard names to live up to.

Maybe I should bring my laser pointer to the wedding. I could make Mindy and Richard crazy during their first dance. "What do you think of that, Goosey?" From her look, I believe she approves of the idea.

As far as the blessed event goes, I'm exhausted just listening to Mindy talk about all the wedding stuff she has to do. Yesterday, she and our cousin Toni and I finally went to Gigi's Cupcakes to deal with cake stuff. The damned event's still five months off, and Mindy's dealing not just with cakes but with florists, DJs, photographers, officiants, making plans for the rehearsal dinner, and reception details. I told her I'd help with the rehearsal dinner. She's also ordering invitations and dealing with save-the-date cards.

Everywhere Mindy goes, she brings a red two-inch ringed binder with divider tabs. She's completely organized about getting hitched, I'll give her that. But I'm thrilled that she took my suggestion about Gigi's. They do nice wedding cakes, in layers, in addition to cupcakes. Mindy thought my idea of a cupcake table at the reception was good, and I even volunteered to work with the ladies at Gigi's, some of whom have apparently sampled their own wares, on the details. Those details will certainly include my tasting samples. They have more than three hundred gourmet cupcake recipes, and we can get both full-size and mini-size cupcakes. We can even get cupcakes for the damned bachelorette party that I'm responsible for.

The Kentucky Bourbon Pie cupcake is my all-time Gigi's favorite—bourbon cake with pecans and chocolate chips, and cream cheese frosting with caramel and ganache. *Yum!* I also love the Lemon Dream Supreme—

lemon cake with lemon filling, lemon buttercream frosting, and a candied lemon slice on top. Thank you for *that* one, too, sweet Jesus!

When Mindy first asked me to be her maid of honor, she gave me a printout from a website listing all the possible duties of that esteemed position. Oh, my *God*! I almost fainted from all the possible tasks: scouting wedding locations, helping with the invitations, dress shopping, helping with seating chart stuff, hosting the bridal shower, hosting the damned bachelorette party, keeping a list of gifts received. And then there was an equally long and tedious list of all the maid of honor duties on the wedding day.

But, as it turned out, Mindy wants to do most of the pre-wedding tasks herself—not that she doesn't trust me, but because she's a little blond control freak. I thank sweet God above that my sister's so compulsive about handling all this stuff herself and isn't asking me to do more than I'm doing, which isn't much, even though I feel overwhelmed with the little I have to do.

Still, when we'd been at Vera's dress shop, I'd overheard one of the consultants telling another customer that it was a good idea for the bride to have a separate personal attendant to do a lot of the wedding day stuff instead of leaving it to the maid of honor. That way, the maid could "enjoy the day more" and not be overwhelmed with all the crap jobs—even things like putting the bride's clothes in the car after she gets dressed at the church, bustling the bride's dress, carrying gifts out to the car or up to a hotel room at the reception, carrying tissues in case the bride gets overly emotional, and the like.

So, when we were at Gigi's yesterday, I remembered what the lady at Vera's had said and had the idea to suggest to Mindy, when I can, that Toni should be her personal attendant. Toni would do it. Hell, she'd love it. She's a mini-Mindy. They're close in age, they sort of look alike—both thin, blue-eyed blondes with cute upturned noses and nice firm butts—and Toni's a people pleaser. It would make her feel needed. Plus, Toni's just as orgasmic as Mindy about weddings and all the nonsense around planning them and making them happen. She'll be thrilled to haul the stupid gifts out to the car or find a pin to attach the guys' boutonnieres if the florist loses one.

I, on the other hand, want to do as little as possible. My main goal from now until the wedding day is to do the absolute minimum I can without offending or alienating my sister and my mother, and then to have many stiff drinks at the open bar at the reception.

And I'm sure that Aunt Grace will be just *thrilled* that Mindy asked her perfect little daughter, Toni, to be the personal attendant. That witch is probably upset that Toni isn't a bridesmaid, much less the maid of honor. I can just imagine her talking to her daughter while sitting on that spotless expensive white-upholstered sofa in her huge Enchanted Valley Estates living room, with the vaulted ceilings and the chandeliers, sipping a crème de menthe. "Well, really, Antoinette, I can't understand why your cousin would want her sister to be the maid of honor rather than you. God knows that you're so much more attractive and vibrant, and would look so much better than that oversized Maggie waddling down the aisle and standing beside the altar." She'd pause and take a delicate sip of her drink, staining the little liqueur glass with red lipstick. "Well, I suspect that mousy Lillian insisted on it and Mindy felt she had no choice. But I know that you'd have been who Mindy wanted, in a perfect world."

A perfect world. *Hah!*

St. Patrick's Day is coming up in a week or so. "Maybe Gigi's will do a special cupcake for the occasion, Lucy. Maybe something in the shape of an Irish potato with corned-beef-and-cabbage-flavored frosting. What do you think?" She doesn't seem too excited at the prospect. "Wouldn't it be nice, Goosey, if Frank had a CD of Irish songs that we could listen to on that day? 'I'll Take You Home Again, Kathleen' and the like? Maybe 'When Irish Eyes Are Smiling' and 'Molly Malone' and 'I'll Tell Me Ma.' 'Carrick Fergus,' perhaps. The album could be called *A Wop from Hoboken Croons the Great Mick Melodies.*"

Lucy, the little priss, stares at me disapprovingly from her toilet seat lid. "That's not okay with you, huh, Lucy? Well, how about just *Ol' Blue Eyes Sings Nice Irish Songs*? Is that bland enough for you, Goose?"

But we'll just have to make do with the music we have. Right now Lucy and I are listening to one of our Sinatra favorites:

When somebody loves you
It's no good unless he loves you all the way.
Happy to be near you
When you need someone to cheer you, all the way.

Yes, Frank, I'd be happy to be near you. I'd be happy to cheer you. We could cheer each other.

When somebody needs you
It's no good unless he needs you all the way.
Through the good or lean years
And for all the in-between years, come what may.

"Nice sentiment, huh, Lucy? 'It's no good unless he loves you *all* the way.' What if he just loves you *part* of the way? What if you just *sort* of love each other, but it's not all the way? What if there are way more lean years than good years or in-between years? What if you're just totally worn down dealing with all the lean years and you need to stupefy yourself with booze every night?"

I don't think Alex loved me or needed me all the way after the initial bloom wore off, and I sure as hell didn't uphold that silly sentiment from my end. Do Mindy and Richard love each other all the way? If not, as Frank says, "it's no good." I wonder. Are you just settling if it's less than all the way? Can't you be satisfied with just *some* of the way? Wouldn't that be good enough?

"Don't worry, Lucy-Goosey. I love *you* all the way. I love you up to the sky and back again and all the way from here to Dublin." She looks at me with just her left eye open.

Maybe instead of her harp music, I'll leave some of my Irish music CDs on next week, on St. Patrick's Day. Lucy and I like The Clancy Brothers and Tommy Makem. We enjoy The Irish Rovers too. Her favorite is "The Unicorn Song." She likes those nice images of green alligators and long-necked geese and humpty-backed camels and chimpanzees. Me too. But I think the little priss finds tin whistles annoying. "Some bogtrotter feline *you* are, kid."

As to Irish stuff, Mindy was glad when I told her that I'd definitely help plan the rehearsal dinner the night before the wedding. *That* I can do. My idea is to have it at Claddagh Irish Pub and Restaurant in Middleton. I hope she'll agree. She probably will. I think she was there once. Alex and I went there a few times, and we liked it. The shepherd's pie is amazing—ground beef and lamb and simmered peas and that incredible crisp mashed potato topping. And the Gaelic Chicken. *Yum!* They have an Irish Mac 'N Cheese dish, too. If I'm PMSing on rehearsal dinner night, macaroni and cheese will be good. It's comforting. That and a few bottles of Guinness.

Fly Me to the Moon

"MORE AGGRAVATION and expense, Lucy. This morning we got our damned bras. Oh, Lord." Mindy and Katie and Julie and Diana and I met at Victoria's Secret at West Towne Mall, and, of course, Mindy decided that we'd get their most popular bra for strapless dresses, the Very Sexy Multi-Way, in "nude." Patty, the sales chick, explained that it's "a gradual pushup bra, so it's not obnoxious. It has no stiff padding. *Wonderful* technology."

My boobs are the biggest of the bunch—36DD. The damned thing set me back fifty-five dollars—the most I've ever paid for a bra, since I usually get them at Walmart or Target. Then, to top it off, we all got no-show seamless panties, also "nude," which cost another $11.50. I can get a *three-pack* of panties at Target for that. Well, if I ever have another boyfriend those hoity-toity panties may come in handy. I'm going to have to wear that silly bra and the wedding shoes at the second visit to Vera's, when the dresses come in and they figure out what alterations have to be made.

Patty must have an interesting work life, focused, as it must be, on other women's boobs: measuring chest sizes, making recommendations, talking about support issues or straps cutting into you, and the like. She herself is fairly well-endowed.

I might like a job like that.

While we were there, I had a fantasy of coming into Victoria's Secret sometime and asking for advice. "This may sound weird," I imagined saying, "but I have an eighty-five-year-old grandmother and I want to get her something *very* special for her birthday next week. She's had a hard life, poor woman. Her husband—my grandpa—was a major jerk and treated her horribly. Thank God he tipped over a month ago, and now she's free. So she's *out* there now. I want to get her something sexy, perhaps some cute lingerie, so she can prance around her house and look at herself in the mirror and have fun. And who knows? Maybe she'll even meet someone that she can wear it for." Patty would smile and nod and make suggestions. "Well, how about our Very Sexy Satin and Chantilly Lace Babydoll? It comes in six colors. Or maybe our lovely Dream Angels Lace Bustier. Or our Very Sexy Lace Corset. Do you know her size?" I'd purse my lips. "Well," I'd say, "that could be a problem. She's five-two and weighs 279 pounds. Would you have anything sexy for . . . a senior citizen of her dimensions?" Patty would cringe and make a face. "HEY!" I'd yell. "Listen, honey, Grandma may be old and fat and ugly, but she's not dead yet and girls just want to have fun, right? She wasn't bad before she let herself go, you know. Now show me some sexy teddies and don't give me any attitude."

Well, my actual grandmother isn't that big. Grandma Liz is short and maybe a bit stocky. She has a huge wart to the left of her bulbous nose. I remember being frightened by that when I was little. She has good, thick silver hair, though, I'll say that for her. We don't see her much, since she lives in Arizona. She has terrible rheumatism, which has gotten worse in the last few years. She has to use a walker a lot of the time. She's nice enough, though I don't know what the hell she and Grandpa Earl, before he expired, did wrong to produce such a self-centered jerk as Dad and such a spiteful bitch as Aunt Grace. I don't know if Grandma Liz will be at the wedding, what with her aches and pains. I doubt it.

I always wish I'd known Grandma Violet better, though. It would be nice to talk with Mom about her. Mindy was too young to remember her at all. I remember that she was quiet, like Mom.

As to boobs, Alex liked mine. He said so once: "Hey, nice bazooms, Mags." I don't know if he ever noticed that one sagged a bit lower than the other. If so, he never mentioned it and I didn't go out of my way to point it out to him. He did ask me once why I had boob sweat. *That* he noticed. I said it was congenital. "All the women in my family, going back to Ireland, had sweaty breasts. It came from an overly starchy diet—too many potatoes and the like." He said he believed me.

Alex. I have to admit that I sometimes miss him. Maybe he was boring, but he wasn't mean.

If he and I'd had a baby, I wouldn't have wanted him in the delivery room. He'd probably have either been one of those guys who faints during the delivery or one who leans over the poor woman and yells, "Push! *Push!*" When I see guys doing that on *A Baby Story*, like I did this morning, it makes me crazy, makes me want to reach through the screen and grab the guy by the throat and say, "Hey you! Yeah, *you!* Shut the hell up. You got her into this mess, and now she's lying there on her back with her legs spread, in big-time pain, and you're just all so nice and comfortable and well-fed, and you have the damned *nerve* to be yelling 'Push!' at her? *Really?* Just sit down and zip your hairy lip."

Maybe the only thing more obnoxious on the show is people taking videos of the baby being born. If it's the baby's father doing it, they stick a little sign on the screen that says "DADDY CAM." Oh, puke. Are you kidding? If I'm lying there in misery—legs spread wide, privates on full display, and an eight-pound child snaking its way out of my stretched-out vajayjay just because it's tired of hanging out in my boring dark womb and wants a little change of pace—the last thing I'd want is the baby daddy or my mother or sister or aunt or some other rubberneck standing at the foot of the bed, pointing a camera or camcorder or phone at my crotch and saying things like, "Oh, what a *miracle!*" and smiling like a fool. "Hey!" I'd yell. "Get that damned thing away from my cooch!"

On *A Baby Story*, they never show the baby actually coming out. It's usually a shot from one side or a view from behind the mother's head, her knees high and far apart and sometimes covered with a blue paper sheet.

Babies. They're everywhere!

Prince William and that way-too-thin Kate Middleton, with those perfect white teeth, are getting hitched later this month. Yet another hoity-toity royal wedding. Yawn. Of course, they'll have kids, and when they do it'll be another huge royal event. Bells will ring all over the kingdom, and limeys everywhere will dab at their eyes and raise a pint and sing "God Save the Queen." Those royals sort of *have* to reproduce, to keep their silly lineage going. Kate can't say, "Well, I certainly understand that Bill and his whole high-falutin' family, including that dowdy little queen, want me to get preggers to make more little princes and princesses, but, frankly, I don't want to. I'm not at all keen about having brats. I quite enjoy shopping and playing croquet and watching polo, but I don't fancy any little pisspots crawling around the palace soiling their disgusting nappies and putting demands on my royal time. Nor do I fancy morning sickness or stretch marks or sagging boobs from breastfeeding. So *sod* off, everyone!"

I guess I'm luckier than Kate. If I don't want kids, it's no big deal. Who's to care? The world will keep on turning quite nicely whether or not Maggie Mullen reproduces.

I'm glad that Alex and I never had a kid. I'm glad he never knocked younger me up. That would have been terrible. I would've been a horrible teen mom. I don't know if I'd have been as scary as Amber or Jenelle or Maci, but it wouldn't have been pretty. Those chicks at least seemed to like being mommies well enough once they were, even though they hadn't intended to get pregnant so young. But I don't think I would have. I'd probably have been resentful and taken it out on the brat: "*No*, I said! No Cheerios today. You had breakfast yesterday, and maybe you'll get breakfast again tomorrow—*if* you behave and I'm not too tired. Now shut up, and leave me alone. I've gotta take a bath and listen to Frank singing 'Fill my heart with song, and let me sing for ever more. You are all I long for, all I worship and adore...'" A *great* song!

And I can only imagine the fights with Mom, the way Jenelle and Barbara always fight. "Oh, Maggie," she'd have maybe said. "I told you that damned Alex was no good. I told you he'd never amount to anything. He should have kept that thing in his pants. How's he going to pay child support delivering pizzas?"

But then again, Mom and I probably wouldn't have fought. She's not Barbara—not at all. We never argue. She's quiet and calm, though, I believe, sad. I can't think of anything she's ever hassled me about. When I told her I wanted to start a cat-tending business four years ago, she just said, "That sounds nice, dear. Do whatever you want. I know you'll like it. I know you'll be good at it." Dad, on the other hand, gave me a decidedly sour look. "*That's* what you want to do?" he growled. "Jesus H. Christ! I can't believe it."

I wonder if Alex's still delivering pizzas. "What do you think, Lucy-Goosey? Has Alex moved up in the world?" But she doesn't have an opinion; she's just chilling, totally relaxed, on her toilet seat lid.

I wouldn't be surprised if he was. When we were going out, he had even less ambition than I did. I remember that once after we'd had sex, in his old bedroom in his parent's house when they were gone somewhere, I asked him what he wanted to do when he was older. He picked up his baseball cap from the floor and put it on backwards, though otherwise naked, and furrowed his brow. "I dunno," he said. "Maybe, like, a cabdriver or somethin'?"

Alex wasn't a bad lover, I'll say that about him. We met when we were seniors in high school and he was my first and, so far, best lover. Not that my experience—seven since him, two of them one-night stands—is that vast.

I was fifty pounds lighter when he and I first started sleeping together. He was a decent kisser, and didn't insist on jamming his damned tongue as far down my throat as possible, like some do. He also didn't object when, the fourth or fifth time we did it, I told him that I wanted to "try doing cowgirl." Sheila had told me about it and said that it was good because if a girl moved a certain way she could control the pressure on her clit, the friction, better than in missionary or doggy or other positions. She was right, as it turned out, though it didn't always work. Maybe half the time. I remember that I asked Alex if he liked cowgirl too, and he said he did but wondered why it was called that. That was maybe the first time I realized how dumb he was.

Sometimes I wonder what my life would be like if Alex and I'd stayed together longer. He moved in with me about two years after graduation, and we lived together for six months. I remember that I sort of felt "in love" with him for a little while. The cymbals clashed. That was an okay feeling, though it didn't last very long.

I'd gone to college at Edgewood, thinking to major in English, but dropped out, totally bored, after a year and got my own place. College wasn't for me. I was working checkout at Sentry, and Alex was making more money and paying half the rent and buying most of the groceries, including his beloved Heineken six-packs. At first it was okay, even nice, to live with him. It felt grown-up. We ate dinner together every night and it was nice to have someone to cuddle with in bed. It was nice, at first, to wake up in the morning and have a man sleeping beside me, even if his mouth was usually partly open and he drooled. But after a while I grew bored. After a while, nothing he said seemed new or interesting, and he began repeating his stories, and I remember not feeling excited anymore when he walked in the door. The sex, too, began to feel repetitive and predictable, and even though I usually liked it, sort of, I remember sometimes—more as time went on—wishing he'd just get it over with so I could go to sleep. I even remember that now and again when we shtupped, I'd close my eyes and pretend it was Ol' Blue Eyes I was doing the deed with. The weird thing was that, in my fantasies, Frank kept his fedora on all the while.

Of course, I never told Alex that I sometimes had to get myself off after we'd done the deed, sometimes in bed but usually in the bathroom after he'd turned over and fallen asleep and commenced snoring.

So if we'd stayed together much longer, it probably would have been bad. I'd probably have started giving him crap about things. "Alex," I'd have said, "didn't you wear that same shirt yesterday?" Or, "I thought you said you were going to clean the toilet." Or, "Did you, like, totally drink the last beer and not get more?" Or, "Why were you talking to that girl yesterday in the Kwik-Trip?"

And if we'd had a kid together, it might have been a disaster. I'd have been on his case about his not changing diapers or not getting up in the middle of the night to see to the screaming brat, or not looking hard enough for a better job to support us—the usual teary-eyed complaints of exasperated young chicks on *16 & Pregnant* and *Teen Mom* who've had to grow up too fast, ragging their sullen and resentful baseball-cap-wearing teenage boyfriends.

But Alex and I broke up after a party when I was tired and a bit drunk and relaxing in the tub, and he came in the bathroom without knocking and sat right down and took a smelly dump in front of me. That was bad enough. But when he wiped himself and examined the soiled toilet paper before tossing it into the bowl, that was it for me.

Well, Alex was usually easy-going enough, I'll say that for him. I remember one occasion after I'd re-read *Sense and Sensibility* and got the DVD of the movie, the one with Emma Thompson and Hugh Grant. We watched it in the bedroom one night after we'd made love. I'd made some microwave popcorn and added extra salt and melted butter. I adore that movie, and was surprised that Alex not only stayed awake but actually said he liked it. Well, what he said was that Kate Winslet, as Marianne, was "totally hot." When I started sniffling at the scene toward the end when Edward tells Elinor that he loves her—"I've come here with no expectations, only to profess, now that I am at liberty to do so, that my heart is, and always will be, yours..."—and Elinor actually showed some emotion, Alex patted my upper arm and handed me a tissue from the bedside stand. Later, he even looked at the Jane Austen books in my bookcase. "So you've actually, like, *read* all these?" he asked, scratching the side of his head.

"What do you think, Lucy-Goosey? Should I have stayed with Alex and tried to make it work? Was I wrong to break up with him? Would you want a daddy?" She just yawns and rests her head on her folded paws, either indifferent to my concerns or, like a good little feline therapist, throwing the question back at me: "Well, what do you think? Do I *need* a daddy?"

Lucy's never had a male human in her life. I got her from the Humane Society eighteen months after Alex and I split up. Getting that girl was the absolute *best* thing I've ever done. A couple of guys have spent the night with me, and I think Lucy mostly resented that because it disrupted her routine and they took up her space on the bed. So we're fine. We're happy. We don't need anyone. If someone comes along—a Larry, perhaps—maybe it'd be okay. But I'm not desperate.

"Relationships, Lucy, they're weird."

They are. Even when you meet someone who seems nice enough, it's a crapshoot. You don't know what's down the road. For that matter, how *do* you ever meet someone who's nice enough, much less someone who's your soulmate, the love of your life? Maybe it's just a matter of luck. Maybe you're standing in line at a Starbucks waiting to order your grande triple-soy sugar-free vanilla latte and you start talking to some guy next to you in line who looks okay, even good—taller than you, nice teeth, wavy hair, a strong face, decent shoulders, dresses okay, acceptable hygiene—and seems at least mildly witty and intelligent. He doesn't have a wedding band on his finger. Your blood runs warm, and you look up at him with big friendly eyes and a coy little smile, and then maybe when you get your coffees you somehow arrange to sit together and talk for a while, and it's nice. You think of a way to give him your phone number and he accepts it, and you go home and hope that he'll call or text, thinking he probably won't. But then he does and, lo and behold, good things happen—maybe even wonderful things. But what if you'd gotten to that Starbucks fifteen minutes earlier or later? Then you'd never have met him, and that damned little dark-haired skinny barista with the perky boobs and Cameron Diaz face and obvious hair extensions and that annoyingly lilting little-girl voice would have maybe snagged him.

Or, let's say you're registering for college classes and you really want to take, say, Shakespeare: The Tragedies. But it's full. In fact, it filled up just ten minutes before you tried to register, and you can't get in, so you sign up for a different course, maybe Nineteenth-Century American Literature, and you miss meeting up with some guy who *did* get into the Shakespeare class—some guy with nice blue eyes like Sinatra or even, dear God, Paul Newman. The two of you might have sat next to each other in a lecture class or discussion session and started talking about *Hamlet* or *Othello*, and you'd have been enchanted. Maybe he would have even been a skillful and considerate and well-endowed lover with whom you regularly had incredible, or at least decent, orgasms. But you missed out on meeting him—*bad luck!*—and now you're alone on a Saturday night eating stale Papa John's pizza and writing a paper on the symbolism of the white whale in *Moby-Dick*.

It's all just chance.

But suppose you and Mr. Shoulders had, indeed, met at Starbucks and he had, indeed, texted you, or vice versa, and you'd have gotten together, and after a while—a few dates—the cymbals would have clashed for both of you. Maybe once you'd gotten to know each other a little better and found you each actually *liked* the other, you would have started to fantasize a future with him. You would have started thinking of him as your boyfriend and you'd have really hoped that he thought of you as his girlfriend, and the sex would stay good enough. And then at some point you'd become an official couple, and there'd be talk of moving in together, and then you would, and next there'd be domesticity.

Soon his razor and shaving cream are in the bathroom next to your tampons and makeup remover. His Hanes briefs and your bras and panties are mixed together in an unruly pile on the bedroom floor. While out grocery shopping together on a Saturday afternoon, you buy refrigerator magnets with cute images of kittens. Maybe you even start thinking that he's your soulmate, that you were meant for each other, that he's the love of your life. For the first year, or maybe a bit longer, you're happy and not usually bored, and it's still exciting. The cymbals haven't completely quieted yet, though somehow they're fainter, and you still think he's The One.

Then you're in a class or at a party or a bar or at work, and you meet someone and make eye contact and talk to him, and he seems interesting enough and seems interested in you, and just then you realize that it's a big world out there with lots of possibilities. Even though you're not really unhappy or dissatisfied or bored with Mr. Shoulders—not yet, anyway—you think about how it might be to be with someone else. You ask yourself if things would be different with this new guy. Might life be better? You like that feeling of the cymbals clashing, and now you have the idea that even though you may like someone a lot and be comfortable enough with him, the cymbal-clashing inevitably dies down after a while. Sure, you still have something nice with him—nice enough, anyway—but it's different than what it was, and things that were once exciting now feel routine, even boring or tedious, and there's a strong part of you that wants to again experience that nice chemical rush that you had before, though, admittedly, with someone else. Oh, that nice rush that makes the world seem just right, that makes you feel like Dorothy stepping out of the monochrome world of her broken, dingy, tornado-tossed house into the Technicolor world of

Munchkinland—an amazing blue sky and yellow and green flowers and a clear blue stream and cheerful little people wearing brightly colored clothes and shoes, dancing and singing happy songs in high-pitched voices, and a yellow-brick road that leads to your heart's desire.

Soulmates. Well, I don't know about that. Alex definitely wasn't my soulmate, even when I felt in love with him. He was just some guy who was good enough for a while, and then that while ended, and I moved on and so did he.

Still, I sort of miss him.

I don't know if I even believe in soulmates—someone who's the one person for you out of all the people in the world, who totally understands and appreciates and cherishes you, and vice versa, and with whom your heart is so in tune. It sounds like a lot of crap. Maybe instead of that, the best you can expect, if you *want* a partner, is to find someone who's good enough, who you can stand being with for more than a few hours after the cymbal-clashing has quieted, who doesn't mind talking about things, who hopefully makes you chuckle once in a while, and who your friends don't think is a doofus. Someone who has more-or-less the same goals as you, including about whether or not to have brats. Someone who isn't a rummy or a cokehead or a wacko. Someone who remembers that you like chocolate -frosted cake doughnuts from Dunkin' and brings you one or a few now and again without your having to ask. Someone who remembers your birthday and the anniversary of the day you met. Maybe even someone with whom you can sit quietly and watch Andy and Opie and Aunt Bee as they sit on the front porch of their Mayberry house on a quiet Sunday afternoon after church, eating homemade ice cream while Andy strums his guitar. Someone who throws an afghan over your feet on a cold night when you're sitting together on the couch watching *Dancing with the Stars* or *America's Got Talent*. Little things.

That's *if* you want a partner. Maybe that's settling for "good enough." Well, hell, maybe settling is what most of us do. What I do I know? Not much, I guess.

I wonder if Marianne in *Sense and Sensibility* felt she was settling for Colonel Brandon. She was crazy about Willoughby until she learned he was a cad, and eventually married Brandon, who was way older. Plus, the reason that Brandon liked Marianne in the first place was that she reminded him of his orphaned cousin, Eliza, for whom he had the hots. That doesn't sound like a great reason to be with someone. I wonder if there were cold nights in

Delaford when Marianne couldn't sleep and looked over at Brandon snoring away, his mouth open and yellow teeth showing, and said to herself, "Oh, sweet Jesus, I should have stuck with Willoughby. He may have had his faults, but, damn it, he was my *soulmate*."

"What do you think, Lucy? Are there soulmates? Would you like one?" She looks thoughtful but doesn't answer. "Am I your soulmate, Lucy -Goosey? You're mine. You're my furry little feline soulmate. You're my one true pointy-eared Valentine kitty."

I wonder if Mindy really thinks of Richard as her soulmate. I doubt it. I imagine she thinks that he *should* be because, after all, he's going to be her husband, and the big idea seems to be that the guy you marry is the absolute love of your life, that you're clearly meant for each other. That's the standard line, and I suspect Mindy will blather words to that effect during her vows: "Oh, yes, Richard, you totally complete me. You're my best friend and the absolute *love* of my whole life. You're, like, totally my soulmate. Out of all the people in the big wide world, we were so lucky to have found each other." She'll utter such nonsense, and maybe some of the guests looking on will dab at their eyes at the sentiment, but I don't know if she believes that herself or has even thought that much about it.

Her big goal since we were little has been to have a glorious wedding where she can be a princess for a day. She's obsessed about her "special day" and planned for it for years, poring over magazines and websites and making lists. She has at least thirty wedding sites bookmarked on her Dell laptop. She has a white cardboard box with at least fifty manila file folders full of wedding stuff, each folder labeled in big capital letters with colored Magic Marker: "INVITATIONS," "REHEARSAL DINNER," "BRIDAL GOWNS", "FLOWERS," "CAKES," "PHOTOGRAPHY." And more. The folders are crammed with cut-out pages from magazines like *Brides*, *Weddings*, *The Knot*, and *Martha Stewart Weddings*, along with printouts from websites and Mindy's notes on light-blue lined paper. She started doing that long before she had a serious boyfriend. Hell, I think she started before she had her first period. So, at some point, given that getting married and having a wedding was her big goal, Mindy had to find a candidate to fill the slot of boyfriend and then fiancé and, ultimately, husband. That's where Richard came in.

They've been going together for three years and living together now for fifteen months. He's nice enough, I guess, but I don't know if she really gives him a lot of thought—Richard the actual human being, as opposed to

Richard the guy out of many possible guys out there who Mindy just happened to meet and started going out with, and at some point decided he was a good enough choice to be the male person she needed to fulfill her big dream.

If it hadn't been him, it certainly would have been some other dude.

Right now, Richard's job description title is *fiancé*, the guy who's agreed, one way or another, to marry my sister and is slated to stand beside her at the altar during her moment of glory when she's dressed in her beautiful gown with the veil and the train, her hair and makeup gorgeous, and everyone looking at her and thinking, *Oh, what a beautiful bride!* Richard's the man who'll dance the first dance with her at the reception as everyone looks on with goofy smiles and the photographer clicks away. On that Saturday in August, his job title will be groom, and Mindy'll be the bride for that happy day that she's dreamt of daily, obsessed about, since before she stuck her first tampon in.

But what about *after* the wedding, when his job title will be *husband*? What about actually being married to this particular man, Richard, for maybe a lot of years when they're husband and wife instead of just bride and groom? Being married to someone is a lot of grueling work. It's a time-consuming business. Hell, *it* is a business. That's just what it is. What about actually sharing a life with him, along with all the daily challenges and tedium that involves? What about having kids with him and going through all the endless hassles and expenses and worries and demands on their time that go with that? What about actually growing older with this guy and seeing his gut get bigger and his chins increase and his hairline decrease and listening to him snore and pass gas at night? What about when he loses his job and gets all down in the dumps and starts drinking at ten in the morning, and now she's worried about how they're going to pay the rent? What about when the marital shtupping gets boring and routine and less-frequent? What about when he needs Viagra or Cialis to get it up? What happens when one of the kids turns into a psychopath and the vice-principal calls the two of them in to discuss educational alternatives? What happens when the kids are grown and gone and Richard and Mindy sit at the breakfast table sipping coffee, trying to think of what to say to each other?

I don't know if Mindy's given all that much thought. If she has, I haven't heard it. I'm guessing she's given a lot of thought to the joys of someday being a mommy and everyone in the world drooling over her darling children, that being the other big role she's certainly dreamt about.

But I just wonder if the prospect of being someone's wife—being in an actual marriage with an actual flesh-and-blood person, as demanding as that is—has taken up much room in her fevered little fairy-tale brain. I doubt it.

"Who knows? Right Lucy-Goosey? How in the hell do you really know anyone, even your own sister?"

Sometimes I think that I understand Lucy and the cats I tend—many of them, anyway—better than my own kin: my sister or parents. I like Mindy well enough, I guess, but sometimes I look at her and wonder, *Who is this person?* Like yesterday. We were having lunch at Panera Bread with Julie and Katie. Naturally, both bitches are thin and pretty, though Julie's maybe *too* thin. We were talking about the invitations for the bridal shower and Katie was saying that the invitations should have information about where the bride is registered, to make it easier for the guests to order gifts. "Good idea," Julie said. I'd ordered Panera's thick tomato soup in a sourdough bread bowl—*delicious!*—and a Classic Grilled Cheese Sandwich. I'd just dipped the end of my sandwich in my soup and was about to take a big bite when Mindy asked me what I thought about Katie's suggestion. I raised my right index finger to indicate "one moment, please," and then, after I'd chewed and swallowed, I said, "Sure. Whatever." For some inexplicable reason, Mindy got red-faced and her chin started trembling and her eyes puddled up. What was *that* about?

But Lucy? Lucy I get. She and I are in tune. I know each of her little moods, and she knows mine. Like tonight, just before my bath. Lucy and I were sitting on the couch, and I was re-reading *Little House on the Prairie*, and had just finished the part where Pa Ingalls gets horribly sick with the fever and ague and has tummy troubles, and I was sad for him, and Lucy looked up at my face and held eye contact for a moment as though saying, "Don't be sad, Mommy. It's okay. I'm here with you. Let's just try to be happy together."

Pa likely had a healthy appetite, at least when he wasn't puking his guts out. Probably all those hard-working Midwestern farmers in the old days did, what with all the planting and threshing and harvesting and fence-building and milking the damned cows and shoveling manure and whatnot. Too bad they didn't have pizza back then. I'm sure Pa would have enjoyed a big sausage-and-pepperoni pie with extra cheese after a hard day in the fields. If Alex had been around back then, maybe he could have delivered it. "Here you go, Mr. Ingalls," he would have said, smiling his crooked smile. "Enjoy. Have a nice day."

Maybe little Mary would have looked up curiously at Alex—before she went blind, that is—and, after Alex left, she would have asked, "Hey, Ma, why did that man have his cap on backwards?" Ma would have shrugged.

Maybe Laura, perceptive as she was, would have immediately intuited how dumb Alex was. Probably she would have agreed with my mother about him. "Pa," she would have maybe said, "if that man gets his girlfriend pregnant, how's he going to pay child support delivering pizzas?" Pa would have taken the occasion to have a heart-to-heart about being safe. "Listen, Laura and Mary, I advise you girls not to have sex before marriage. Your mother and I didn't, of course. Well, maybe once or twice. But if you do, always be sure the guy wears a condom. If he won't, keep your knees together. No rubber, no rub-a-dub. And even that's not enough. You should use something, too. The Pill is good, or a diaphragm, or maybe an IUD. They have these sponges that you can stick in there. Estrogen patches. *Something.* You don't want to be one of those girls who doesn't know they're pregnant and one day, *boom*, here comes a baby when you're sitting in the outhouse shivering on a freezing-cold prairie morning."

I wouldn't mind a pizza tonight. Lucy and I sometimes like to eat in bed at night when we watch TV after my bath, particularly when we watch one of our revenge movies. Peanut-butter-and-banana sandwiches are probably our favorite, and I think she agrees with me that Reduced Fat Skippy Super Chunk goes the best with bananas. Smooth peanut butter's a bit too bland, but still good. The chunks and the banana slices together, though, are a wonderful combination. They're soulmates—perfect together. We like oat-bran bread.

But now and again we like a pizza. Lucy isn't at all particular about that, so I get to choose. I'm usually partial to thin crust with extra cheese, light sauce, pepperonis, and onions. Sometimes, if I'm in the mood, we add anchovies. Lucy doesn't care for those. "Do you, Goose?"

As often as not, the delivery dude from Papa John's is Manuel, a short Hispanic guy with a perpetual three-day growth of whiskers. He has one of those little tattooed teardrops under his dark-brown left eye, which, I believe, signifies gangbanger or prison. He likes seeing Lucy, who always comes out of the bedroom to see who's here. I tip Manuel more than I probably should, because I'm scared of him. I'm scared he might stick a knife in me and steal Lucy and take her back to the gang headquarters, where they'd do unspeakable things to her as part of one of their stupid rituals. "To be a member of thees gang, hombre, you must first deesembowel a *gato*."

If I recovered from the knife wound, I'd dedicate myself to seeking revenge against Manuel and his homies, maybe with the aid of the Legion of Overweight Cat Avengers. Oh, the things we'd do. One option might be to tattoo an image of a sweet, smiling kitten next to their stupid teardrops. I'm sure that would earn them big-time street cred. Or maybe we could borrow a fierce African lion from the Vilas Park Zoo and bring it to their gang headquarters. "So you guys like mutilating cats, huh? Well, let's see you try that on *this* guy."

But Manuel's always non-threatening and polite and smiles nicely, showing a gold upper tooth, and thanks me after I pay him. "Have a good evening, Mees. You and your keety." Maybe I should offer him a Thin Mint or a Caramel deLite before he leaves each time, just to stay on his good side.

Sometimes if I'm horny, I wish Alex would be the delivery guy. I have zero desire for him to be my boyfriend anymore, but a little roll in the hay would be okay. "Hi, Alex," I'd say. "Nice to see you again. How've you been? Listen, I know you have to do more deliveries, but any chance of a quickie first? For old time's sake? Yeah? Great! Let me put the pizza in the oven." Maybe he wouldn't want to do cowgirl because I'm too heavy now. Maybe he'd comment on how much weight I've gained since we broke up. "You know, Maggie," he'd say, "my cousin Shelly did the Atkins diet. It worked pretty well for her. Maybe it'd, uh, work for you, too."

But that's okay. I don't care anymore what he thinks. I just want to use him for a little while. Maybe he wasn't a Rhodes Scholar or a Mensa member, but he was an okay lover. He seemed to know what he was doing, and his thingie was a decent size—neither too big nor too little. I didn't come all the time when we did it, but that's okay. I know how to take care of myself. When we're done, he can leave and finish his deliveries, and Lucy and I can happily go back to watching TV and pigging out on our pizza, even if it's a bit dried from the oven. I'll drink a Diet Pepsi along with my chardonnay. Of course, Lucy will only get a bit—a tiny bite of sausage, a little string of cheese, and certainly no sauce or pizza crust.

Lucy and I are going to watch *Carrie* tonight. "Aren't we, sweet Goose?" It's one of our all-time favorite revenge movies, but we only like the original, not any lame remake. We've seen it at least three times. We can't wait until the prom scene when the bucket of pig blood falls on Sissy

Spacek's head and she goes apeshit and, wide-eyed and blood-soaked, uses her telekinetic powers to wipe out everyone who was mean to her, including Nora, that obnoxious chick who always wore a red baseball cap, even to the prom.

Well, I can't wait. Lucy's probably too nice to like it when bad things happen to anyone, even when they deserve it. Like Rodney King, she wishes we could all just get along.

In the Wee Small Hours

"I'LL TELL you, Lucy, I felt bad for Blue at first. The poor girl didn't have a good beginning." She didn't. She was a six-month old stray, a Siamese, when someone found her living in a corner of a garage in winter and brought her to their veterinarian. She was one of three cats who lived in the vet's office for part of a year before the Drakes adopted her. They said she was a quaking mess at first. Now she's a four-year-old that I take care of twice a year when the Drakes go to visit their bland blond grandchildren in Pennsylvania for a week or so each time.

For the first year I tended Blue, she was an only cat and a bundle of nerves. I'd never see her at all for the first twenty minutes, and then she'd usually make an almost ghostlike appearance from wherever she'd been hiding, slithering silently into the kitchen when I poured some Blue Wilderness Duck Recipe kibbles into her bowl. She'd always look up at me almost fearfully while eating, a bit cross-eyed, unsure of my intent, and then she'd run and hide again. Sometimes I never saw her at all except when she ate, and now and again she didn't even come out for that. I tried talking to her soothingly when I saw her, but to no avail. I even tried a technique I've used before with nervous cats, which is to lie quietly face-up on the floor and let the cat climb on my chest if she wants to. Blue declined.

But that little Siamese underwent a personality transformation when the Drakes got her a companion from the Dane County Humane Society, a huge black cat named Gus. He must weigh close to twenty pounds, but he's a complete and total wuss. Mrs. Drake told me that for the first week Gus was at their house, he hid under a bed. Then when he came out, he never asserted himself in any way. He'd slink against the walls and try to make himself as small and unobtrusive as possible—no mean feat, given his bulk. Blue observed him for a few days, disapprovingly, and then quickly assumed the dominant role of authority figure in their relationship. She took it as her solemn duty to whip poor Gus into shape and became partly a mother, partly a drill sergeant, and partly a nagging, henpecking wife. I never saw anyone change so quickly.

"So this morning, Lucy, Blue and Gus and I were watching *I Didn't Know I Was Pregnant* at the Drakes' house. You'd like Gus. He's just a big old clown. But my God, Lucy, that poor boy is pussywhipped!" He is. We were sitting on the couch and Blue was on my lap and poor Gussie jumped up to say hello, and that little Siamese bitch screamed at him and batted him upside the head and he jumped down and slinked away, tail down, looking defeated. I don't know why he doesn't just pounce on her once in a while and smother the hell out of her. She's a little bully.

Lucy opens her eyes to look at me. "Fine, Mom," she'd maybe say if she could talk. "Whatever you say."

So Blue's horrible a lot to poor Gus. But at other times she's good. After we watched the show, I scooped out the litter boxes and changed the water bowl and watered the plants, and when I came back to the living room the two cats were on the leather recliner in the corner. Blue was furiously, even maniacally, washing Gus's head. Her blue eyes were half-closed and she worked that little pink tongue over the furry surface of his ebony head with the ferocity of a blitzing linebacker trying to get to a quarterback on third and long. I couldn't tell if Gus liked it or just tolerated it. No matter. She imposed her will on him in this as in everything, and he, big wimp, submitted. At one point, he tried to raise himself up so as to maybe jump down from the chair, but Blue hissed and pinned his shoulder down with her left forepaw, and he gave up immediately. What a pair.

I don't know about those Drakes. They make me nervous. Well, *he* does. I met both of them when we had our initial meeting, and Mrs. D—Kathleen—did all the talking. She told me Blue's sad story in a sing-song, high-pitched voice, her small hands fluttering. All the while, Mr. D—Robert—stood to her right, still as a corpse, not saying a word and not even blinking or nodding or moving his long, narrow head—a head that put me in mind of that older priest in *The Exorcist*, Father Merrin, the one who poor little possessed Regan causes to expire shortly after she's projectile-vomited pea soup on his face and cassock and that lovely purple silk sash with the fringes on the bottom. Mr. D. just stared at me with big dark-brown eyes like a hardened detective sizing up an alleged perp in a nasty child abduction case. I half-expected him to say, "So, Ms. Mullen, have you ever had fantasies of kidnapping children and keeping them in a locked room in your basement and feeding them stale bread and corn flakes and making them use a tin pail for a toilet?"

The only time I even recall hearing his voice was when he came into the house about ten minutes after I'd arrived and yelled out a greeting to his wife. "Hi, Kathleen, I'm home," he called from the front entrance, in a mildly bored baritone voice.

"Oh, *hi*, Robert," she chirped back. "I'm in the kitchen with Maggie."

Robert and *Kathleen*, they called each other—not Bob and Kathy, not snookums and honey. I wonder if they're that formal in bed. "Oh, Robert," she might say, "that's good. A little to the left, Robert. Oh, yes, Robert. Right *there*, Robert. Oh, that's nice, Robert." He'd pause from his labors and wipe the sweat from his brow. "I'm glad you like it, Kathleen," he'd say. "Now what about *this*, Kathleen? Is that *good*, Kathleen?"

As usual, I wonder how this pair got together. "What do you think, Lucy? What was the attraction?" But she has no opinion on the matter. She could care less about Robert and Kathleen. She has zero curiosity about them and is, I believe, indifferent to their existence. She's perfectly happy right now in our bathroom, quiet and warm and comfortable on her folded turquoise towel on the toilet seat lid. She's safe and well-fed and sleepy and content. She likes our routine. I believe she does. She lives in the moment.

I look at her, her eyes closed and head resting on her forepaws. The world outside our apartment is of little interest to Lucy. It never occurs to her to speculate about how someone met someone else, what they saw in each other, what they see in each other now, whether or not they're happy enough together or feel trapped, or what the future might hold for them. Those things don't matter to her. I don't think they do. But, of course, I can't get inside her little feline head to really know what's going on there. Nor, I believe, can she get inside mine. We're together and we love each other and we're happy enough with the quiet life we have, but how much can we know each other? It's hard enough to know someone in your *own* ridiculous species, including your pathetic kin. It's hard enough to know yourself. We're in tune, Lucy and I, but there's always a gap.

I guess I'm getting to know my fellow bridesmaids better, though. I knew Katie and Julie a little from Mindy's high school years, but hadn't seen them for a while before all the wedding crap commenced. Now I've seen them at Vera's, at Rocky Rococo afterward, and then again when we had lunch at Panera.

Julie's rail-thin. She looks like she's lost twenty pounds since I saw her when she was younger. She's practically lost her hips and breasts. I don't know how she's going to keep that damned strapless bridesmaid's dress up, with no boobs to speak of. Her face is drawn and pale, and it looks like she wears too much makeup, particularly on her cheeks. She has pretty eyes, though. Sometimes she's animated and talkative and even funny, and she spends more time than she maybe should looking at her iPhone and texting. That damned phone's attached to her left hand. I wonder how she'll get along without it during the wedding ceremony. But at other times she sort of spaces out and doesn't talk much and now and again just stares into the middle distance. I wonder what's going on inside her head then. I'm a little worried about her.

Katie, though, is the same chick she was in high school—giggly, funny, sarcastic, sometimes annoying. She has a habit of tensing her shoulders and opening her brown eyes wide and going, "Oh...my...GOD!" when she wants to make a point. When we were at Rocky after choosing the bridesmaid dresses, Katie was going on and on about her mother-in-law. "That *woman*!" she said. "She is, like, *so* controlling. Scott practically can't take a *dump* without consulting her. Oh...my…GOD!" But I guess I like her.

Diana's my favorite of the bridesmaids. She's short, maybe five feet, and kind of squat and solid. She reminds me of Carla from *Cheers*—that great Rhea Perlman. She has amazing greenish eyes and dark hair. She told me she's thinking of dying her hair bright-red. I love the tattoos on both of her upper arms: a big colorful butterfly on her left, and some Japanese or Chinese character on the right. I'll have to ask her what that one means. She's the middle child, between her brothers—Richard, who's the oldest, and then Mark. When we went to Rocky Rococo, I asked her if she had a boyfriend. She pursed her lips and furrowed her brow and looked at the ceiling for a moment before answering. "I had one. Adam. We went together for about two years. We broke up last New Year's Eve. He turned into a pain in the ass. He wanted me to wear short skirts when we went out, and do other things, too. I'll tell you about *that* sometime. Plus, he had a little dick. He kept saying it was average, but that's a load of crap." She paused. "Anyway, I'm done with men for a while."

I like Diana. I don't have many friends, but maybe she could be one. Maybe she and Sheila and I could do stuff now and again. I'd like to ask her sometime how she feels about her brother and my sister getting hitched, and what she thinks of her brother Mark, the best man. I don't have a high opinion from the little I know him, but maybe I'm wrong. Maybe he's a true prince. He at least needs to change his hairstyle and do something about that horrible goatee.

Diana said, when we were at Rocky Rococo, that she's getting a turquoise bracelet for her mom for Mother's Day, which now is in two days. Mindy and I are taking Mom to brunch at Captain Bill's—great steaks and seafood. I like the Bourbon Glazed Chicken and also the Captain's Tenderloin, which I usually order medium-well. It's topped with lobster tail meat in a lobster-and-mushroom cream sauce. *Yum!*

Part of me wishes I could just be alone with Mom so I could talk to her away from the house, away from my father. I'd like to ask her a few things. She's quiet a lot and just seems unhappy. She doesn't smile much. I want to know about that. Is that how she really feels—unhappy, depressed? She's never been one to talk much, at least to me. I'd like to know why she's stayed with Dad all these years when he treats her so badly, so rudely, and at times almost contemptuously. Has she thought about leaving him? Does she imagine a better life, either alone or with someone else?

Or am I wrong? Maybe she's not as unhappy as she seems to be. I know she likes doing her paintings of ponds and streams. Maybe that's enough for her. Since I was in middle school, she's had the habit of sitting alone late at night in the dark and quiet living room, drinking gin or vodka or, now and again, scotch and soda. When I'd ask if she was okay, she'd always quietly say, "Yes, honey, I'm fine. Everything's okay." She'd *say* that, but I never quite believed it.

It frustrates me that Mom's so closed, so quiet. Maybe she opens up more to Mindy. I don't know. It just makes me sad to think of my mother now, living in that house with just Dad, her daughters grown and gone, and her sitting in the living room night after night with her drink while he's in his damned study upstairs, probably texting cute little history graduate students.

What goes on in Mom's head? And I'd like to know how she'd feel if I never have kids, never give her grandchildren. As of now, I don't think I will. But who knows?

"Speaking of kids, Lucy-Goosey, the episode we watched this morning was weird." As usual, it was about a chick who didn't know she was preggers. She started feeling poorly and wasn't sure what was wrong and sought help and—*oops!*—squeezed out a kid, a girl, and was shocked. Shocked! But then it turned out that her married sister gave birth to a planned baby girl that same day, which the chick found out about later. I didn't see the end of the episode because I had to go potty, but I imagine it ended with the sisters, months later, sitting together on rattan chairs on a nice wooden deck on a sunny summer day, drinking sweetened iced tea in tall glasses through transparent plastic straws while holding their adorable sleeping babies, and talking about how happy they are and how much they look forward to their darlings growing up together and being not just cousins but best friends forever.

So that made me think. Suppose Mindy gets pregnant down the road and is all excited to have her baby and, of course, she has everything planned out and executed down to the smallest detail: a well-thought-out written birth plan specifying, among other things, whether or not she wants an epidural; a room for the baby prepared by her and Richard, probably with twinkling stars and sunflowers and rainbows decorating the walls and ceiling; an IKEA crib with safe side rails; and a matching IKEA changing table. She'll have an ultrasound to find out the gender—*it's a girl!*—and then they'll pick out a fashionable name like Sophie or Olivia or Isabella. She'll buy a whole feminine wardrobe for the kid. Then she'll go into labor and, of course, get to the hospital in plenty of time, maybe with a competent midwife or doula there to help her, and the birth will go smoothly and undramatically. She'll pop out a perfect little girl. Richard, his raised fist pumping high in the air, will dash out to the waiting room to announce the miracle. Everyone will squeal in delight.

I'll be among the crowd in the waiting room, and while Richard is making his announcement I'll feel a nasty pain in my tummy and think I have to go number two. "Excuse me," I'll say, and find a bathroom. I'll sit on the toilet, doing what I can, and finally hear that satisfying plop. I'll feel better, and look into the bowl, and there will be my daughter.

Having seen such situations many times on *I Didn't Know I Was Pregnant*, I'll be nonplussed. I won't get weirded out. I'll calmly extract the kid from the water and dry her off and wrap her in a towel. I'll competently cut the cord with a penknife and tie it into a little knot at her navel. I'll bring the baby out to the waiting room to meet her kinfolk, but most of them will have gone to Mindy's room to see her and her baby. I'll go there too. "What do you have there, Maggie?" Mom will ask. "It's your granddaughter," I'll reply. "Mindy, here's your niece. Corinna. Your baby's cousin." Everyone will just stare at us.

Maybe having babies on the same day would make me feel closer to my sister. We'd have something in common. In summer, we'd pack the brats in strollers and go down to the UW Memorial Union and sit on the Terrace and watch the sailboats on Lake Mendota and eat Babcock Hall ice cream. My favorite's mint chocolate chip in a dish, not a cone, even though the flimsy white plastic spoons they give you sometimes break when you're trying to penetrate the cold ice cream. We'd let the girls have tastes. Students would approach and drool over the kids. "Omigod!" one would say. "They're, like, so *cute*. Oh, what are their *names*?"

We'd tell them that we're sisters and we've always been close and we love each other, and now our daughters, Sophie and Corinna, will be close and love each other too, and we hope they'll both grow up to be strong, capable women, like us, who'll be happy and successful and realize all of their dreams. Those are our hopes.

Hah!

But more likely we wouldn't be all that close. Mindy will certainly have more kids—two, maybe three—and she and Richard will always have a fairly new minivan or SUV with good tires and high-safety-rated car seats for all the children and lots of cupholders and a built-in DVD player in the back seat. As the kids get older, she and Richard will spend a lot of time hauling them to play dates and soccer practice and Mandarin lessons.

Corinna and Lucy and I, on the other hand, will live a fairly quiet life in my apartment. I'll buy a used crib at St. Vinny's, and my baby will have to sleep in my room with Lucy and me since we only have that one bedroom, a small one at that. We won't get out much. We'll watch our revenge movies and I'll certainly read to my child a lot; she'll come to love the Little House books. And I'll talk to her about the cats I tend and maybe tell her stories of heroic toddlers throughout history. But I doubt she'll do Mandarin lessons. Ours will be a quiet life.

Every night, I'll sing my girl to sleep:

I love Corinna, tell the world I do.
I love Corinna, tell the world I do.
I pray at night, she'll love me too.
Corinna, Corinna
Corinna, Corinna
Corinna, Corinna,
I love you so.

But that's only if I get preggo without intending to and decide to keep the kid. Otherwise, being a mommy isn't what I want now. I keep thinking it's what I should want, that somehow I'm not a legitimate woman unless I want to be a mother. I'm an outcast in the great sorority of females throughout the world who mark their sisterhood with morning sickness. Sometimes I worry, too, that I'm not doing my part to keep up with reproduction of the species, which seems to be the main point of all this screwing and swollen bellies and squeezing out babies. But, hell, there're too damn many human beings currently putzing around this world, and what have we done to make the planet such a wonderful place anyway? I don't know if the world needs more cats, but I'm pretty sure we don't need more people.

That aside, I just don't feel that I *want* to have a baby. I feel weird for not wanting that, since most do, and sometimes I wonder if I'm missing something in my brain that so many other women have, if I'm somehow deficient. I probably am. It feels like I am. Well, hell, I know for absolute sure that I'd sometimes like to have a hot fudge sundae with a cherry on top, or a meatloaf sandwich with gravy and yank fries and a butterscotch malt at Mickie's Dairy Bar. But I don't feel the same about having a needy, messy infant.

And I don't get this whole madness about kids, anyway. Aunt Grace once said that being a mother was the best thing in her life—the most important thing she'd ever done. But she didn't say why. Did she feel she had to squeeze out a baby in order to be a real woman? Was it to give her status or acceptance in the eyes of other people—family, society, whatever? Did she need to feel loved by her offspring, or need to feel needed by them, to feed her ego? Did she just want to re-create any good family stuff from when she was young? Or if she had a crappy childhood and a lousy mother, was she trying to make up for that by being a good mom herself? Or was it just for the tax deductions?

Maybe it's mostly instinct. If so, why don't I have that?

Mostly, sitting in my tub with Lucy beside me, I think about all the reasons not to have kids instead of the other way around. Maybe I'd resent Corinna for any bad outcomes of pregnancy and childbirth: swollen, painful boobs that eventually sag from breastfeeding; leaking urine every time you cough or sneeze; sags, bumps, wrinkles and lines; libido out the window. Maybe I'd have horrible post-partum depression and hide my head under my blankets all day and ignore my poor baby.

I don't want to be tied down, not free to come and go as I want. I don't want all the expense and responsibility of a kid. I dread the prospect of feeling overwhelmed and unhappy. I worry about being a bad mother. Maybe I'd resent my poor child for taking up so much of my time and energy. Perhaps I'd be one of those frazzled moms you see in Walmart or Piggly-Wiggly, pushing around a cart piled high with Cocoa Puffs and Pampers and yelling at her brats who are begging for candy and pouting and crying and throwing tantrums when she says no.

And then, of course, I always think of the bad things that could happen to my child—accidents, assorted disasters, diseases.

What's wrong with me? "Can you tell me that, Lucy-Goosey? Why can't Mommy be more optimistic?" But my cat's non-committal. She doesn't see a problem. She likes me the way I am. "Bless you for that, my dear."

Well, I don't know. Maybe I'd be happy with Corinna, at least most of the time. Maybe we'd have fun and I'd be proud of her and I'd love her hugely, like those dewy-eyed new mothers on *A Baby Story* always say they do, and like the new, though unwitting, moms on *I Didn't Know I Was Pregnant* eventually say they do.

I wonder if Mom feels the same as Aunt Grace about motherhood, about how being a mother was the best thing she's ever done. Maybe she's *okay* with being a mother but feels that her paintings are the best things she's ever done. She's never said one way or the other.

Anyway, my prospects for getting pregnant on purpose or otherwise are slim unless I either go the turkey-baster route or do nasties with someone of the male persuasion, which right now I'm not. No one's currently a candidate to fertilize my precious little eggs. If good old Alex isn't available for a little old-friends-with-benefits shtupping, I suppose I could fix up my face and hair and put on something a bit alluring, big though I am, and go bar-hopping with Sheila to see what happens.

But I can't say I'm too motivated. I'm certainly horny now and again, but with all the wedding aggravation I don't have much energy or drive to find a man to scratch my itch. So for now I'll handle my horniness on my own, either right here in the bathtub with my fat fingers or in bed with my trusty purple vibrator, with its three speeds and four pulsating modes, that I bought for $36.95 at A Woman's Touch—best money I ever spent. "Surging" is my favorite mode.

Maybe I'll meet some available stud at the wedding, most likely at the reception. But until then I'll just lie here in the hot soapy water, my sleepy cat nearby, and fantasize about Frank gazing at me lovingly with those amazing blue eyes while he croons just to me, the song that's playing now:

In the wee small hours of the morning,
While the whole wide world is fast asleep,
You lie awake and think about the girl
And never ever think of counting sheep.

Oh, sweet Jesus! Those eyes, that face. I close my eyes and touch myself and imagine Frank, between verses, sweetly and softly kissing my neck and throat and even my earlobes and murmuring, "Oh, Maggie, my sweet little Maggie," and, OH! it's all very nice. My, oh my.

Of course, it's probably weird to be fantasizing about someone who was seven decades older than me and who's been dead for thirteen years and is now just dust. If he were still alive, he'd be ninety-six. I read that they buried him with some Tootsie Rolls, which he'd liked in life. That's something Frank and I have in common. I like the little ones—Tootsie Roll Midgees—best. I always carry a bag of them, along with those little York Dark Chocolate Peppermint Patties and plastic-wrapped butterscotch hard candies, in my purse to snack on during my cat-tending rounds. The chocolate Tootsie Rolls standby is best, but the flavored ones are good too, particularly the lime and cherry. Vanilla's okay.

And it's absurd to think that Ol' Blue Eyes could have ever liked a girl like me. I can't imagine he'd give me a second glance. Who am *I?* No one. Here's this world-famous guy who was married to Ava Gardner and Mia Farrow and probably boffed Marilyn Monroe and no doubt hundreds of other thin bitches, and he'd be in any way interested in chubby old Maggie Mullen from Wisconsin who takes care of cats? Hah! Well, so what? I'm just as entitled to my fantasies as Taylor Swift or Paris Hilton or Jennifer Aniston or any other famous skinny chick, or even that bubble-butt Kim Kardashian. Who are *they*, anyway?

I wonder if Robert and Kathleen like Sinatra. I hope they're having a good time in Pennsylvania with their grandchildren. They have a gaggle of photos in expensive silver frames on a hutch in the living room. Most show the grandkids—two boys, both garden-variety blue-eyed blondes—smiling into the camera. A few photos show the kids posing in blue-and-red soccer uniforms with high white socks on green grass on a summer day. Sometimes it's just the two of them and sometimes they're with their equally bland parents. *Yawn!* I don't know for sure which of the parents is the Drakes' kid, but I suspect it's the daddy because he has Robert's long, narrow Father Merrin head. Maybe his name is Thomas and his wife's name is Elizabeth, and they call each other that all the time, even in moments of passion. No Tom or Liz or sweetie or baby.

Maybe the Drakes would like one of my paintings in their house, if and when I get around to doing that, to balance out the absolute boringness of their family photos. I'd be happy to sell them one. Maybe they'd like a callas lily or a blush hibiscus. "Oh, isn't it *lovely*, Robert?" Kathleen would ask. He'd study it for a bit. "Yes, Kathleen," he'd answer. "I guess so. Very colorful. But, gee, it sorts of looks like...a *vagina*, doesn't it? A nice, moist, budding vagina. Yes, it's very nice, Kathleen. Very nice indeed."

I'm glad Robert and Kathleen have provided Blue and Gus with good homes, I'll say that for them. Whatever faults or shortcomings or eccentricities they may have, at least they've done that. They may be communists or devil worshippers or members of a doomsday cult. Or maybe she dresses in a black leather corset and fishnet stockings and thigh-high boots with stiletto heels and he wears nothing but a studded collar with a leash, and she belittles and insults him and whips him as he crawls on the floor, tethered to the leash, and he calls her "Mistress Kathleen" as he begs for punishment, and she calls him a worthless scumbag. No matter. They've given good homes to two sad, needy cats. So good for them. Maybe they secretly can't stand each other, but they've done right by those felines.

Just before I left this morning, I told Blue and Gus a joke. "Hey, kids," I said. "How come the leper couldn't speak?" Blue looked up at me, cross-eyed. "The cat got his tongue. Get it?"

Come Fly with Me

"WHO SAYS that you can't learn good things from television, Lucy? A person can learn a lot." Today on *A Baby Story* a pregnant young woman had food cravings for Oreos and strawberry milk and french-fried onions. She separated each Oreo and dipped the halves into the milk before eating them. After every few cookies, she'd scoop a handful of onions from the bag and shove them down her gullet. When I saw that, I said aloud, "Oh, what a lovely idea." So I stopped at Sentry on the way home and bought four packages of Oreos and six containers of French's French Fried Onions—original, not cheddar—and a half-gallon of strawberry milk. I sat at my kitchen table before I even took off my jacket and went at it with pretty much the same enthusiasm as the preggo lady. I suspect that chocolate milk would be a marvelous choice as well, and I'll probably try that, but there's no question that Oreos and strawberry milk are delicious soulmates. It brought me back to my middle school days, when I used to come home from school and immediately go to my room and pull a package of Oreos from my bottom dresser drawer. I'd pull each one apart and squirt Hershey's Chocolate Syrup over the white frosting, then put the cookie together and scarf it down in one big bite—sometimes two. I should do that again, for old time's sake.

At least I have more self-control when it comes to eating than some. Last week there was an episode of *I Didn't Know I Was Pregnant* about this black chick who didn't know she was preggers and said that she ate five cheeseburgers and drank a huge Mountain Dew, and then later that day chowed down four slices of pizza. So there's that.

Today was the first time I cat-tended for a pair of lesbians, Annie and Giselle. They'd seen my flier at Steep & Brew and called to ask if I could care for their cat, Meepers, while they went to a music festival in Michigan. I talked with Giselle, and asked her my usual questions: Does your cat nip or claw? Does your cat use the litter box when you guys are away? Is your cat on medication? If so, is he receptive to being medicated by a stranger? "All good," she said. "No problems."

Then I met with them last week to give them my paperwork and get the key and met their guy, a silver-colored Persian of some sort. I love those serious little flat faces. The women were funny. Giselle greeted me at the door with a big hug and a bigger smile. "Maggie!" she said. "Nice to meet you. Want a beer?" I nodded and she shouted to Annie in the kitchen. "Hey, assface. Maggie's here and she's thirsty as hell. Bring some beers. *Hurry!*"

"Miller Lite okay?" Annie yelled back. "It better be, since that's all we have."

The three of us sat and drank our beers in the living room while Meepers padded from one lap to another, including mine. Annie told me they'd gotten got the cat two years ago from a friend of theirs, Lacey, who'd had to give him up when she got a new live-in girlfriend who, sadly, was allergic to cats. "Tough deal," Giselle said. "And now they're probably gonna break up. But Meeps stays here. That's it. End of story." Annie nodded and let out a huge burp.

"Why, what a pig you are!" Giselle said. "It's just a shame that a refined person like me has to be with someone like you. I certainly deserve better." Annie gave her a look, arched her eyebrows, shrugged her shoulders, and burped again, louder than before. Giselle giggled.

They're an interesting pair. Annie's shorter and a bit thick, with short brownish-blond hair and beautiful hazel eyes. She plucks her eyebrows. Giselle's taller and thinner, more athletic-looking, with long brown hair tied back in a ponytail, held in with a red knit scrunchie, and a strong face with big, dark eyes. For all I know, she's a Cherokee.

To my surprise, I heard myself asking how they met. "On-line dating," Annie said. "Zoosk. I didn't come out until I was twenty. I tried Match.com and OkCupid first. They were okay. Got a few dates. But Zoosk is better. Finally, I hooked up with this one. She's acceptable, I guess." She looked over at Giselle and winked.

It's good that Giselle and Annie found each other. They seem to like being together. I like them. I'm glad for them. It's good to have a beer with a client. I'd be okay if more clients burped and farted when I met them. They seem like a good couple. It's interesting how people find each other. On-line dating worked well for them.

But I can't get my mind around this whole deal of so many people working so hard all the time to couple up, like through online dating sites. I guess I can understand meeting someone somewhere and liking them and feeling some chemistry and then maybe starting a relationship, if one's so inclined. That's okay. But I don't get all this *seeking out* someone to have a relationship with. Tens of thousands do that. What do they get that I don't?

"What do you think, Lucy? Why are so many people so into that? Doesn't it seem a little desperate?" As usual, she couldn't care less. "Are people so afraid of being alone, Lucy-Goosey? Is it mostly for the sex? Or do people just want the status of being part of a couple? Do they think the world will feel sorry for them or look down on them if they're single?"

Maybe that's it. Or maybe we're just hard-wired to seek out and have mates in order to keep the species going. Like birds. When it's mating season, like in the early spring, and even now in mid-June, birds call out to each other for a mate. Many do. They sit on a tree branch or a telephone wire and do their little call—the birdie version of "Come fly with me, let's fly, let's fly away..."—and hope that another bird on some other wire hears them and is interested and comes winging around. Birds don't, I imagine, look for great matches, compatibility, shared interests—all the stuff that people go for on dating sites. They don't interview each other as to their views on having children, religion, family values, and so on. They don't check out mate prospects on Facebook to see about their status and their interests and how many friends they have. They don't check out the other bird's Instagram or Twitter accounts. They just need a candidate to make more little birdies with. Probably any bird of the other gender with minimum qualifications will do. Romance doesn't seem to be an issue with them. It's a simple system with simple goals.

Maybe we should be more like birds. Maybe instead of all this furious seeking to couple up with whoever—straight, gay, other variations—people should just sing out to one another when they want or need a partner, short-term or long-term. There could be different tunes for different purposes. If you just want to hook up with someone for some zipless no-strings sex, you could stick your head out the window and belt out a particular song—perhaps "Hot Stuff" or "Afternoon Delight" or Marvin Gaye's "Let's Get It On" or even "I Want Your Sex." If you want romantic doings instead of just a quick hook-up, you could maybe croon out "Love Me Do" or one of Frank's great songs—that nice "Come Fly with Me" or perhaps "Hello, Young Lovers." And if you have bigger things in mind, like a spouse, you could do "Going to the Chapel."

Of course, everyone would have to be on the same wavelength as to the import of the selections. It would be a shame if some guy eating his lunch on a park bench on a nice spring afternoon heard a girl like Mindy a block away singing "Going to the Chapel" and jumped up and ran over to her, all excited, thinking her song to be a booty call and hoping to just get some quick nookie and then come back and finish his ham sandwich and oatmeal cookie, only to discover that what she's seeking is a Richard to someday stand beside her at an altar. Of course, the nookie would happen, and he'd be thrilled at first to be getting that, and certainly grateful for it, and he'd keep coming back for more. Then, in a while, before he knew what had hit him, he'd be trapped and renting a tuxedo and on his way to the chapel. "How the hell did *this* happen?" he'd mutter to himself while walking up the aisle with his new wifey on his arm, she clutching her bouquet to her tummy and grinning proudly and giving out darling little self -satisfied waves to all the guests on either side of the aisle and maybe even sniffling a bit. "Hell, I just wanted to get a little *poontang*," he'd complain to anyone who'd listen.

And it would be just as important the other way around: You wouldn't want some horny broad like me who just wants to get laid now and again singing out for a short-term stud, and then have some dude come sniffing around who mostly wants a wife and kids and a house with a mortgage and a Viking stove and a double-door refrigerator with one of those ice water dispensers, and deck furniture, and a life of tedium, and, after a while, total boredom in the bedroom. Well, the boredom isn't what he'd want, most likely, but it would inevitably happen anyway, sooner or later.

Maybe they could post the song rules in prominent places so as to minimize confusion, like on billboards next to main thoroughfares in every town and city. Maybe the president could appoint Oprah to somehow be sure that everyone in America is aware of what to sing to get just what they want. She could do that, and maybe she could recruit her tall, blah boyfriend, Stedman, to help. What else does he have to do? He has a good mustache, though, I'll say that for him.

I don't know if Stedman's a daddy. I'll have to look that up.

Well, as to that, next Sunday is Father's Day. I'll have to get a card at Walgreens or CVS and think of some lame-ass present for Dad. Coming from me, the card will be disingenuous because they all have warm, positive things to say: "Oh, you're just the most wonderful father in the entire universe, and I'm so *happy* you're my daddy. I'll love you forever and ever." Hah! If I were honest, I'd get a blank card with a picture of a dead fish on the front and write what I really think: "Thanks for raising me and paying for my one stupid year of college, but in my opinion, sir, you're a self-centered jerk and I don't like you much. You treat your wife, my *mother*, like crap. You're rude and dismissive and disrespectful. I don't know why she puts up with your raggedy ass. I wouldn't if I were her. Happy Father's Day. Love, Maggie."

Sometimes I wonder if Mom would be happier if they'd divorced sometime after Mindy and I were born. Maybe it would have been better if she'd been his starter wife. They met and started dating when he was a graduate student at Ohio State and she was a secretary in the history department. They got married after a while and she helped put him through school. Then when he got a job at UW, she worked as a secretary at Madison Area Technical College for a while. After he made full professor and started making good money, she didn't have to work full-time. But at some point, I'm not sure when, things turned sour. He was a big shot tenured prof, a big Civil War expert with well-regarded articles and books to his name. He presented papers at big-time academic history conferences. And who was she? Some mousy little secretary. Whatever they'd once had in common, they didn't anymore. He started treating her like shit at home and in public. I hated it!

So maybe he should've done what other bigshots like him sometimes do: dumped his boring little nothinghead first wife and hooked up with some younger, long-haired beauty from the halls of academia—one with perky boobs and good legs, who'd look up at him with big eyes and laugh at his jokes and feed his ego. "Oh, Professor Mullen, that is so insightful! I just never looked at the Emancipation Proclamation *quite* that way." He'd take her to faculty parties and maybe out-of-state conferences, where they'd shack up. He'd send her witty and suggestive texts and e-mails. In time they'd be an item, and he'd finally ask Mom for a divorce. "I've met someone new, Lillian. You can keep the house."

It might have been hard for a while, but in the long run it would probably have been better for her. She could have moved ahead with her life. Now she's stuck and sad, as far as I can see. I don't know why they stay together. Probably just inertia.

Meepers is a friendly, mellow guy. When I went there this afternoon, he seemed happy to see me. He's a head-butter. "Hi, Meeps," I said. "Aunt Maggie's here. I'm going to feed you and then clean your litter box and bring in the mail and water that weird plant in the living room, and then we'll watch a little TV. Is that a plan?" He listened attentively with nice eye contact, and then butted his head twice against my left leg. I took that to mean that he was okay with my plan.

After he ate his wet food—Friskies Mixed Grill—he went to get a drink and I noticed that he's one of those cats who sticks his paw in the water and swishes it around a bit before he drinks. Lucy used to do that too, but I haven't seen it for a while. "Maybe you'd like Meepers, Lucy. The two of you have something in common."

I think they'd get along. Meeps seems to be one of those fortunate felines who takes everything in their stride. He accepts what comes and seems happy with what each day brings. Maybe he missed Lacey at first, but he seems fine now with Annie and Giselle. They also have a golden retriever, Arthur, who's being boarded while they're gone, and Giselle said that Meeps and the dog are good buddies. They sleep together every night at the foot of the queen-sized bed. So I imagine that Meepers misses Arthur, but maybe not. Who knows what goes on in the feline mind?

After my chores and before Meeps and I watched TV, I checked out the house. It's a modest older dark-green ranch house with two bedrooms, a small kitchen, a living room, and a tiny dining area. The living room's comfortable and has three big stuffed chairs and a small and battered dark-red couch with four assorted throw pillows. None of the chairs match. The best item is a dark-brown wooden glass-covered coffee table with ornate carving on the legs and all four edges. There's not a scratch on it. It looks like an antique, but what do I know? There's a small glass vase with one pink rose in it on the coffee table and a book of photographs, *Immediate Family* by Sally Mann. I've never heard of her. The book has great black-and-white pictures of Sally's three young kids—two girls and a boy—frolicking around the family property in Virginia, often naked and looking directly and unsmilingly into the lens. I really like those pictures. Sally's my idea of a good mother.

There's a built-in wooden bookcase at one end of the living room. It's filled mostly with tattered paperbacks piled up every which way, including a lot of science fiction—Robert Heinlein, Ray Bradbury, Ursula Le Guin. I wonder which one of them—Annie or Giselle—is into that, or if both are. Maybe that's one of the things they had in common on Zoosk. "Oh my God!" Annie maybe said when she saw on her computer or phone screen what Giselle likes to read. "She's into Ursula! Oh, *happy* day."

The kitchen has an old-fashioned wooden table covered with a green-and-white-checked oilcloth. The stove is a pink electric Westinghouse with push-button controls. It looks like it was in-style during the Korean War. It's even older than my relic of a stove.

Their one bathroom is unremarkable, except for the toilet paper. It's simple white paper, but each square has a light-red image of a seated and smiling Mickey Mouse. His big, round ears are prominent. Mickey Mouse toilet paper! How lovely. The first time I saw that, I giggled and I remember thinking that it would be almost sacrilegious to use that paper to wipe one's self. What would Walt Disney think?

Their bedroom is small but tidy. The bed has a lime-green bedspread and six pillows piled up at the head and, surprisingly, two Barbies propped up against one of the pillows. I would have guessed that lesbians would have Carpenter Barbie or Rugby Barbie, but both dolls were dressed in fashionable short dresses and high heels and had painted nails, just like most of Mindy's stupid Barbies.

Three framed photos hang on the wall opposite the windows. In one, Annie and Giselle are standing together on a hilltop in autumn, with orange and red fall foliage in the background. Both are grinning, and Giselle has her arm around Annie's shoulder. That's the only picture of them together. Another shows Giselle and an older woman with silver hair, maybe her grandmother, sitting at an outdoor picnic table. The third is of a group of about a dozen women seated at a long table in a bar or restaurant somewhere, all looking up at the camera, most of them grinning and holding their raised glasses. Annie was one of them, though her hair was blonder and shorter then.

I like checking out the houses of all my clients. It's interesting to see how people live and what they have. But for some reason, I was particularly fascinated by this pair's home. I don't know why.

After looking around, I lay down on their bed and closed my eyes for a few moments. The room was comfortable and relaxing. After a bit, I opened my eyes and saw Meepers standing at the foot of the bed, staring at me. "Come here, Meeps," I said. "Let's take a nap." He hesitated a bit, but then sauntered over. I picked him up and set him down gently on my chest. Happily, he stayed and made himself comfortable. I don't know how long we slept—maybe ten or fifteen minutes—but it was nice there on Annie and Giselle's bed. Their bedroom has good vibes.

"I wonder what it's like to be a lesbian, Lucy?" What's it like to make love with someone who has the same body stuff as you? A man's a different thing than a woman—usually bigger, more muscular, and all angles instead of curves. No boobs. Hair all over, including his butt. Skin isn't soft. His equipment down there's totally different, and strange; that thing keeps getting bigger and harder and then smaller and softer. It keeps changing from a worm to a dragon and back. It has a life of its own, it seems. Sheila once joked that a penis is a handy thing to have at a picnic. I nodded, remembering the awkwardness of trying to pee in the woods when I was a kid. Then he has those ugly testicles hanging down in that wrinkled hairy sack of skin. Yuck! Plus, he's all closed up down there, which seems weird. A man's stuff is interesting for a little while, I guess, and it can make you feel good, but it's still strange.

A woman's different. She's all softness and curves and, "down there," mysterious folds. A man can just look down anytime, like when showering or peeing or whacking off, and see all his stuff, but we have to lie back and use a hand mirror to see our vajayjays. Cooches live secret lives. They hide out down there between our legs, like ground squirrels. But they can get all soft and wet and enthusiastic. They open like flowers. That's a good thing.

It might be nice, I think, to be with a woman—at least to try that. It would be interesting to see if someone who has the same body parts as me would be a better, more sensitive lover considering that she has those same parts. Would she be better at making me feel good than your average man? Could I do the same for her? And what about kissing? Kissing is good. I like softer, gentler kisses, but a lot of the guys I've been with aren't into that. They kiss too hard, like the Nazis blitzkrieging Poland, and some of them shove their damned tongues as far down my throat as they can. It's like they're drilling for oil. I've noticed that the hard kissers are also usually the ones who do that uncomfortable jackhammer thrusting during sex. And not many of them spend time doing soft, slow kisses on my neck, face, ears, nose, and shoulders. I like those. I fantasize about Frank doing those. I have to think a lot of other women are like me in that way and would be better at giving and liking to get softer kisses.

Alex was a pretty decent kisser, except that he liked to lick my teeth with his tongue. Maybe he thought there'd be traces of Oreos stuck between my teeth.

I have to think that a lesbian or a bisexual woman would be better at finding a clit, for that matter. Some of the men I've been with couldn't find mine with a GPS. They fumbled around like Ponce de León trudging through the Florida swamps searching for the Fountain of Youth. One guy I spent a night with, Anthony, kept saying, "Where is that damned thing?"

When I asked him what he was referring to, he said, “You know, the whaddyacall, the man in the boat.” I don’t remember if he found the damned thing.

And what about the G-spot? If you have one of those elusive dealies of your own—and I’m not sure I do—can you find another woman’s more easily?

Well, I don’t know if I’ll ever do that—be with a woman, or even just kiss one—but it’s interesting to think about. Maybe I’ll ask Sheila what it’s like. She once told me she’d crossed that bridge a few times in college.

I wonder if Annie and Giselle were always lesbians or if either of them liked men first. “What do you think, Lucy-Goosey?” But she’s a sleepy girl on her turquoise towel.

I think they’d tell me if I asked them. They’re open, I think. They seem forthcoming. With a lot of my clients, I fantasize about asking them about their personal lives, but that’s as far as it goes. I’d like to interrogate them and find out what they think, what they feel, what their inner lives are. I want to know if they’re okay with their lives, desperately unhappy, or somewhere in-between. I want to know their dreams, their frustrations. I’m too damned nosy, I admit. Way too nosy. But I’ve never felt that interviewing, probing, was ever an actual option with any clients, except maybe Larry some day—professional boundaries and the like. Plus, I’m shy when sober. It’s a business relationship to them, nothing more. I’m just there to care for their cats when they’re gone. That’s it. Who am I to them?

But with this pair, based on our first meeting, I feel like it could be more than just business. Maybe we could be friends. Maybe I could stop over after they came back from the music festival to return their key and get my check, and they’d invite me in. “Want a beer, Maggie?” Giselle would ask again. We’d guzzle a few Miller Lites and play with Meepers and Arthur and make small talk, and maybe after a while Annie would pull out a stash. “Hey, Maggie, do you, uh, smoke weed?” I’d nod enthusiastically. Pretty soon we’d get the giggles and then the munchies, and one of them would toodle off to the kitchen and come back with a big bag of Keebler Chips Deluxe Chocolate Lovers cookies or Little Debbie Honey Buns, which we’d quickly polish off.

“So tell me,” I’d say. “Have you guys always been carpet munchers?” I’d probably phrase it better than that. They’d both laugh and tell me their stories. Maybe Annie would say that she used to sleep just with guys, having lost her virginity in her junior year of high school, and then discovered girls one magical moonlit night when she was nineteen, and for a while did both, and finally decided to go just with women and came out to her parents the next year, which was awkward at first. Eventually her mother came around, but her father—they're divorced, most likely—had a tougher time with it. Giselle, on the other hand, would maybe say that she'd known she was a lesbian since she was five years old and has never known a man in the biblical way. "I've never even *kissed* a man," she'd assert. "And I doubt I ever will. *Yuck!*" Then she'd lean over and plant a soft wet one on Annie's lips while gently stroking her hair.

"So let me ask you guys something," I'd say. "What do you like about each other? What do you get out of being a couple?" We'd start with that and see what happened. I bet they'd yak quite a lot.

"Hey, Lucy-Goosey," I say, taking a big sip of my chardonnay. "Here's a little tune for you."

Bells will ring,
The sun will shine.
Oh, I'll be his and he'll be mine.
We'll love until the end of time,
And we'll never be lonely anymore.

Because we're going to the chapel,
And we're gonna get married . . .

She seems to like it. "What a crock, huh Goosey? They'll 'love until the end of time.' Hah! If they get two good years, I'll be surprised." After that they may stick together but one or both will eventually start peeping around corners to see who else's around.

And they'll "never be lonely anymore"? Oh, give me a break. Everyone's lonely. Me and everyone else. That's just how it is. Maybe being with someone good can make you feel a little less that way for a while, and that's fine, that's good, but you're still basically lonely in the long run, even if you're part of one of the greatest love affairs the world's ever known: Romeo and that little twit Juliet, Antony and Cleopatra, Prince Edward and Wallis What's-Her-Name, Bogie and Bacall, Amber and Gary. Well, not them.

And it's like they say: If you're lonely and single, tomorrow's another day; if you're lonely and married, tomorrow's the same day.

Anyway, I hope that Annie and Giselle help make each other a little less lonely for a while. Hopefully a long while. I hope they're winners in the crapshoot of relationships. I hope they're even soulmates, if things work that way. I'll drink to that. "Right, Lucy-Goosey?"

After leaving Annie and Giselle's and before going home, I stopped at Hubbard Avenue Diner for a piece of their magnificent key lime pie. I was sitting at the counter when that interesting Kat Grammy came in and sat next to me and ordered lemon meringue pie and decaf coffee. I recognized her from the PDQ. Her dyed hair looked to be even redder than when I'd seen her then. She wore a purple dress with a yellow scarf. When our orders came, she and I ate in silence. I wanted to ask her about herself, what she did. I was thinking what to maybe say when our server, Vivianne, came by and asked us how our pie was. In a lower voice than I would have expected, Grammy said, "Way better than I deserve, honey, I'll tell you that."

I was trying to work up the nerve to talk to Grammy when some ugly little doofus on the other side of her started giving lip to Vivianne. "Hey," he said, "I ordered this burger medium-rare. This is rare, for Chrissake. Take it back and cook it some more, huh? And I'm in a hurry here, too, so c'mon." Vivianne mumbled something—I couldn't understand what—and took the man's plate away and headed toward the kitchen.

"Excuse me, young man," Kat Grammy said, leaning toward the doofus and staring directly into his eyes. "Your manners are significantly in need of improvement. I suggest that you learn to talk to people more politely and respectfully. Do you understand?" His face turned red, and he nodded. "Good," Grammy said. "Enjoy your medium-rare burger."

After he ate and left and she was about to leave, she turned to me and said, "If any of my cats behaved that badly, they'd get a lecture and maybe a well-deserved time-out."

We talked briefly, and it turns out that she does what I do. She's been doing it for thirty years. "And I don't intend to stop until I drop dead or my mind goes. My cats need me. And I need them, honey. I *really* do."

She had to go, but we exchanged phone numbers and agreed to get together some time after my sister's ridiculous wedding. Maybe I can learn from Kat Grammy.

The Nearness of You

"WELL, LUCY, at least the damned bridal shower's over. Thank *God*, huh, Goose?"

At least it wasn't horrible. I didn't have to do much except show up. Aunt Grace planned it and handled all the details and hosted it, leaving me off the hook entirely. Bless her soul for that, though I've never had any use for her otherwise. Mindy worships the ground Grace stomps on, but I know her for who she really is: a controlling, sanctimonious, spiteful, thin rich bitch who'll smile at you so very nicely, with professionally whitened teeth, while twisting the knife she's just plunged into your back. I wish I had a dollar for every little cutting passive-aggressive remark about my weight that she's made to me over the last few years. "Oh, Maggie, where do you get your clothes? Do you know about that wonderful boutique for bigger girls near the Middleton post office? Oh, what's it called, anyway?" Or, "So what diets have you tried, Maggie?" I should have said, "Well, Aunt Grace, I don't recall that I've ever indicated to you that I've *been* on any diets. So why do you ask?" But, overall, I try to have as little to do with her as I can. What would be the point?

The shower was okay. It was at Grace's huge four-bedroom house in that hoity-toity Enchanted Valley Road neighborhood, the house she kept when her lawyer husband, Uncle Edgar, finally wised up and ditched her. Now she and Toni and Grace's sallow-faced boys, her two youngest kids, live there.

Besides the bridesmaids and Toni and Mom, there were maybe thirty assorted women at the shower. I didn't know most of them. My main job was to get there early and then greet the guests as they arrived, with a big phony smile on my face and a disingenuous, "Oh, nice to see you. Thanks so much for coming today."

A good thing about the deal was the catered sit-down plated dinner from Gaylord's. I had the Ranch Stuffed Chicken Breast, which was filled with a wonderful herb cheese, bacon and broccoli filling, and covered with an amazing champagne cream sauce. *Yum!*

After the meal, during coffee and dessert, it was time for the gift orgy. Toni helped Mindy open each one and kept a written tally in a blue spiraled notebook. Mindy said she liked my gift, a set of toasting flutes with intertwined crystal and silver hearts and an engraving with the names of the happy couple and their wedding date. I got it at Things Remembered at West Towne Mall. It set me back $118, after which I went to Auntie Anne's Pretzels and treated myself to a jumbo soft pretzel with cheddar cheese dipping sauce. When I'd finished that off, I considered getting another but thought better of it. I don't know whether that set of toasting flutes was the right choice, though Mom said that she loved it.

I'd toyed with the idea of having the people at Things Remembered engrave something special on the glasses: *Let's hope and pray that you two don't get sick and tired of each other too soon—that you have at least a few good years before everything goes to hell.* When I told that to Diana at the shower, she laughed. "I gave them some stupid linens," she said. "But later I thought I should have gotten them a bagel slicer. You can get 'em at Bagels Forever, and they're handy little dealies. Did you ever try to slice a bagel with a knife? Half the time, you cut your damned fingers and you can never slice both halves evenly. My blah brother likes bagels, but he's so dull that he always gets plain ones—not onion or egg or sesame or chocolate chip. I bet your sister's the same. Maybe a bagel slicer would expand their limited horizons." She paused. "Or a heated toilet seat. That would be a good gift. There's nothing worse than getting up in the middle of a cold winter night to pee and having to plop your bare ass on a cold hard toilet seat. Am I right?" I nodded.

The best part of the whole silly event, though, was meeting Grace's new cat, Nefertiti, an Egyptian Mau. Naturally, Ms. Enchanted Valley *would* have an expensive purebred cat; no commoners or no-account strays for *her*. That aside, I liked Nefertiti. She's a smaller, sturdy girl with bronze-colored fur and black spots on the tips of the hairs on her coat and incredible green eyes that appeared to change to turquoise from time to time as I looked at her. She has a long dark stripe that runs along the length of her spine from head to tail.

Nefertiti rubbed against my leg during the gift orgy as I sat by myself in a corner, and I reached down to stroke her head and neck and back. As I did, she closed her pretty eyes and vocalized loudly with little chirps and chortles, and wiggled her striped tail furiously. I laughed out loud when she did that, and half the women turned to stare at me, some with their brows furrowed. One, a tall and thin strawberry-blonde with visible dark roots and a face like the wicked witch's in *The Wizard of Oz*, turned to whisper something to Aunt Grace. I can only imagine what she said: "Oh, Grace, isn't that the maid of honor, Maggie, your brother's strange older daughter? And she's sitting alone in a corner laughing at nothing during her sister's bridal shower? Well, that's a pity. Poor Warren and that pathetic Lillian must be mortified. What a shame that your lovely Toni isn't the maid of honor."

Well, maybe I am strange, maybe I'm heavy, and maybe my face isn't ever going to adorn the cover of *Glamour*. But at least it isn't hideous, like *that* broad's. "Am I right, Lucy-Goosey? Hmm? Do you think Mommy's hideous? No? Oh, good. I think you'd like Nefertiti, Goose. She's funny."

As to other wedding events, thank God Mindy agreed with my idea of having the dinner for her upcoming bachelorette party at Johnny's Italian Steakhouse in Greenway Station in Middleton. The food there's great, but the main selling point is its Rat Pack theme. They have a bunch of framed pictures on the walls of Frank and Dean and Sammy, most of them either singing or yucking it up, usually with Sammy grinning hugely—that lopsided grin of his—and doubled over with laughter, sometimes holding a lit cigarette in one hand. His white teeth and oiled hair gleam. Some pictures are stills from their movies, like the original *Ocean's 11* or *Robin and the 7 Hoods.* I've seen both multiple times and, of course, the magnificent *From Here to Eternity*. I always get misty when Frank's character, poor Angelo Maggio, expires in Private Robert E. Lee Prewitt's arms.

Robert E. Lee. Dad would like *that* name, I'm sure.

A few photos also include guys like Peter Lawford and Joey Bishop. I don't know what their contribution was, but it must have been something. I think Lawford, with his Kennedy connection, got women for Frank—"broads," in Sinatra's parlance. So why didn't Lawford give me a call?

And, of course, Johnny's plays a lot of the famous Rat Pack songs—"That's Amore" and "New York, New York" and "I've Gotta Be Me" and the like. So if I have to go through this nonsense with Mindy and her bridesmaids and other friends, I at least want to be able to listen to Ol' Blue Eyes and look at his sweet face. The only sadness is that all the photos are black and white, so I won't get to see those amazing eyes in their natural glory.

We'll likely start off with an appetizer, maybe grilled focaccia bread or Johnny's Toasted Ravioli, and then have our salads and entrees. I like the nine-ounce Chubby Cut Top Sirloin or the Johnny's Filet Medallion trio, all with parmesan crusts. I know that Mindy likes the Johnny's Chicken Parmigianino, with focaccia crumbs and fresh mozzarella. And, of course, we'll have a few stiff drinks. I'm going to need a *lot* of stiff drinks for that occasion—maybe a half-dozen vodka and tonics, heavy on the vodka and light on the tonic. And then, of course, dessert. Johnny's has a Roasted Banana Cheesecake that's to die for, and the tiramisu cake and crème brulee are also heavenly. *Yummy!*

I'm curious to see how Diana handles her liquor at the bachelorette party. Mindy, when she drinks, gets either weepy or sarcastic, depending on the topic and her mood. If it's anything sentimental, like nonsense about romance or babies, she gets that misty-eyed, blubbery-faced look with the trembling chin I've seen so often, and commences sniffling, and her voice escalates to a higher register. She does this thing where she blinks her blue-gray eyes about a hundred times a minute when she's emotional. It makes me want to vomit. I like her better as a mean, snarky little drunk. I remember when she and Richard had been to Katie's wedding reception, and Mindy was half-plastered at the end of the night, and she was ragging him about how he didn't slow-dance with her enough. At one point, red-faced and eyes half-closed and her hair askew, she slurred, "Well, at least I didn't have to shmell…*smell*…your stinking armpits…or have you shtomping on my damned toes every two seconds, you big hairy *ape*." *That* I liked!

My guess is that Katie's an obnoxious or funny drunk, and Julie's probably a sad drunk, but I wonder about Diana. Ever since her "pain in the ass" remark at the bridesmaid dress session at Vera's, I've liked her. Maybe she's one of those women who gets quiet and sinks into herself when she's had a few, and you don't know what's going on inside her head, and she just stares at you unblinking for the longest time and finally blurts out some cutting remark. "Well, well," she might say to one of the partiers, her upper lip curled into a sneer. "*You're* a pretty little thing, aren't you? Are those boobs your own or did your *daddy* buy them for you?" Or she might be the type who'll get all ribald later in the evening, after the dinner and when we're bar hopping. "So, Julie," she'd say, giggling, "what's, like, the weirdest place you've ever done it? Does your boyfriend have a huge one or is it one of those little *golf pencil* dealies?" And if Mindy wants a male stripper as part of her bachelorette party, maybe Diana, with a few drinks in her belly, will be the boldest of our merry group. She'll be the first to volunteer to grind and hump with him, all the while shaking her chest and wiggling her little butt and waving her arms and yelling "*Woo-hoo!*". She'll stick multiple dollar bills down the front of his thong, each time gazing seductively at his face, her eyebrows arched and her sexy little tongue running over her pouty lips.

Anyway, the damned bachelorette party will be in three weeks, so I've got to finalize our plans. Mindy said she wants the last place we visit to be Plan B, a gay dance bar on Williamson Street. But I have to work on the gag gifts, the limo, and maybe other bars to go to. The whole deal's a pain in the butt. At least it'll be an occasion to have a few drinks. More than a few.

Well, hell, I'd much rather think about the cats I take care of than the silly bachelorette party. As to cats, Lucy and I saw an interesting new show on Animal Planet called *My Cat from Hell*. "Didn't we, Goose? It was good." It just started in May. It's about a weird guy, Jackson Galaxy, who's a musician by night and a cat behaviorist by day. He goes into people's homes and helps them with their tough cat problems: cats who snarl at and bite their owners and visitors, cats who pee all over the place, cats who can't get along with other cats or dogs in the house, and the like. Difficult, frustrating situations. Jackson talks to the people and analyzes each situation and gives them advice and homework assignments. He understands cats—what they need, how they feel, what goes on in their heads, their motivations—and knows how to change their behavior.

The first episode was about a young couple, Hannah and Johnnie, who had trouble with one of their cats, Bear. Bear was aggressive and unpredictable and acted hostile and threatening to their other cat, Monkey, and their dog, Frankie. Hannah and Johnny's relationship was in big trouble because of the stress Bear was causing all of them. Jackson came up with a plan. He advised Hannah and Johnny to play with Bear with cat toys in order to use up Bear's "predatory energy" and also to create high places for him to spend time—cat trees and, even better, elevated walkways so he can "circumnavigate" the living room and not always have to be on the ground, where he was, according to Jackson, overly vigilant and unrelaxed. He also had them talk to Bear more soothingly and attentively and to touch and stroke him a certain way, on the cheeks, so the cat could spread his smell to its humans. After Jackson did his thing, Hannah and Johnny and Bear and Monkey and Frankie all got along much better. Their troubles were behind them. They were a happy little forever family with nothing but blue skies ahead. *Hah!*

I like Jackson. He's a strange dude. He shaves his head and has sculpted sideburns and a great pointy, well-trimmed beard. There's a little horizontal unshaven area between the bottom of each sideburn and the upper edge of the beard on his cheeks. He has earrings and incredible heavily tattooed arms. He wears glasses with thick green frames. He carries a battered guitar case to every house, and it's filled with cat treats and toys. He's great with people and their cats. I wonder if "Jackson Galaxy" is his real name. If not, he chose a good one. I can learn more about cats from his show. What's interesting is that this guy seems so comfortable with his weirdness, how he looks. He goes into people's homes and helps them with their cats, and his bizarre appearance doesn't seem to matter at all. He's fine being who he is; he doesn't need to be different than who he is. I like that.

"So, Lucy, Jackson calls people who have cats the 'guardians' of their cats—not 'owners' or 'masters'. So I guess that's what I am to you—your guardian. I don't own you. Are you down with that?" She seems to be. She doesn't want to be owned, and doesn't want to own anyone or anything. She doesn't even want a collar. But can a cat's *guardian* also be that cat's *mommy*? Well, why the hell not?

I probably need to tell Sheila about Jackson Galaxy's perspective on this issue. She always refers to herself as "a responsible pet owner" because she picks up after her ugly little brown cocker spaniel, Hector, when he's pooped on his walks. I like Hector, but he's not the brightest bulb in the canine world. He consistently falls for the old fake-fetch-toss trick and then sits on his haunches with a confused *what just happened here*? look on his face. Well, maybe Sheila can start calling herself a "responsible pet guardian." That has a nice ring to it.

Sheila called this morning and asked if I wanted to go with her and her boyfriend, Lou, to the Fourth of July fireworks tomorrow night at Warner Park. I told her I'd think about it, lying that I haven't felt all that well lately, and that I'd let her know tomorrow. But I don't want to go. For one thing, the traffic afterward's a horror story. It takes half the night to get home. For another, I don't get fireworks. They're interesting for about three minutes and then boring as hell. I can't stand being with all those snot-nosed kids and their parents who are always going, "*Ooooh! Ahhhh!* Oh, look at *that* one. Oh, look, Billy and Susie. Oh, see? Oh, goodness, what wonderful colors! Red and green and yellow! Oh, isn't that one *amazing*?"

Plus, I don't particularly like Lou. He's a sullen guy with an unflattering buzz cut who used to play football at one of the smaller state universities—Whitewater, I think, or maybe Platteville—and I don't think he treats

Sheila all that well. She told me that if he gets mad at her for something—usually something trivial or stupid, like forgetting to pick up his stuff at the dry cleaner—he sometimes gives her the silent treatment for a day or even longer. That's not okay. So the hell with him, as far as I'm concerned. I don't know what she sees in the guy.

More to the point, I don't like to be away from Lucy on the night of the Fourth. People in the neighborhood shoot off fireworks, and she gets frightened. "Don't worry, Lucy-Goosey. I'm not going to leave you alone and scared while these numbnuts make nasty noises. Mommy, your faithful guardian, will take care of you. After our bath tomorrow night we'll close all the windows and get into bed and turn up the TV volume, and you'll get some catnip to celebrate our country's independence. Independence is good, right?"

It is. *My* independence is good. I'm glad I'm not with a guy like Lou. I'm glad I'm independent of controlling jerks like him. I feel bad for Sheila. But maybe there's more to Lou and to their relationship than meets the eye. Maybe he's really sweet when he's not pissed off at her. Maybe he really loves her and is considerate and caring, bringing her breakfast in bed on weekends, even if it's just a Big Breakfast from McDonald's—the one with the three hotcakes and that little plastic syrup packet in addition to those disgusting scrambled eggs and the run-of-the-mill hash browns and that bone-dry biscuit. Who knows? But I doubt it. People who do that silent treatment thing are usually difficult and controlling in other ways too. My father, for example. No, thank you.

On this silly overblown holiday, I worry about the cats I'm tending. I worry that they'll be scared by the fireworks. All they hear are loud, scary noises, and their guardians won't be there to comfort them. The cats don't understand what the noble occasion is. Even if they did, I doubt they'd care much. Ideas of country and government and taxation without representation and chucking perfectly good tea into a harbor don't matter to them. If I told them about Thomas Jefferson and Ben Franklin and George Washington, they'd probably wonder if those guys had been kind to animals. If they hadn't, none of their other virtues or high-faluting ideas about holding truths to be self-evident, blah blah, would matter.

It'd be nice if I could take all my cats from their homes tomorrow and gather them all together in a big house somewhere in the country, far from the noise, until the next day. Or maybe we could all go to the rich old lady's mansion in Maple Bluff, the one who'd take in all the abused cats that my hefty friends from the Legion of Overweight Cat Avengers and I rescued. My cats would mix with the rescued cats, which would, hopefully, expand everyone's horizons. Maybe we'd invite Nefertiti. Perhaps some or all of the Avengers would be there. We could invite Kat Grammy. She'd come wearing one of her colorful outfits—maybe something with a red, white, and blue theme—and her red hair would be bright. We'd celebrate the holiday in our own way. No loud noises. First, all the cats would get a special holiday meal—maybe the highest-quality Science Diet wet food served in individual little dishes with a side of kibbles. Then they'd all take naps on individual pads while digesting. We'd play gentle harp music for them while they slept.

Later, we'd tell the cats the story of the Fourth—what it's all about—but in a very abbreviated way, considering their short attention spans. We'd have to boil it down to about twenty seconds or less: "King George was a naughty man, and crazy too, and we didn't want to be friends with him anymore, so we started our own country and built the Statue of Liberty and welcomed poor, tired kitties from all over the world who were yearning to breathe free. The end."

After that, we'd play a recording of Kate Smith singing "God Bless America" and we'd all—the old lady and the Avengers and Kat Grammy and I—put our arms around each other's shoulders and sing along, patriotically swaying from side to side and waving our right arms high at the end: "God bless America…my home, swe-e-t *h-o-o-ome*!" I think the cats would like that.

Then we'd turn on Animal Planet, and any cats who were interested could watch *My Cat from Hell or Cats 101*. Maybe when watching the latter, some of them would recognize their breeds and learn interesting facts and feel proud of their heritages. And finally, we'd pass out fresh organic catnip so everyone could feel elevated. Then all the felines would go to sleep, exhausted from the festivities, and we members of the Legion of Overweight Cat Avengers would cap our holiday celebration with some alcoholic spirits and pleasant snacks—perhaps those nice little eat-with-a-toothpick cocktail wieners swimming in a hot mixture of grape jelly and barbeque sauce; bacon-wrapped chestnuts; and, certainly, assorted sandwiches on oat bran bread, including turkey and ham, roast beef, and for some, though not me, liverwurst. For those few prissy Legion members on diets, we could have finger sandwiches, perhaps including grilled-cheese-and-pickle sandwiches on pumpernickel bread, as well as tea sandwiches with ham, watercress, and mustardy cream cheese.

Of course, if we're going to mix together a diverse group of cats I'd have to be sure that my charges would be okay. Jake should be fine. He'll just sit on his haunches and stare at everyone, taking it all in. Maria might look around for Carlos, and maybe feel disappointed not to see him. But hopefully, she'd be okay by the time we passed out the catnip. Blue and Gus might have a hard time, though. I imagine they'd be nervous at first and would stick together pretty closely. Blue would have to guide Gus through the whole deal and manage his social niceties. If he got out of line in any way—eating another cat's kibbles, trying to climb the drapes—she'd hiss and her blue eyes would narrow and she'd whomp him upside his black head with her right forepaw. The worry would be that Blue would take it upon herself to supervise some of the other cats as well and make them toe the line. That could be a problem. Suppose Meepers or Bella or Bupkis took a dump on the old lady's Persian rug and Blue got all weirded out and commenced screaming at the offender in that high-pitched Siamese voice, and some other cats took exception to her thinking that she was the boss, and they faced off. All the other cats would choose sides pretty quickly. All those green and yellow eyes would widen and the pupils would dilate. Their fur would puff out so they looked bigger. Ears would turn back, tails would be down, and claws would come out—in those that still had claws. We'd have to turn the harp music up higher to calm them.

Perhaps Miss Kitty, sitting serene and Buddha-like on the best chair in the house, could be a calming influence. Maybe she'd deputize Chester and Festus to keep order.

"What about you, Lucy-Goosey? Would you want to be with all the other kitties on the Fourth of July, far from the nasty fireworks? Or should you and I just stay home, like we planned?" She opens her eyes and glances at me.

When I started my bath tonight I shaved my legs, and Lucy sat up on her toilet seat lid perch and stared the whole time. Something about that ritual fascinates her. Living the quiet, sheltered life that she does, I really don't know how she'd react to being around a bunch of other cats. I imagine she'd be nervous. So we'll just have a quiet Fourth, Lucy and I.

In bed after our bathtime tomorrow, we should watch something patriotic—maybe *Braveheart*, where Mel Gibson and those other fierce, long-haired, skirt-wearing guys from Scotland paint their faces blue and show contempt for their enemies, the English, by bending over and raising their kilts and exposing their pale bare butts. That wasn't a smart move, because the English archers promptly loosed hundreds of arrows, some of which punctured those lily-white Scottish asses. *Ouch!*

Well, maybe we'll watch one of our revenge movies instead. Maybe it would be a good day to watch *Death Wish* again. Charles Bronson's character, Paul Kersey, is a mild-mannered architect in New York City. One day some jerks break into his apartment and beat his wife and rape his daughter. The wife later expires and the daughter becomes catatonic. So Kersey takes the gun he got as a gift from one of his clients and blows away an assortment of thugs and lowlifes—probably nine or ten scumbags in all—before the cops catch him and quietly send him to Chicago. They don't want the public to know that the vigilante's been caught so that the bad guys in New York will keep thinking that he's out there looking for them, and there'll thus be less crime.

Lucy and I are good with the whole concept. If someone broke into our apartment and hurt us, we certainly hope that someone we know—Mindy or Sheila or Larry or even Diana—would be a vigilante and track down the bad guys who hurt us and deliver some serious hurt back. We don't wish death on anyone, but *something* bad should happen—maybe break an arm or a leg.

Well, Lucy probably doesn't even wish that on anyone. She's a softie. She thinks that if you just put some rehabilitation on criminals and psychopaths they'll change their ways and be as gentle as bunnies. "Don't you, Lucy-Goosey?" That's what comes from living an isolated life in a little Midwestern apartment and spending your evenings sitting on a closed toilet seat lid and listening to romantic songs, like the great one that Frank's singing now, and not experiencing the big wide world. Like I do. *Hah!*

Larry's probably not temperamentally suited to be a vigilante. But if he were, maybe he could do interesting things. He might bring his barber's scissors and clippers and razor with him as he stalks nasty assholes on the mean streets, and when he catches them he could handcuff and leg-shackle them and shave all the hair from their heads and bodies, then slather them with some kind of evil-smelling lotion that would make them itch like crazy for two or three weeks. They could make a movie about his exploits and call it *Scratch Wish.* If the cops caught him and made him move to Chicago, I'd visit him. It's only a few hours away. We'd go to Millennium Park and Navy Pier in the summer and watch all the happy little couples strolling about arm-in-arm, so very much in love, and speculate about their bleak futures together. We'd crack wise about their dreary sex lives down the road.

Well, I hope that Mindy and Richard don't have a bleak future together. Their silly wedding's just over a month away, and then their married couple future starts. Yikes!

At least the second bridesmaid dress event at Vera's is done now. The damned dresses came in, and Mindy and we bubbling bridesmaids went to get them pinned so that the seamstresses could "fit" them. I had to plunk down the balance for the stupid dress. We had to wear our new shoes and our new Victoria's Secret bras so they could tell how our bustlines fit. "Not bad," Lydia, the woman doing the pinning, said to me. I don't know if she meant my boobs in general or the way they looked in the dress or my overall character. "Not bad" isn't exactly high praise, but at least it's better than "Horrible!" or "Oh, my God, I've never seen anything so *disgusting* in my entire life."

And the shoes! Mindy chose silver-colored Lyric sandals by Touch Ups for us. They're ridiculous, and I hate them, but at least the heels are modest—they're not four-inch stiletto horrors. And at least Diana and I are on the same wave length about the Lyric shoes. "Do you think your sister will notice if I come to her silly wedding wearing my worn-out moccasins?" she whispered to me as we were leaving Vera's. "I could tell her that some drug-crazed hoodlums mugged me and stole the lovely silver sandals as I was walking around the Square one midnight to break them in. Think she'd believe me?" She paused and shook her little head. "What a pain!" she said.

I prefer being alone in my little home to having to deal with dresses and shoes. Before my bath tonight, I looked around our apartment. I like it. I like that it's small and simple. My living room is about the size of Aunt Grace's master bathroom. My little battered couch and burnt-orange armchair and messy desk and four-shelf bookcase that holds my *Little House* and Jane Austen books and others are all I have in there, not counting one of Mom's nice paintings, of a tranquil pond with about a dozen water lilies here and there and a frog resting on one of the lilies. If I ever do my flowers-that-look-like-vaginas watercolors, I'll hang a few of them in my apartment. I'd like to get one or two framed photos from that photographer whose book I saw at Annie and Giselle's house, Sally Mann. It would probably be weird to have pictures of her naked and unsmiling children in my home, but the black-and-white photos are so great. If the kids were smiling, I wouldn't be interested.

I love my bedroom, too. If I had to fit Corinna's crib in there, it'd be a tight squeeze. And there'd be no room for any fancy-schmancy IKEA changing tables, what with my double bed and my battered brown dresser and my TV and DVD player taking up most of the room. Two more of Mom's watercolors are all I have on my bedroom walls, other than a framed photo of my parents and Mindy and me at my sister's high school graduation. Last year I put a piece of gray duct tape over Dad's face in the photo after he'd been particularly rude to Mom at Thanksgiving. "My God, Lillian," he'd complained, "can't you even cook a damned *turkey* right? And why the hell did you put cranberries on my plate? I've told you a *thousand* times I don't like cranberries. Can't you remember *anything*? Christ Almighty!" Maybe someday I'll get around to removing the tape if I ever feel more generous toward the jerk.

And I like my little kitchen. It's not even a separate room, just a sort of hallway between the living room and bedroom. My electric stove and refrigerator are ancient, and not pretty, but they do what I need them to do, and without a lot of ego or calling attention to themselves either. That said, maybe it *would* be nice, someday, to have one of those stainless steel Viking stoves. It would be a touch of class.

If Aunt Grace ever saw my humble kitchen, she'd probably turn up her nose in disgust—that shnoz that looks better now than it did three years ago, thanks to a nose job. And that wasn't her only improvement. Her face has been tightened, and I believe her ass has too, though I don't know that for sure. I wouldn't be surprised to hear that she's had her labia prettified. Well, no matter. Nothing any plastic surgeon can do could improve that broad's rotten personality. "So, Maggie," she'd said at the shower, "are you going to the gym once in a while before the wedding?"

The hell with you, Grace. And the hell with your huge Enchanted Valley house, with its many obscenely huge rooms and four-and-a-half bathrooms with sparkling-clean toilet bowls and hoity-toity brass fixtures and the toilet paper hung with that ridiculous under-the-roll method. And the hell with your crapload of expensive, well-upholstered furniture and the chandeliers and your walk-in-closets and vaulted ceilings and perfect Oriental rugs and shiny hardwood floors, and the kitchen with the breakfast nook and that ridiculous oval island and the quartz counters and the high-end cookware hanging on hooks. Screw your flawless maple five-piece bedroom set in the master bedroom, where now—*hah!*—you sleep alone, with the perfect matching bed and nightstands and dresser and that huge mirror that you have to look at yourself in, and no doubt the eight-hundred-thread-count sheets on your lonely bed. And the hell with all those many fancy Impressionist prints on your walls, Manet and Monet and whoever-the-hell else.

I'll take my apartment any day. I like its size, and I like it that it takes me maybe ten minutes to clean it—*when* I clean— with the old blue Eureka EZ Kleen upright vacuum cleaner that I bought at St. Vinny's for $10.75.

Aunt Grace, I'm sure, hires a crew of people to clean her damned mansion, and it must take them hours and hours. I'm sure she supervises them and rakes them over the coals, her fixed nose pointing toward the vaulted ceiling, if they don't meet her exacting standards for cleanliness. "Consuela, you've left *streaks* on the living room windows! Now do it again, and this time I want that glass to *sparkle*."

I like having a place that's just mine, that I don't have to share with anyone. I like not having to answer to anyone, not having to please anyone except Lucy. "And you're easy to please, aren't you, Goose? You have very modest expectations, don't you?"

I liked some things about living with Alex, but there were times, I remember, when I resented another person in my living space. And I hated having to share a bathroom with him. That was terrible. If I ever live with a man again, we'll *have* to have separate bathrooms. That's non-negotiable. Any maybe separate bedrooms, too, except for occasional shtupping or cuddling. "I'm happy to share a bedroom with you, Goose, but that's it." Except maybe if Corinna comes along. Well, hell, maybe even separate *residences* with any future partner, as I've thought more than once, would be the way to go.

"Hey, Lucy-Goosey," I say, leaning in toward her while propping my fat forearm on the edge of the tub, my floppy breasts flattened against its side. "This Frank song is for you."

It's not the pale moon that excites me
That thrills and delights me. Oh, no.
It's just the nearness of you.

It isn't your sweet conversation
That brings this sensation. Oh, no.
It's just the nearness of you.

"The nearness of you, my sweet Goosey. That's *just* what it is."

Young at Heart

I WISH I would have been chosen to be on an episode of *What Not to Wear* so I could pay for all this wedding nonsense. It's ridiculous. In addition to paying for that damned strapless Bill Levkoff bridesmaid dress with the stupid ruching and the alterations, I had to dip into my savings for the bra and the shoes. And I'll have to pay for getting my hair done. Hopefully, Mindy won't want us to go to Macy's or Boston Store to get our makeup professionally done on the morning of the wedding by those smock-wearing, heavily-made-up chicks in high heels who work at the Estēe Lauder or Clinique or Chanel counters. Some of them look grotesque, with all that crap on their faces. I don't know how much that'd cost, but I'm sure it's not cheap. Plus, I had to pay my part for the damned bachelorette party earlier tonight—the dinner at Johnny's and my alcohol and the limo and the drinks at the various bars we went to, and my gag gift for Mindy, and all of Mindy's food and liquor. Damn! I'm going to have to pay for our hotel room, mine and Mindy's, even though I chose not to stay. If this continues, I'm going to be eating cat food along with Lucy. Well, yes, the other bridesmaids kicked in, but still.

If you're on *What Not to Wear*, you get $5,000 to buy a new wardrobe. Before you get that, though, you have to be willing to be humiliated. You have to stand inside a 360-degree mirror and explain what you like about your current wardrobe and why you think your clothes look good on you. Then you have to put up with Stacy and Clinton snarking about your current fashion choices—the what *not* to wear part. "So, Maggie," Clinton would say in his mildly condescending, affected tone. "I understand that when you go to meet with your clients for the first time, you often wear a blue denim jumper or blue jeans. Is that right?" I'd nod. "And your idea is that blue is a comforting color, that your clients will think of you as the girl next door?" Again I'd nod.

"*Well*," Stacy would say, looking down her nose, her plucked eye-brows arched, "the idea of blue jeans is to make a girl's butt look good. You know that, right? But Maggie, that is *not* working for you. You're a bit too, uh, well...*full-figured* for those jeans that you squeeze yourself into."

After unceremoniously tossing my unacceptable jeans and denim jumpers into a trash can, she'd suggest something more flattering for my future client visits—perhaps a gray-striped pantsuit and a sensible pastel-colored blouse. I'd have to go along with their critiques and suggestions for my improvement and admit that, yes, they're right: I *desperately* need to change the way I dress and the way I wear my hair, along with my makeup choices, in order to advance my career and be a better woman all the way around—the kind of woman people would love to hire to care for their cats and, more to the point, a woman who'd be more likely to land a man and not be alone for the rest of her pathetic life.

I'd put up with their nonsense and with the camera crew following me around just so I could get the five-thousand-dollar gift card. I'd use it to buy a nice wardrobe in the various New York stores they'd suggest—Ann Taylor, H&M, Bloomingdale's, Montmarte, New York & Company—and I'd put up with the hair and makeup styling makeovers. The hairstylist would probably gag over my usual brown ponytail and suggest chopping off most of my hair and doing a short, stylish bob with subtle blond highlights. I'd also have to endure that little angelic makeup artist's running commentary about what shade of lipstick I should wear to go with my skin tone, and how nicely I'd profit from plucked eyebrows and a little foundation and blush and lip gloss, and how such-and-such a shade of eyeliner will just *perfectly* accentuate my lovely brown eyes. I'd even have to put up with the finale of the show, wherein all my family and few friends would gather together in a hotel or restaurant and I'd sashay in wearing one of my new outfits and maybe a pair of Jimmy Choo heels while showing off my updated hair and makeup—*Here's the new and improved Maggie Mullen!* —and they'd all clap their hands to their mouths and jump up and down and some would pump their upraised fists and scream and they'd go, "Oh, my God! Oh, Maggie, you are *so* beautiful!" And I'd smile proudly and pose and primp and slowly turn my body so everyone could see how great my ass looks, thanks to Stacy's and Clinton's well-informed suggestions.

But then when it was all over, I'd go back to my old nondescript hair style and I'd quickly schlep all, or at least most, of my new clothes and shoes to a high-end women's clothing consignment store—maybe The Pink Poodle on Odana Road—and dump them off. I'd use whatever money I got to buy a few more pairs of blue jeans and denim jumpers and to pay for my share of my sister's ridiculous wedding. I'd also buy Lucy a special treat, maybe some high-end catnip.

I'd also like to bring some special treats to poor Bella. She looks like she doesn't have much time left. Her brown fur's matted and ragged, and her yellow-green eyes seem more listless all the time. She looks like Grizabella in *Cats*. I half-expect her to break out in a poignant verse of "Memories." She's seventeen and has lymphoma and digestive problems. I have to give her liquid medicine every day, sticking a syringe into her mouth and squirting a milliliter of Lactulose down her throat, which she understandably hates. Plus, she has to take daily steroids, prednisone, and some kind of cancer med, all packed into little brown chewable tuna-flavored treats that were compounded at Hoey's Pharmacy. Poor girl. I feel bad for her. She's so frail, just skin and bones. If she weighs six pounds, I'd be surprised. When I go to her house—Mr. Randall's house—I spend as much time as I can sitting with her and stroking her bony back and talking to her. When I first met her three years ago, she had a fine appetite and loved her little meals and always scarfed down her food as fast as she could. Now when I put her stainless steel food bowl on the floor, she sniffs at it and then looks up at me for a moment, thinks about it, and then takes a few bites, almost reluctantly, almost as though she's eating to please me.

After she eats, I lie on my back on the brown leather couch and Bella crawls onto my chest and we chill. She closes her eyes and I gently stroke her head and thin back and tail. I talk to her and sometimes sing to her. I sang quietly to her this morning:

Fairy tales can come true
It can happen to you if you're young at heart.
For it's hard, you will find,
To be narrow of mind if you're young at heart.

You can go to extremes with impossible schemes,
You can laugh when your dreams fall apart at the seams.
And life gets more exciting with each passing day,
And love is either in your heart or on its way.

Bella may still be young at heart, but her poor little body's old and sick and tired. Still, she closes her eyes and seems content when I stroke her and sing to her. I love Bella a lot, and tell her that many times at every visit. I know

I'll miss her when she goes, but even so I hope she goes quickly, one way or another, before she starts suffering too much, before her quality of life diminishes too much. I wouldn't mind if she just faded away quietly one day while lying on my chest as I sang Sinatra to her. That would be an okay way for her to go. She'd ascend to the Heaviside Layer, like Grizabella, to be reborn. Everyone should die with someone who loves them touching them, stroking them, and singing lovingly to them. Well, I probably won't. I'll probably expire alone in my apartment or some miserable nursing home—neglected by the aides, soaked in my own urine. But not dying alone is a nice thought.

"I'm angry at Mr. Randall for leaving Bella alone now, Lucy. It's just so wrong."

I don't know what the hell's so important that he has to leave her alone for a week or so twice a year. He never told me where he goes, but one of his trips is always around this time of year, late July. Maybe he has an almond-eyed, long-haired girlfriend in Rio de Janeiro who has one of those great Brazilian butts, and they stroll the beach at sunrise and sing samba songs. She'd likely wear a skimpy lime-green string bikini, with the lower halves of her sweet round cheeks spilling out, and he'd wear a disgusting black thong bathing suit that, with his gut bulging over and his pasty skin on full display, would nauseate all the girls from Ipanema toasting themselves on the beach.

Or maybe he's a Civil War re-enactor and goes down to Virginia to be a Confederate soldier in the Second Battle of Bull Run. If so, I hope some Union re-enactor sticks a bayonet in him, though avoiding any vital organs. Well, I don't hope that, but at least they could take him captive and send him to some horrible prisoner of war camp where he'd get fed one stale baloney sandwich a week and have to wear the same raggedy clothes for a year, and where he'd get bit by thousands of flies and mosquitoes and gnats and have to deal with brutal, sadistic Yankee guards who'd make him stand naked in the rain and sing "Dixie." Probably it's mean for me to think that, but it's just wrong for that man to leave such a sick cat alone for so long. I'd *never* do that if Lucy were that sick. I couldn't live with myself if I were that self-centered and inconsiderate.

If Mr. Randall at least e-mailed or texted me each day to ask how Bella was doing, I'd have some respect for him. But no. His poor aged cat's apparently out of sight, out of mind. Well, who knows? Maybe he's actually a good guy who's visiting his ill mother in Nebraska or some other godforsaken place. Or maybe he's a divorced daddy who's going to visit his two sad children in Oregon or Texas. I should give him the benefit of the doubt. I should take the high road. But that's hard. I keep thinking about poor Bella, sick and alone except when I go there twice a day for a little while each time.

I look over at my sleepy Lucy on her turquoise towel and think that she's a lucky girl. "You are, Lucy-Goosey. Don't worry. If you get sick, I'll never leave you alone."

I wonder if she'd be okay if we took Bella to live out her days with us. I think she would be. I'd be fine with that. It'd be hard, in a way, because maybe Lucy would get attached and then Bella would be gone and Lucy'd be alone again. But maybe she'd accept that and feel comforted that she'd done what she could to brighten the last days of a poor fellow feline.

Perhaps when Mr. R. comes back, I'll broach the subject with him. "I have an idea, sir," I'd say. "How about if I take Bella to live with me? I'd be *glad* to." He'd look at me askance, his brow furrowed, and ask why I wanted to do that. "Well," I'd say, smiling, "it would free you up to spend more time with your Brazilian friend. Wouldn't you like to do that? I'm sure she's a lovely person. Maybe the two of you could even take a nice side trip to Peru to visit Machu Picchu. Oh, wouldn't that be special?"

Of course, what I'd *like* to say is, "Look, Randall, you're a crappy cat daddy, so maybe you should just get your pathetic ass on a plane down to Rio and shack up with that dusky bitch with the big tush and pork her until she gets totally bored with you, which won't be long, and dumps you for some younger dude with wavy hair and good shoulders and pecs, whose gut isn't hanging over his bathing suit and who can actually get it up once in a while without Viagra. A thong's the last thing you should be seen in, buddy! By the time you get back, poor Bella will be gone and it won't matter that she was with Lucy and me."

Anyway, I'm *so* glad that damned bachelorette party is behind me. What a *relief!* It's lovely to be home now, in my clawfoot tub, soaking the alcohol out, with Lucy next to me. I put a little Aura Cacia Body Soak Soothe with lavender and sweet marjoram in the tub. It smells and feels nice. I like lavender. I'm smoking a joint to relax. It's three in the damned morning. I just got home half an hour ago. It was so lovely to see my Lucy-Goosey when she greeted me at the door. But I'm exhausted.

The dinner at Johnny's was good, except that we had to wait at the bar for fifteen minutes until our table in the back room was ready. There's a wall of liquor bottles behind the bar and, for some reason, the whole deal's illuminated by obnoxious blue lights. Plus, the same color lights are on the underside of the bar, so that when you sit or stand there your lower legs and feet are bathed in blue. It's just a sea of blue, and by the end of my second vodka and tonic I thought I was hallucinating a thousand bluebirds flying around looking for places to nest. But the meal was wonderful. I had the Johnny's Filet Medallion Trio, medium-well, all with the parmesan crusts, and garlic mashed potatoes. Diana, who sat next to me, thank God, actually ordered the Johnny's Veal Sinatra. Bless that little woman's precious little soul. She and I mostly talked to each other while Julie and Katie and Toni and the other six fluffheads bantered with Mindy. One of them, Jessa, asked Mindy if she was going to get a bikini wax job before the wedding, as a "special treat" for Richard on their wedding night. Mindy said she was thinking about it. "Oh, *do* it," Jessa urged. "I got one, a full wax, and Randy *loved* it. He said it was a whole new me."

Diana looked toward me and rolled her eyes. "If I ever think about ripping the hair off my twat to please some man, shoot me," she whispered. "Don't ask any questions, just shoot me and dump my body in Lake Mendota."

I don't understand what's so special about a wedding night anyway. It's not like anything will be new for Mindy and Richard when the reception at the Concourse is over and they take the elevator upstairs to the Governor's Club Room, their precious little honeymoon suite. It's not like she's a virgin—a desired prize, that he's been waiting so very patiently for the opportunity to finally deflower, all the while taking cold showers and reading the Bible to divert his lustful thoughts. That pair's been boffing for years. Just because some witch doctor mumbles words over them and they sign some papers, and the Catholic Church and the State of Wisconsin gives them their solemn blessings, how will that make their wedding night sex special—different from all the other hundreds of times they've shtupped? Even if Mindy wears nothing but crotchless thong panties and does an alluring bump-and-grind in the middle of their hotel room, waving their marriage certificate in her little left hand, now adorned with her lovely gold wedding band, how can anything be all that novel?

As usual, I wonder what it is that I don't get that everyone else seems to.

Aside from the food and drinks, maybe the best thing during the dinner was that I got to stare at a large framed black-and-white photo on the far wall of Frank and Dean and Sammy and Lawford. I believe it's from *Ocean's 11*. Sammy's standing at the far right, bent over a bit, intently examining something. Maybe he's reading a racing form or even a book. The other three are standing behind a pool table holding upright cue sticks in their hands and Frank, at the far left, is saying something to Lawford and Martin. Frank is *so* handsome. He's probably saying, "Hey, either of you guys know where we can get some broads?" I wonder what Sammy's reading, if that's what he's doing. I don't imagine it's a biography of Winston Churchill, but what do I know?

While staring, I fantasized about playing pool with Ol' Blue Eyes. "What do I *do*, Frank?" I'd ask innocently. "It's easy, sweet Maggie," he'd say, his amazing blue eyes warm and sparkling. "The object is to put the ball in the pocket. Here, let me help you." I'd bend over the green-surfaced table with my cue stick in hand, and Frank would lean over me from behind and put his hands over mine as I positioned the cue. His body would press softly against mine and I'd feel his sweet breath on the back of my neck. Our faces would be close. "That's it," he'd murmur, pushing the cue forward slowly. "Just like this, Miss Maggie. We want a smooth, steady stroke here, right?" Yes, Frank. A steady stroke. That's certainly what we want. "Thanks so much, Frank," I'd say, smiling sweetly and looking directly into his eyes while subtly chalking the tip of my cue for the next shot. "I think I've got it now." But then I'd deliberately muff that next shot, sending the cue ball directly into a corner pocket, for a "scratch." "Oh, Frank, what did I do *wrong?*" I'd ask, my brow furrowed and nose crinkled and mouth curled downward in a feminine little pout. "No problem, my love," he'd reply. "Here, let me show you again how to hold the cue."

A funny thing was that one of the servers came in while we were eating and saw me staring at the photo. Somehow she got onto the subject of Sinatra, and told us that there's an eccentric silver-haired older woman who always comes to Johnny's every year on Frank's birthday, December 12th, with her son. They have dinner. The son is always dressed in a blue suit, crisp white shirt, and a red tie. The woman goes around to every table in the place to enthusiastically announce the joyous occasion to the patrons. Many people, the server said, find her annoying—an intrusion, I suppose, into their precious dining experience. Well, the hell with those people. I'd love it if I were there and that woman came around. We could talk about our favorites of Sinatra's songs. Maybe we'd sing "Happy Birthday" to his ghost.

Hell, maybe I'll *be* that old woman someday.

And of course, the other good thing was the music they piped through the place while we ate. Frank sang "Chicago" and "Come Fly with Me," and Dean did "You're Nobody 'Til Somebody Loves You"—a sentiment that, in my opinion, is a major load of crap. Hearing Sammy sing "Candy Man" made me miss my Lucy, though. It's one of her favorites. "Isn't it, Goose?" I raised my glass and blew a little kiss in her honor when they played her favorite verse:

Oh, who can take tomorrow,
Dip it in a dream,
Separate the sorrow and collect up all the cream?
The Candy Man.
Oh, the Candy Man can.
The Candy Man can 'cause he mixes it with love
And makes the world taste good.

Some of the other six fluffheads, not including Toni, had been high school friends of Mindy's, like Julie and Katie had. The others were friends from college. "Oh, my God," one of her high-school BFFs, Kiersten, said. "Remember how *drunk* I got at prom? I, like, totally threw up all over my boyfriend's car. He was *so* pissed!" I remember Kiersten. She apparently has many fond memories of upchucking because I recall her once talking about how drunk she got and much she puked when she turned twenty-one, and she and Mindy and a few others had gone out drinking and dancing at the Crystal Corner. It had been a momentous occasion in her life, a rite of passage, because she could finally get into places without her fake ID.

"Maybe later she'll choke on her own vomit and we can go home early," Diana whispered to me. "I wouldn't mind that."

I understood. Diana's an outcast, pretty much excluded in this crowd. These other chickies have a history together with Mindy: in-jokes and glorious stories of shared youthful good times and wild adventures and high dramas. The only reason Diana's a bridesmaid is because she's the groom's sister. I'm only slightly less of an outcast. But I don't think our status bothered either of us. Diana was happily munching her dessert—a turtle cheesecake with chocolate ganache frosting, creamy caramel and chopped pecans. *Yum!* I'd ordered the magnificent Roasted Banana Cheesecake, which was topped not just with an unbelievably delicious brûlée of fresh bananas but also—*thank* you, dear God!—with salted rum butterscotch. "Let me tell you something," Diana whispered, licking her lips. "This is better than sex."

The rest of the evening after Johnny's was exhausting.

"For what it's worth, Lucy-Goosey, I'd rather have been here with you." She opens her eyes and looks at me, as though to say, "Thanks, Mom. I missed you too. Please don't go away in the evenings anymore. It's our time together, you know. Do what you have to do during the day, but we should be together here in our bathroom and then our bedroom, you and me, every night of our lives."

After the dinner, we all piled into a white limo bus and went bar-hopping. Mindy had by then donned a green sash with "BACHELORETTE" in red letters, along with a cute little plastic crown with a veil. As soon as we were all seated, facing each other, one of the fluffheads, Brooke, passed out plastic necklaces with little flesh-colored rubber penises strung on them, which we all had to wear. Penises and other things that go into vaginas were a big theme of the evening. Lauren, a short chick with a silver nose ring and a streak of purple on the left side of her light-brown hair, announced that we were going to play "hot potato," and immediately produced a huge rubber dildo from her purse and waved it around while going "*Woo!*" Lauren explained the rules and started the music. We passed the dildo around, most of the chickies giggling and one, Sammi, opening her mouth wide and sticking the thing in and licking it with her ugly little tongue. Yuck! When the music stopped, Kiersten was holding the dildo and was "out." It went on like that until we were all out except Kimmy and Katie. Lauren started the music and the two of them furiously passed it back and forth between them for twenty seconds or so. When the music stopped, Katie was holding the dildo. "Oh, yay for *me*. I *win!*" Kimmy squealed in a high-pitched Betty Boop voice.

Lauren announced that Kimmy's prize would be the dildo. "What are you going to *do* with it?" Julie asked.

Kimmy looked at her, then stared out the window and furrowed her brow and pursed her thin lips and thought for a moment. "Well," she said in her little girl voice, "I'm just gonna pleasure myself all night, every night, until I, like, can't walk anymore. *That's* what."

Almost everyone was glad when I opened the big flat box of Gigi's mini-cupcakes and passed them out. "Here you go, ladies," I said, taking a big bite of a Triple Chocolate Torte. "Here's to a long and happy life for

Mindy and good old What's-His-Name." Julie was the only one who declined. That worried me. Why in the world would anyone *not* accept a free cupcake, mini or maxi? It seemed unnatural. Kiersten took two cupcakes, an orange-frosted one and a chocolate one with chocolate buttercream frosting and chocolate chips on top, and held one in each hand and took little ladylike bites, first from one and then the other.

Brooke offered the cute curly-haired limo driver, Nick, a yellow-frosted cupcake. "Would you like to eat something tasty and *sweet*, sweetie?" she asked coyly, batting her lashes at him. I noticed that she stuck out her chest and drew her shoulders back when giving him the cupcake. She looked good in that little black dress, I'll say that. She has good legs.

It must be nice to have thighs that don't rub together all the time when you walk.

Our first stop was The Merchant on Pinckney Street, where we had more drinks and ate popcorn and cheese curds and a few final mini-cupcakes, as well as brussels sprouts in a nice smoked-bacon sauce. Mindy ordered warm marinated olives with ricotta cheese. Yuck!

We played more games, including one with "stud scoring" flash cards, and gave Mindy her gag gifts. Mine was *The Kama Sutra Bath Book: Sudsy Fun in the Tub for Grown-Ups*, which featured saucy suggested positions for tub or shower sex: Lotus, Climbing the Tree, Camel's Hump, Hanging Bow, Tigress, and others. I'd like to experiment with some of those down the road if I ever have sex again, though it would have to be done in a very big tub. A *huge* tub. Even then it might not work. The cartoon couple in the illustrations aren't porkers like me, and they fit quite nicely, with room to spare, in the tub and shower. The dark-haired cartoon guy's tall and muscular—great shoulders and biceps—and the red-haired chick is, of course, thin and pretty. Her cartoon boobs are firm. They stick out and don't sag and the nipples are quite erect. Unlike the boobs of most real human beings, such as me, hers are perfectly symmetrical; one doesn't hang lower than the other.

Both cartoon characters are smiling like simpletons as they contort themselves into their bizarre positions. The contorting might be a problem for me. It might be an even bigger problem if my partner was hefty too. Oh, sweet Jesus!

Mindy opened the book and paged through it. "Oh," she chirped, "what great ideas. I can't wait to do some of these." As I watched her studying the pictures—her forehead wrinkled, stuffing cheese curds and olives into her mouth and washing them down with Southern Comfort and Coke—I imagined her and Richard in a tub somewhere, trying out the Tigress position or Kiss the Yoni Blossom. I envisioned them in a shower stall doing Camel's Hump. I felt momentarily sickened, but also nostalgic. I remembered sitting together with her on the living room couch while Dad read *On the Banks of Plum Creek* to us, and Mindy crying over Pa's trading Pet and Patty. I recalled my sister as a cute little blue-eyed, blond-haired five-year-old about to start her first day of kindergarten, nervous but excited, wearing a new light-yellow dress. And now it's come to this: Mindy bare-ass naked, leaning back in some strange tub with her legs resting on either edge, and bland also-naked Richard between her thighs, kneeling in the tepid water, his hairy butt saluting the ceiling as he rubs his bristly face against her precious yoni blossom.

Maybe someday their tub sex will lead to a tub birth. Some of the women on *A Baby Story* do that. They have well-thought-out birth plans calling for a water birth in a tub. We'll see a woman lying back, usually with a bra or halter top on, her face contorted in pain and her hands desperately grasping the edges of the tub, legs spread and moaning and groaning, until the water turns dark and the kid oozes out. "What the *hell!*" her baby's maybe muttering. "I thought I was finally getting out of that yucky moist womb and onto some dry land, and here I am in Waterworld again. Damn!"

So you can screw and conceive in a tub and give birth in that same tub, and maybe eat your meals in the tub, and, if you're like me, spend the best hours of your life in the tub with the one you love best relaxed on the toilet seat nearby. "Right, Lucy-Goosey? This is *our* time and *no one* can take it away from us. No, no, they can't take that away from us."

Of course, it would be sad if I didn't know I was pregnant, and, one night while taking my bath, I felt horrible pains and squeezed out a kid. I imagine that'd compromise the loveliness of our nightly routine. Lucy would be alarmed by my moaning and would probably raise herself up and peer over at me and be amazed at what she saw. "Who's *that*, Mommy?" she'd wonder aloud if she could talk. "I thought you said it would just be us two forever."

It was disgusting watching my sister stuff those marinated olives with ricotta cheese down her gullet. She chowed down at least a dozen. I have no respect for people who like olives.

Mindy seemed to like her other gifts too. Kiersten gave her fruity-flavored penis gummies, and Katie gave her a garter with pieces of sugary candy stuck to it. Toni had splurged. Her gift was a red teddy open at the nipples and crotch. "Maybe that's more of a gift for *Richard*," Mindy murmured, looking coy. Diana's gift was a set of jumbo playing cards with fifty-two sex games for couples on their wedding night. She looked pained as she handed it to Mindy, but put on an apparently well-practiced phony little smile. "I thought of giving her a subscription to *The Weekly Reader*," she whispered to me. "She does know how to read, doesn't she?"

I wonder if Mindy still likes having sex with Richard. I wonder if she's bored with him yet in bed. The newness for them, that thrill, has to be long-gone. They'll have their silly wedding night, but then what? Maybe she appreciated his doing his stud duties at first in their time together, and maybe she still does now and again, but my guess is that at some time after the wedding his bedroom job description title, in her little mind, will change from *stud* to *sperm donor* so she can move on to her next big phase: Mindy the Mommy. Maybe not right away, but sooner rather than later.

And what about him? I suspect that he appreciates having a steady sex partner so that he doesn't have to go sniffing around the neighborhood or go online to dating sites for nookie. But does he find Mindy boring in bed sometimes? I have to think he must. And what about her genital yeast infections? That's a problem she's had now and again. Thank God, I've only had that once, three years ago around Christmas. Has he experienced that particular loveliness up close? Has he ever noticed her Monistat in the medicine cabinet? "Honey, what's this for?" he'd ask. "Well," she'd murmur, "it's to make my precious little hoohah even sweeter than it already *is*, snookums. Just for you!"

At least Mindy doesn't get PMS like I do. She has maybe part of a day before her period starts where she gets just a little moody, a bit blue and weepy, but nothing too bad. And then she breezes through her periods, and never has to slow down and never even complains. She probably doesn't even have those miserable heavy-flow days. I don't think she gets nasty cramps, like I always do. Or if she does, they're not bad enough that she gripes about them. And the only pre-menstrual craving she's ever mentioned is for spaghetti and meatballs with grated parmesan cheese and garlic bread.

Our last bachelorette party stop was Plan B on Williamson Street, per Mindy's directive. It was crowded—Saturday evening being weekly drag queen night—and we had to mill around one side of the rectangular bar. The bar has a plexiglass surface that was lit up with most of the colors of the rainbow, and TV sets were mounted high on each of the four sides. Mindy and Katie and Julie got to sit on bar stools, and the rest of us gathered around. We started with a round of shots, and after her second one Julie yelled out, "Body shot!" At that, one of the bartenders, Joey, took off his silky black shirt with the Plan B logo and grinned and lay supine on the bar, and another bartender poured a shot of tequila, with salt and a lime, into his hairy belly button. Mindy raised herself from her seat and leaned over and slurped the liquor from Joey's navel. Katie loved it. "Oh…my… *GOD!*" she squealed.

We got to hear a little bit of the drag queens before the DJ came on at eleven o'clock. The best was Davina DeVille, wearing a neon-green leotard, six-inch pink heels, and an amazing whitish-blond wig. She lip-synched to Nicki Minaj's "Super Bass." A few of us drifted from the bar to the dance floor to watch for a few minutes. Diana leaned over to me and whispered, "Oh, sweet Jesus! I *so* want to be Nicki Minaj in my next life. Or at least Cyndi *effin'* Lauper."

I had my answer as to how Diana would be with a few drinks in her belly. She wasn't quiet or sarcastic or ribald. When the DJ started, Mindy and Julie led all of us to the dance floor, where the twelve of us boogied together for a few minutes before splitting off into smaller groups. Diana, by then, was on her third or fourth White Russian, plus what she'd downed at Johnny's and The Merchant, not to mention the shots so far at Plan B. She was feeling no pain. When the DJ played "Firework" by Katy Perry, she went, "Oh, *yes!*" and grabbed my hand and pulled me to the middle of the dance floor where she immediately commenced gyrating her squat little body, waving her arms high, swishing her backside, and animatedly mouthing the lyrics: "Do you ever feel like a plastic bag…drifting through the wind…wanting to start again? …"

Pretty soon five gay guys formed a circle around us, clapping and dancing happily. One of them yelled, "You *go*, girl!" Brooke bopped over to us and faced Diana to dance with her, sort of nudging me aside. For a moment I considered knocking her down and stomping on her face. "Take *that*, you prissy little bitch!" I imagined yelling as I ground the heel of my shoe into her forehead. I envisioned some of the gay guys clapping their hands to their mouths and going, "Catfight! Oh, my goodness, *catfight!*" But that moment passed, and I caught a glimpse of Mindy about ten feet away, dancing with Julie and Katie, all three pleasantly inebriated. Julie looked way too thin. Mindy bent over and shook her butt seductively and Katie slipped behind her and grasped Mindy's hips and ground her pelvis against the bachelorette's buttocks. I noticed Toni off to one side, laughing hugely. Just then, just for a moment, I felt an affection for my sister that I hadn't felt for a while.

The dancing was good. I didn't care about being fat. I didn't care what anyone thought. It felt good to move my body to the loud music. It was good to dance with Diana. *Maybe*, I thought, *I'll even dance a little with my sister*. Usually I feel self-conscious about that, since I think I dance as awkwardly as Elaine on *Seinfeld*, though without that little kick and the backward thumb thrusts.

I glanced over to the other end of the club beyond the bar, where three guys and an amazingly beautiful tall black woman—possibly a transvestite—in a skin-tight orange dress that barely covered her crotch, with huge curly reddish hair, were shooting pool at the red-covered pool table. Above the table there was a big white plastic deer head with antlers. The blank white eyes seemed to be staring right at me. It was spooky, and for some bizarre reason, while looking at the deer, I suddenly worried that a plane would crash into the roof of Plan B or that an errant eighteen-wheel truck speeding down Willy Street with the driver asleep or drunk or dead would crash through the front windows, causing mass casualties. *What a shame*, I thought, *if poor Mindy and her bridesmaids were wiped out just a few weeks before her big day.* If I survived the disaster but my sister didn't, at least I wouldn't have to worry anymore about the damned wedding.

In the limo on the way back to Courtyard by Marriott, the hotel near Johnny's where Mindy and the inebriated ladies would be spending the night, Kiersten got sick. "Oh, my God!" she squealed to the driver. "Pull over, Nick. I have to barf." We'd just exited the Beltline onto Greenway Boulevard. Nick pulled over under the bridge, and Kiersten jumped out and puked on the sidewalk. There was a gutter right there, but she chose the sidewalk. Jessa and Toni held Kiersten's hair back as she upchucked in three huge waves, each accentuated with a loud and disgusting "*W-A-A-G-H!*" Between the second and third waves, Kiersten held her flushed face in her hands and said, "Oh, sweet mother of Jesus, *never* again. I, like, totally swear to God."

The funny thing was that I didn't feel at all grossed out by Kiersten's throwing up. I didn't feel sorry for her. I didn't care. I was thinking just then of poor Bella, hoping that she was warm and comfortable in Mr. Randall's house, hopefully sleeping and not scared of being alone on a dark Saturday night, and not feeling poorly. I wondered if she'd liked the song I'd sung to her when I was there. I decided that I'd sing more of it to her, gently, when I go to take care of her later today.

Don't you know that it's worth
Every treasure on earth to be young at heart.
For as rich as you are,
It's much better by far to be young at heart.

And if you should survive to a hundred and five,
Look at all you'll derive out of being alive.
And here is the best part, you have a head start
If you are among the very young at heart.

I hope Mindy believed me when I told her that I couldn't spend the night at the hotel because I was having terrible cramps. That was a lie. "I just wanted to come home to you, Goose. Enough is enough with these girls." Mindy gave me a look, but she was too happy or tired or liquored up to make an issue of it. As to that, I probably shouldn't have driven home myself, considering my alcohol intake over the course of the evening. Maybe I should have asked Nick to drive me home. But here I am. It worked out. I suspect that Sister Agnella wouldn't approve of either my lying or driving with high blood alcohol. If I ever go to confession again, I'll try to remember to mention both transgressions.

"Am I a terrible person for lying to my sister, Lucy?" She opens her eyes briefly to look directly at me, with a sweet expression. Her green eyes look warm and accepting. I take that to mean that she thinks I'm not terrible. Then, after a moment, she carefully washes her left paw with her tongue. I wonder if she finds it strange that we're doing our routine so much later than usual.

"Thank God that damned bachelorette deal's over with, right, Lucy-Goosey? Thank God, thank God. But the dancing was good. And now it's just us." She breaks off her grooming to again look into my eyes. "Poor Bella, though, huh, Lucy? Poor sweet little Bella."

Fools Rush In

SOME DAYS are more aggravating than others. Today was one. The first aggravation started at the Fergusons' house. Mrs. F.—Doris—had instructed me to give Princess two peeled shrimp each day. I did, and Princess wolfed down the shrimp and seemed quite happy. After feeding her, I watered the plants upstairs and downstairs and scooped out the litter box and opened the windows and put bird food in the feeders. I was about to sit down with Princess and watch TV for a while when I stepped in a pile of cat puke on the throw rug in the foyer. But I didn't realize that right away, and tramped through several rooms of the house before I noticed. Apparently, the shrimp didn't sit well with Princess's little tummy. The vomit had gotten into the treads of my right sandal. I cleaned it out as best I could in the stationary sink in the laundry room, using hot water and a butter knife, then I cleaned where I'd stepped on the carpets using Resolve and paper towels. It wasn't a major tragedy, like a war or an earthquake or your period being two weeks late, but it put me in a bit of a sour mood.

Princess is a Russian Blue. She's beautiful, with amazing emerald-green eyes and thick bluish fur that looks like it's been frosted with silvery powdered sugar. She knows she's royalty, but doesn't put on any airs. She's gentle, almost shy. Whenever I go there, she greets me at the door and looks up with those incredible eyes. She likes to sit quietly next to me on the white couch when we watch TV. And she loves to play fetch. The Fergusons have a wicker basket in a corner of the living room filled with assorted cat toys, including little mice and birds and chase toys. Princess's favorite seems to be a little yellow cloth duck with beady black eyes and an outsized orange beak. She has three of them. When I'm at her house, I toss one of the ducks a few feet and Princess runs over to get it and brings it back clamped in her mouth, then drops it at my feet. She'll do that over and over. Only a few cats I've known like to play fetch, but Princess does. Once when I came there, I noticed that she'd deposited one of her cloth ducks in her water bowl. What was that about?

She also loves stories of heroic royal cats. "Once there was a beautiful Russian Blue princess," I told her, "and she rode in her silver coach throughout Russia to distribute kibbles and catnip to poor peasant cats. She also gave advice on proper grooming, especially face washing. 'Hooray for the princess,' all the peasant kitties said happily, their tummies full and their paws and faces and whiskers so very clean. 'Oh, how we love her!' The end."

The Fergusons seem like a good couple. They're older and are both short and stout. They don't look like they've missed too many meals. Mr. F. —John—has a wonderful brown handlebar mustache that twists upward at the end, and he always wears baggy khaki or gray trousers held up with wide red suspenders. Doris usually wears her whitish hair in a long braid that hangs down to her butt, and she favors Wisconsin Badger T-shirts in warm weather and Badger sweatshirts in colder weather. The last time I saw her, she was wearing a red T-shirt that said "TEACH ME HOW TO BUCKY" in bold white letters.

John and Doris smile and laugh a lot. They seem to get a kick out of each other. They also love licorice. There's a plastic tub of Twizzlers Strawberry Licorice Twists on one end of their kitchen counter, and, next to that, another huge container of Red Vines Black Licorice Twists. Then they have a smaller container with those little bite-sized pieces of licorice, both red and black, and a box of red-licorice saltwater taffy. Plus, there are always boxes of Good & Plentys on a hutch in their dining room. The first time I went there, Doris was munching on a red Twizzler. "Have some, Maggie," she said, pointing to one of the plastic tubs. "Have as much as you'd like." Every time I've gone there since, she's left a note on the counter about food. The latest one read: "Maggie, plenty of licorice for you. I know you like the red best. And potato salad in the fridge. Help yourself." That's nice of her, though I'm not sure if potato salad and licorice go well together.

I like it that they have a roomy and friendly kitchen, with no island or huge stainless steel stove or granite countertops. The kitchen cabinets are some kind of cheap wood—pine, maybe—and not cherry or oak or maple or hickory or any of those other hoity-toity woods. The refrigerator door's covered with Badger stuff: a 2011 football schedule, starting with UNLV; an outdated basketball schedule from the 2010-2011 season; a photo of the volleyball team—mostly tall, serious, athletic women wearing tight shorts, with their hair in ponytails; various Bucky Badger images; and twenty-three assorted red-and-white refrigerator magnets, seven of which say "GO BUCKY."

After I cleaned up the mess from the shrimp, Princess and I watched an episode of *A Baby Story*, and that added to my sour mood. It was about a dark-skinned couple with two girls, one maybe eight years old and the other about five or six. The mother's pregnant with a third child. Her husband is a huge guy, tall and heavy, with a head the size of Gary's and close-cropped hair. His eyes are squinty because his face is so fleshy. He works long hours at his own business—a restaurant, I think—seven days a week. The wife is much smaller and quiet, even mousy. She has her baby boy two-thirds of the way into the episode and then, back home a month or so after the birth, she speaks to the camera, in an emotionless monotone, about how tired and overworked she feels. "But it's okay," she says, unsmiling and with a flattened affect, resigned. "This is my life now." The girls are similarly joyless. At the end, the whole family's relaxing in the parents' bed, the mother holding the baby, flanked by her girls, and she says that she's glad they now have all the children they're going to have. The gigantic husband says, "Well, maybe one more." She looks down and says, softly, "No, this it." He pauses and repeats, this time more definitively, "Maybe one more."

I felt bad for her. I imagined this huge controlling dipwad on top of his sad little wife in that bed, crushing her, hoping to plant the seed of their fourth meek child. I imagined the years ahead of her, taking care of three or four children day after weary day while her beefy husband's at work, not much time for herself, dreading his return home, wondering what happened to her girlhood dreams. Maybe she had hopes of being a dancer. Perhaps she wanted to write poignant short stories, like Alice Munro. Maybe she wanted to be a scientist and spend her quiet, focused days in a lab wearing a white coat and recording data. "But it's okay," she says to herself now and again while staring at the overflowing baskets of laundry to be folded. "This is my life now."

Then I went to Jackie's apartment to take care of her two cats, Bupkis and Groucho. "Hi guys!" I yelled out as I entered. "Aunt Maggie's here." They both came running, and Bupkis immediately sniffed my sandals and rubbed the side of his head against the right sandal. Groucho followed suit and rolled against my right foot and began furiously licking my toes. I don't know if it was the shrimp or the vomit that tickled their fancies. Maybe both. It was amusing, but I was still in a nasty mood because of the *Baby Story* episode. Plus, I almost gagged when I fed the cats in the kitchen because of the smell from the Panasonic microwave when I warmed up their wet food. Jackie'd inadvertently overheated it a month or so ago while trying to defrost an onion bagel from Gotham Bagels, and the inside of the machine had turned yellow, and now there's a persistent acrid smell. Yuck.

Plus, even though I like Jackie, I never feel comfortable in her place. There's a sadness, a loneliness. She's a probation officer, in her mid-fifties, and has been married and divorced twice. She's been alone for twelve years. She told me that she has one child—a grown daughter who lives in Evansville, Indiana, from whom she's estranged. She didn't say why. There're no photos of the daughter or any other family members in her apartment. There are, though, a few prints of African scenes: a group of lazy, yawning lions lounging near some scrubby bushes; a herd of strolling elephants; and a bunch of anxious, hyper-vigilant wildebeests. But no people pictures.

I like Jackie's cats, of course, but there's a gloom in the air. If her apartment were messier, a bit more cluttered, I think I'd feel less glum. But it isn't. Everything is neat and in its place. When I come over the first time while she's away, there are never any dishes in the sink. The kitchen garbage can is always empty, and there's never even a crumb on the counter. The carpets are always vacuumed. I know she's a rabid duster because I always check picture frames and the tops of cabinets and bookcases. No dust. There's not even any dust on her many knick-knacks: porcelain owls and bluebirds and elephants and camels and the like, arranged with perfect spacing and at symmetrical angles on glass shelves in every room except the bathroom. Her bed's always well-made and covered with a midnight-blue bedspread that's folded just so under the pillows, like in a freshly made-up hotel room. The edges of the spread hang down perfectly evenly on either side and at the end of the bed. Even the *Cat Fancier* and *National Geographic* magazines on her well-polished wooden coffee table are in perfectly neat little piles. I was surprised, given her fastidiousness, that Jackie'd been careless with her microwave.

I always like to leave a place a little better than I found it, but with Jackie's apartment that's not possible. Plus, I'm afraid to eat there. I'd brought along a bag of Famous Amos bite-size chocolate chip cookies and a few Thin Mints to munch on, but I didn't eat them; I was afraid to leave any crumbs. Fortunately, I also had my plastic bag of butterscotch hard candies and Tootsie Rolls and Peppermint Patties, none of which leave crumbs.

I'm also afraid to poop there. I'd hate to inadvertently leave brown streaks in her sparkling-clean toilet bowl. I can only imagine what Ms. Immaculate would say if she came home and saw *that*. Plus, Jackie has one of those annoying toilets where to flush it, you have to turn around and press a metal button in the middle of the top of the tank lid. It doesn't have a little handle on one side of the tank or the front of the tank, like most toilets do. A toilet with a front or side handle's usually not a problem; you just sort of reach around and press the handle while you're sitting there. But with that damned button, that's hard to do, especially if you're big like me. I usually have to raise my butt off the seat and stand up and turn around to press it. That's okay if you only need to flush once; you can pull up your panties and jeans and then flush while dressed. But sometimes, of course, a girl has to flush more than once, so for any flushes before the final one you have to stand up and turn around, bare-assed, with your clothes bunched around your ankles. It's a minor aggravation on the great scale of things, but still an aggravation.

Her toilet paper holder is in a recessed axle on the wall to the left of the toilet. Jackie uses Angel Soft with Pretty Prints toilet paper, which seems a nice choice. It's quality, like everything else about that woman. There are four packaged rolls in a pretty wicker basket on a glass shelf above the toilet. Jackie uses the under-the-roll method of hanging toilet paper. She's the only person I know who does that, except for Aunt Grace.

I wonder if Jackie has obsessive-compulsive disorder. Everything in her place is in such perfect order. She uses part of her second bedroom as an office, and there's a big dark-brown wooden desk with, of course, not a speck of dust anywhere on it. There's not much on the desktop, but what's there is in perfect order. There's an iMac directly in the center and, to the left of that, a Hewlett-Packard printer and a small shredder. To the right of the computer there's a gray Swingline stapler, a letter opener, two silver-colored ballpoint pens, one perfectly sharpened number-two pencil, and a small white notepad. None of those items were placed carelessly. They're all in straight lines, each item parallel to the next, and evenly spaced. The tops of the two pens and the pencil are lined up, and each is about an inch, neither more nor less, from the next item. Her desk bears absolutely no resemblance to my little desk in the corner of my living room, which looks like a tornado just ripped through.

Now and again, I have an urge to mess up Jackie's desk—maybe move her stapler and the pens and pencil to random positions, at horrible angles.

I'd shift the base of the iMac so that it faced slightly to the left. I'd move the shredder to a precarious position at the far edge. I'd wad up a couple of sheets from the notepad and leave them scattered on top of the desk. But I won't do it. Jackie'd likely have a panic attack. Maybe she'd call me when she got home, perspiring heavily, her voice trembling. "Maggie! Oh my God, Maggie. Oh, dear Jesus! What happened to my desk? Oh, this is just *terrible!*"

I'd listen and talk serenely and confidently, in a low voice, to try to calm her. "Well," I'd say, "it must have been the cats. Now take a deep breath, Jackie. Breathe in and out slowly and evenly. It'll be okay."

I wonder if Groucho and Bupkis are sensitive to the same thing I pick up on: the sadness of Jackie's place. They're always happy and playful, always up for a little playtime with my shoelace or one of my cat toys on a stick. Bupkis is a tawny orange guy with streaks of white, and Groucho is brownish with one white paw, the front left. He has a little black mustache-like tuft of fur under his nose, like Hitler. *Adolph* would be a fitting name for him, maybe shortened to *Dolph. Der Führer* might be too much.

"You and Groucho are the same color, Lucy. Isn't that nice? They live in a nice apartment, but it's too sterile. It needs to be a little messier, like our place. Am I right?"

Well, it would be lots worse if Jackie were one of those people you see on *Hoarding: Buried Alive*, where every room of the house is filled with saved crap from floor to ceiling, and you have to crawl over piles of junk to get from one room to another. The hoarder often has to sleep on a cot or a blanket on the floor because her bed is piled high with stuff. She can't cook anything because the kitchen is unusable. Empty pizza boxes are scattered everywhere. Sometimes rodents run free. At best, there's a narrow path in a room that allows a person to stumble their way to the next horrible room. That would be a terrible deal for a cat. They'd hate it. Hopefully, the hoarder would have seen Jackson Galaxy's show and would have put up plenty of elevated walkways.

Whatever shortcomings I may have, at least I'm not one of those hoarders.

Lucy likes to hear about Groucho's nap habit. He prefers to sleep on a blue cloth pad high up on top of a tall bookcase in Jackie's bedroom. He gets on top of her dresser and jumps from there to the top of the bookcase—a leap of almost four feet. What's funny is that when he's on the dresser, poised to jump, he totally concentrates and fixes his focus on the top of the bookcase and tenses his little body, gauging the distance, and then in a mighty spring he propels himself upward with his powerful rear legs and lands perfectly softly, with room to spare. Amazing. Then he settles himself on his pad and looks down from his high vantage point with a smug, self-satisfied expression. "I'll bet you're pretty impressed," he seems to be saying. "I'll bet *you* can't do that."

Bupkis seems content to spend his time below. Unlike Groucho, he apparently has no need to perch high above the madding crowd.

I like it when Bupkis sits next to me and lets me know that he'd like to be stroked and petted. But he has limits. Now and again when I'm petting him, he'll suddenly lunge and scratch or bite my hand. It's never terrible, but it hurts a little. Sometimes there's blood. It's like he's saying, "Thanks for the attention, but hey, enough is enough." After I learned he was that way, I tried to look for little warning signs—a stare, a tensed body, ears flattened, a little throaty growl. Sometimes he does one of those, but not always. I wish I could train him to be a better communicator about his needs, his limits, his boundaries. I wish I could teach him to, say, shake his furry little head when he's had enough. Maybe I could call Jackson and get some advice. I'm sure he has a handle on that particular feline behavior.

While Bupkis was relaxing next to me, I told him that I thought he was great. "You're an *amazingly* wonderful cat, Bupkis," I said. "You're perfectly beautiful, and you have a *wonderful* personality. You're the absolute envy of every feline in the neighborhood." But I said it in a harsh, scolding tone with my brow furrowed and eyes cold and shoulders hunched. He looked up at me and studied my face, unsure, maybe a bit scared. "What did I do wrong, Aunt Maggie?" he maybe would have said if he could talk. "Am I bad?"

I don't know if Jackie's much of an imbiber. If she is, it'd be nice if, when she's home, she and I could down a few drinks. Maybe that would loosen her tongue, and she'd tell her sad story. I'd like to know what happened between her and the daughter. What caused their estrangement? Whose fault, if anyone's, was it? Does Jackie wish things were different? Or is she resigned? How will she feel if she never talks to or sees her child again? I wonder if she has other relatives that she's close to, or even many friends. Or is she content living a quiet, pretty-much-alone life, like I do, and doesn't need many others? And I wonder what she sees for herself as to future relationships. At her age, is she interested or has the boat sailed?

Maybe she and I could smoke some weed and she'd tell me about her two marriages. I imagine it might be hard for a guy to be married to a probation officer. Those people are all about laying rules on others and keeping a hawk's eye on them to be sure they're following the straight and narrow, and hammering them with consequences for violating the rules. I'm sure it's bad enough to be a criminal and have a PO always on your case. You can't drink or do drugs. You have to try to get a job. You can't go here and you can't go there. You have to keep regular hours. You have to account for your whereabouts. You can't associate with certain lowlifes. POs get to search you when they want to and make you pee in a cup. And if you don't follow the rules, they can slap a violation on you and ship your noncompliant ass back to the pokey.

But maybe it's even worse to be *married* to a probation officer. From what I can see, too many relationships in general and marriages in particular are like being on probation, or, in some cases, like being in jail. There are tons of rules and regulations, though not formalized or written down, like they are if you're really on probation or parole. You have to do this, and you have to do that; you can't do this, and you can't do that. It starts out fine. You meet someone and have fun and sex, and it's all sweetness and light, and the cymbals may be clashing, and the object of your affection's not yet laid expectations on you. You're happy at first, and not critical toward or annoyed or bored with the other person. Then after a while, once you're at least a semi-official couple, things change—slowly, not all at once. It probably starts with something seemingly benign, like, "Why didn't you text me when you woke up, like you said you would?" Then, out of the blue, she gets all serious and starts in with the dreaded let's-define-our-relationship discussion: "What am I to you? Am I your girlfriend? Are we a couple? Where's this going?" Then maybe you move in together and there's domesticity, and pretty soon it's, "You're going to George's to watch Thursday Night Football? No. You were there on Monday night. Once a week with your friends is enough."

Then you're arguing about who does more housework or other domestic stuff, and before you know it the harping gets more specific. You're on his case for leaving the toilet seat up. He's nagging you about how often the two of you have sex, or what kind of sex you have or don't have. The two of you argue about how much time the other spends on the computer or phone. You don't like the shirts he wears. He thinks you've let yourself go, that you've gained too much weight in the last year. Soon there's constant scolding or bickering. "Please put your napkin on your lap when you eat." "Don't eat so fast." "Change your shirt more often." "Don't laugh so loud in the movies." "Don't use that tone of voice with me." "Why don't you ever tell me that you love me?" "Why do you seem depressed so much?" "Why are your bras always hanging on the shower rod?" "I don't like it when you look at other women when we're at the mall." "Stand up straight." "Can't you clean the toothpaste from the sink?" "How often do you change your underwear?" "Stop using so much hair gel." "I need you to stop watching that TV show that I know you like so much and do something else that I want you to do instead." "Don't drink so much on weekends." "Please don't tailgate." "I've told you that a *thousand* times." *Argh!*

And then you're looking at his phone when he's asleep to see who he's called or texted, and you're checking his Twitter and Facebook accounts. You need to see the pictures in his Instagram account.

Pretty soon he's laying down control: "I know three kids is a lot, but I think we should have one more. Maybe one more."

And then, of course, the suspicions start. There she is after work having drinks with her girlfriends. "Oh, my God!" she's blubbering. "I think Eddie's cheating on me. Oh, boo hoo. Oh, poor me. Poor sad little betrayed me." Her friends nod and rub her shoulders and their heavily made -up faces harden in shared sisterhood outrage over horrible, unfaithful men. "Oh, that *bastard*," one says. "*Cheating* on you! Oh, how terrible. He doesn't deserve you. He just does not deserve to be with a true princess like you."

So all that's bad enough, but it's probably much worse when one or the other partner's a probation officer. Maybe that's what drove Jackie's husbands away. "Toe the line, Willy," she maybe said, "or your ass is grass. I told you that you had to call if you were gonna be later than six, but you didn't call until six forty-five. That's a violation of the rules, bucko. So you're cut off until next month. I certainly hope this'll be a lesson to you."

I hope she didn't make either of her husbands submit to random urine tests.

Of course, I don't know about much of this from my own experience. I only lived with Alex for a while, and neither of us nagged or whipped the other. I don't think we did, anyway. Probably that would have happened if we'd stayed together longer. He eventually bored the hell out of me, but that's different. But I've seen enough discord in my parents' marriage. It irritates me to think about it. My poor mother's sort of like that dark little mousy woman on *A Baby Story*—quiet, resigned, and oppressed by her jerk of a husband.

"What do you think, Lucy? You met my father that one time when he and Mom came over. What was your opinion?" But she's too polite to speak her mind on this—too well-mannered to speak ill of her guardian's daddy. If she did speak up, though, what would she say? "Well, Mommy, I must say that my impression of your father is that he's rather self-centered. He's quite impressed with himself. He's a muckety-muck history professor, right? He's on the UW Faculty Senate, huh? A very important guy, right? Well, maybe so, but he's still kind of cold-hearted. He likes things his way. And I hate to say this, but I don't think he likes you much. I don't think he approves of you, Mommy. He seemed disgusted when he was looking around our apartment. He couldn't wait to leave. And I don't think he likes your mom much, either. He was so rude to her. 'C'mon Lillian, let's go. I have a faculty meeting to get ready for.' And, of course, he didn't say anything to me. Mr. High and Mighty couldn't condescend to say, 'Oh, hi Lucy. How are you today? Nice to see you.' Not even a pat on the head."

But that's okay. I wouldn't expect my father to show any concern or caring for my cat. He's too important, of course, to care about that. And I'm past caring what my father thinks of me. It's an old issue. It used to bother me that he so clearly preferred Mindy, approved of her, and found me … well, weird, I guess. Mindy was always his golden girl, the one he could be proud of, the one who measured up to his idea of what Warren Mullen's daughter should be like. She's pretty, did well in school, was popular, had lots of friends, got decent grades, played soccer, was on prom court, blah blah. She was even a *Girl Scout*, for God's sake. His only issue with her that I know of is that she wants to be a paralegal. He thinks she should go to law school. And then, I imagine, he'd want her to get in as an associate with some hoity-toity corporate firm in town—Axley Brynelson, say, or Foley and Lardner, or Habush Habush and Rottier—and work obscene amounts of time, including evenings and weekends, to rack up billable hours until she makes partner and can really rake in the dough. He'd probably put on his disapproving stern face if she wanted to be a public defender or work in a public interest law firm representing screwed-over tenants, or maybe for Greenpeace.

Of course, he very much disapproves of my pathetic career choice. I can just imagine him talking to his colleagues at a faculty party. "So how are your kids these days, Warren?" some professor of East Asian history would ask while eating a chocolate-covered strawberry. "Well," he'd say, sipping sherry, "my younger daughter, Mindy, is thinking of going to law school. Maybe she'll want to go here to Wisconsin, but, frankly, I'm hoping she'll consider Harvard or Yale, or at least Columbia." The other guy would nod approvingly and then, at some point, ask Dad about his older daughter. There'd be a pause, and Dad would purse his lips and scowl. "Maggie," he'd say. "Yes, Maggie. Well, she's, uh …still trying to find herself."

No, I don't care what he thinks of me anymore. I did when I was younger, but not now. I used to feel bad that he seemed to have such a low opinion of me, but not now. The hell with him now. I just don't like how he treats Mom. That's what grates on me. He's a mean bastard to her. He dismisses her. He ignores her. I don't think he likes her much anymore. Lucy's right about that. He's rude.

"I'll tell you the truth, Lucy, sometimes I wish bad things for him. Sometimes I wouldn't mind if he'd trip while walking down Bascom Hill and roll all the way to the bottom, clunking his head on rocks and tree roots and coming out with some brain damage. Not horrible brain damage, but some." Or maybe one night, while drunk, he'd climb the statue of Lincoln at the top of Bascom and fall off and mess up his head. Maybe the brain trauma would make him less of an arrogant, self-centered, controlling jerk. It would alter his frontal lobe for the better. Maybe he'd be nicer to Mom. But if that didn't happen, then at least he'd maybe turn into a vegetable and have to be placed in some brain trauma ward for a while—a year or two—and Mom could get a break from him, get out from under his yoke, and have a life and not have to sit in her living room at night, in the dark, drinking and ruminating.

Well, that's pretty mean for me to think. It really is. I should be ashamed of myself, I guess. I should. "All right, I *am* ashamed, Lucy. Okay? There, I said it." He's my own father, after all. He did his part to give me life, though I'm sure he wasn't giving the future me much thought during my conception. I'm sure he was focused just on his own pleasure. But he is paying for his golden girl's wedding, making her happy. There's that. And speaking of his pleasure, I keep wondering if he's fooling around with some twiggy little history graduate student. I wouldn't be surprised. "Oh, Professor Mullen," she'd say innocently, looking up at him with big brown doe eyes. "Thanks ever so much for your wonderful help on my dissertation about the significance of the Missouri Compromise. I don't know that I could have done it without you." He'd smile subtly and nod and wave his hand dismissively. "Oh, you're most welcome, Dierdre," he'd say. "Glad to help out …Say, why don't you come by my office later tonight and we can talk about your dissertation. Lots of, uh, issues to discuss—abolitionism and so on. Maybe around nine o'clock? I have wine and cheese."

Well, I don't know why I keep thinking those thoughts. I have no reason to suspect my father of fooling around. There's no evidence that I know of. So why do I always have such mean suspicions?

I wonder what Dad will think when he sees me at the wedding in that damned strapless Bill Levkoff dress that I picked up this morning at Vera's. I don't imagine he'll be saying, "Oh, look, Lillian, isn't our Maggie lovely? Well, yes, she's a tad overweight, but so what? That doesn't matter at all. She's really a fine person, and her appearance is insignificant. Oh, we're so proud of *both* our girls, aren't we?" Hah!

Vera's. "That was another aggravation, Lucy-Goosey. Oh, my God!"

The alterations were fine, but my arms and shoulders looked terrible—so big—when I saw myself in that huge mirror. And the ruching! Those damned folds are so wrong for me. Christ! The only good thing was that cute little Amy was there again, again with the cleavage. I wonder why she's always showing off her boobs, since it's mostly women who come to the store. Well, maybe that's the reason. I wonder if her boobs ever itch, like mine do—on top of them being all sweaty sometimes. It's one thing if mine itch and I scratch them. None of my cats would give a damn. None of them would care if I stood naked in their living room and shook my ass like Gypsy Rose Lee and sang "The Battle Hymn of the Republic." But Amy's with people all the time at Vera's: brides, bridesmaids, mothers, her fellow consultants, and lovely silver-haired Vera herself, who's in her seventies and walks around the store nodding and smiling and making happy talk. "Oh, that's one of our very best gowns. Isn't it just lovely?" Vera can be my grandmother any time. And now and again grooms and groomsmen come in to get tuxedos. Maybe, while going on and on with some bride about how the bridesmaid dresses need to flatter and enhance the bridal gown, Amy's boobs would start itching and she'd have to excuse herself. "Uh, I'll be right back," she'd mumble, and quickly retreat to a bathroom or fitting room and pull up her top and unhook or raise her bra and scratch, and maybe slather some lotion on one or both boobies. "Oh, that's better," she'd say to herself. But maybe that's why she always wears low-cut tops and dresses, so that if her breasts itch, particularly on the insides, she can just subtly turn around and stick her fingers in the valley to do a quick fix.

Before leaving Vera's, I bought some two-sided tape to attach my new dress to my old boobs so that they don't slip all over the damned place or fall out. What a pain in the ass! "Whoever invented strapless dresses should be shot, Lucy. That's just my opinion."

Anyway, the thought of wearing that dress in a few weeks makes me need to take an extra-big swallow of my chardonnay and then another. Perhaps Lucy disapproves, but too bad. She's not in my shoes. And that's another aggravation—those silly shoes. I can just see myself waddling down the aisle in those heeled Lyric sandals by Touch Ups, holding my damned bouquet against my tummy, trying not to fall on my butt. If I did, I'd probably clunk my head against the hard edge of one of the pews and lose consciousness and they'd have to call the EMTs. Rubberneck guests would gather around, some clapping their hands to their cheeks, and one of the EMTs would yell, "*Please* move back, people. Give the maid of honor some air, for God's sake." Mindy would be furious at the distraction from her big day.

At least on the way up the aisle, I'll be able to hold onto the stupid best man's arm for support.

Damn! This thing is really happening—my sister's wedding. Now I really need to start working on my ridiculous toast for the reception. Just thinking about it makes my boobs sweat.

Well, as aggravating as this day may have been, now it's done. Tonight, things are better. They're fine. My Lucy and I are alone in our warm bathroom yet again, I'm on my second glass of wine, and Frank's crooning one of our all-time favorites:

Fools rush in
Where wise men never go,
But wise men never fall in love
So how are they to know?

When we met
I felt my life begin,
So open up your heart and let
This fool rush in.

Are Mindy and Richard fools rushing in? Did her life begin when they met? Did his? I hope to hell not. I'd like to think they have lives of their own that started way back and will continue quite nicely—nicely enough, anyway—even if the other one gets sick or crazy or tips over. It's all a crapshoot, anyway. You can't know what's ahead. Maybe they're star-crossed lovers and will stay in love for the next fifty or sixty years and have lovely, healthy, successful children whom they'll dote on and be proud of and then, down the road, lovely, healthy, successful grandchildren. Or maybe they'll turn into my parents, and in a few years Mindy, too, will sit silently in a darkened living room with a Southern Comfort and Coke and think what a fool she was for rushing into a relationship with Richard.

Well, when Mindy and Richard have kids, I'll be an aunt. That might be okay. I can handle that. You can do fun things with a niece or nephew and then, after a while, happily dump them off on their exhausted parents, who can then do all the tedious stuff: filling their bellies; putting clothes on their precious little backs; getting them up and ready for school; packing their lunches; making sure they've brushed their teeth, using an up-and-down motion rather than a back-and-forth one; berating a teacher who dared to give their darling a grade lower than an A; promoting their brats' self-esteem and laying the groundwork for future success; getting them ready for the SATs; or maybe picking them up from juvenile detention. Mindy and Richard can do all that while I'm alone in my apartment, sipping wine and chilling with my beloved cat and fantasizing about Frank softly brushing my earlobes with his warm lips.

"Hey, Lucy, do you want to hear the joke I told Bupkis and Groucho today? Okay, here it is: Why was the leper kicked off the relay team? …He lost the last leg. Get it?" She looks at me askance, one eye half-closed. I forgot that my cat disapproves of unkind jokes. "Okay, kid. I hear you. So why did the kitty cross the street? …To get to the other side. Is *that* better?"

High Hopes

SHEILA TOLD me a sad story about an older couple when we were having lunch at Mickie's Dairy Bar today. They were both in their eighties and had been married for almost sixty years. They never had kids. They lived in the same modest house for most of their time together. They were both quiet and didn't have many friends or relatives—just each other. Then she got bone cancer, and he took care of her for as long as he could before things got tough and she had to be hospitalized. She was in the hospital for six days and he came to be with her all day, every day. He sat in a brown chair in a corner of the room, next to her bed, and talked to her and read newspapers and magazines to her, even as she drifted in and out of consciousness. He commented to her on what he'd read. She had no other visitors. At the end of the sixth day, shortly after eight o'clock, she died. He stayed in the room with her for as long as they let him. Sheila's last view was of him walking slowly alone down the hallway of the ward—a short, white-haired man with black-framed glasses, wearing gray slacks and a dark-brown sweater with a tattered collar. She said his shoes were scuffed and worn-down at the heels.

He was the only person with his wife when she passed. They'd been together for sixty years, just the two of them, and he walked out of the hospital alone, down the long hallway to the elevator and then out of the hospital—quiet now, at night—to the parking structure, where he got into his car and drove home to their house on the east side of Madison, the house where he and his wife had lived together for half a century, where now he'd be alone.

"I can't get it out of my mind," Sheila said.

At least the poor woman didn't die alone. At least her husband was there with her. There's that. Maybe he won't be so fortunate. Well, hopefully, Sheila or someone like her, someone caring, will be there with him at the end. It won't be kin or friends; it'll be someone doing her job. But at least, damn it, it'll be *someone*.

Sheila loves the tuna-and-egg-salad club sandwich at Mickie's. Whenever we get together for lunch—once every three or four months—that's what she gets, along with a side of potato salad and a blueberry shake. I always get the meatloaf sandwich with yank fries and gravy and a butterscotch malt. We rarely vary our orders. Why would we? "If you like something, stick with it. That's what I say. Having new experiences is way overrated. Am I right, Lucy?" Well, Sheila doesn't always get the same flavor of shake. Sometimes she gets strawberry or cherry or mint, and now and again she goes for the old standbys—chocolate or vanilla. Mickie's has nine flavors of shakes and malts.

Sheila and I like to sit on the red-vinyl-covered stools at the Formica-topped counter, rather than at any of the closely packed tables or booths. She likes to study the handwritten, in red and black dry markers, breakfast and lunch and dinner menus on the wall above the kitchen, and the whiteboard on the far right that shows the daily lunch specials. She also likes to look at the old menu on the left side wall that shows items and prices from the early 1950s. Back then, a malt was thirty cents. A hamburger, no cheese, cost the same. A meatloaf sandwich was fifty cents. Now it's $3.50. You could get a breakfast with two eggs, any style, fried in butter, along with coffee or tea or milk, for forty-five cents. Those were the days. My bank account wishes those days were still here.

We both like it that Mickie's probably hasn't changed much since the '50s. It's near Camp Randall Stadium. Athletes and coaches and trainers and equipment guys and the like eat there. No doubt hundreds of great Wisconsin jocks have eaten there over the years, like Elroy "Crazylegs" Hirsch, with his long jaw and unattractive flattop, when he returned to Madison after his pro football career.

When you enter, the first thing you see is a handwritten sign attached to the soda machine on the front counter that says "WE ACCEPT CASH ONLY. THANK YOU FOR YOUR UNDERSTANDING." No checks or credit or debit cards for them. I like that thank you. They could have just said "**CASH ONLY!!**" and left it at that and not cared a fig how anyone felt about the deal. But they appreciate your understanding. Who does *that* anymore?

I also appreciate their honesty about undercooked food. There's another handwritten sign to the right of the kitchen that says that certain items will only be served "upon the consumer's request" because they may be undercooked: eggs prepared over easy or sunny side up or soft boiled, or hamburgers or steaks served rare or medium-rare. Maybe someday I'll go to Mickie's for breakfast. The chick taking my order would say, "Soft-boiled eggs? Are you sure about that? They might be undercooked and then you'll be up all night hurling chunks or having the screaming shits. Is that what you want? I advise you to at least order eggs over medium, or perhaps eschew eggs altogether and go with our banana nut pancakes with hot maple syrup. We've heard that you love peanut butter and banana sandwiches, so I think you'd like them." I'd probably agree and order a side of their homemade corned beef hash, with fried onion slices and cheddar cheese mixed in.

I'd told Sheila a while back my idea about asking Larry to be my date for the wedding. She'd said that she thought it was a good idea. I was thinking about that conversation as I was slurping down the last of my butterscotch malt, so I was surprised when I heard a familiar voice and turned around and there was Larry himself. He was standing beside a shorter guy with curly brown hair and incredible crinkly steely-blue eyes. "Oh, hi, Maggie," Larry said. "This is my friend Jordan. We played hoops together in high school. He was a mediocre point guard." I shook Jordan's hand. After a moment I realized that he was the shorter guy in the basketball photo I'd seen in Larry's bedroom. "Nice to meet you," I think I said. I don't remember just what I said. My heart was pounding. Those eyes! After a bit, I introduced Jordan and Larry to Sheila.

"Oh, you're the barber," she said to Larry. "Chester and Festus, right?"

He nodded. "And Miss Kitty," he said. "Don't forget Miss Kitty."

We made small talk for a minute or so and then Sheila blurted out, "You know, Larry, Maggie's sister is getting married soon. Maggie's the maid of honor. Do you want to go to the wedding with her? Be her date? She'd like that. You'd have a great time. They're having a free cupcake table, from Gigi's. You like cupcakes, don't you?"

I wanted to sink through the floor of Mickie's. I wanted to break my now-empty plate over Sheila's head. But I was surprised again when I heard Larry say, "A cupcake table? Gigi's? Sure. Sounds like fun."

Before we left Mickie's, I had to use the bathroom. It's a tiny room in the back corner of the restaurant, and I had to practically wedge myself in to sit on the toilet. The seat's an ancient and stained white plastic one. I have a vague memory that the seat used to be an even more ancient brown wooden dealie. If that wooden seat were still there, I'd worry about getting a splinter in my butt. A splinter in your finger's one thing; you can usually get it out yourself with a tweezers. But a splinter in your ass is quite another thing; you'd need help to get that thing out. Maybe I'd have to go to urgent care and, with my luck, it'd take a whole team of health care professionals—doctors, nurses, physician assistants—to get the damned thing out. They'd all be staring at my bottom during the procedure. "I see we have a little problem with cellulite," one of them might say. "Maybe a little exercise is in order." I'd turn my head around the best I could to look at him. "Yeah?" I'd say. "Well, maybe a little kiss-my-cellulited-ass is in order."

After lunch, I went to the Bergers' house to take care of Harold. The poor guy has issues. He had a bad start in life. He was a stray from Florida and the Bergers somehow adopted him from there and he was flown to Wisconsin in a cage. Apparently that traumatized him, and when he got to his new home he scooted under the bed in the master bedroom and stayed there all day, except for brief interludes of eating and using his litter box. After a month, he came out at night and spent some time on the bed with the Bergers. But when the alarm went off each morning, back under the bed Harold scampered. It took me three days before he trusted me enough to come out much from under the bed. I had to give him small dishes of tuna and talk to him softly, soothingly. I'd get down on my hands and knees next to the bed. "Hey, Harold. It's me, Aunt Maggie. It's wonderful to see you, my little furry friend. Won't you come out?"

I told him stories of heroic Florida kitties. "Once there was a very nice long-haired tortoiseshell cat, just like you, and his name was Irving. Irving was very kind and brave, and he helped find poor lost kittens all the way from Tallahassee to Key West. If anybody heard about a lost kitten, they'd call Irving and he'd come running just as fast as he could on his funny little legs, and he'd search high and low, and never stop, until the kitten was safe and sound and drinking cream. He even saved kittens who'd fallen into quicksand in the Everglades and couldn't get out. 'Oh, hooray for Irving,' all the cat lovers in Florida said. 'Isn't he just the most wonderful feline hero we've ever known?' The end."

Eventually Harold came out and allowed me to pet him a bit. He didn't stay for long, but at least it was for longer each time.

Harold's other issue is that he sometimes hallucinates. Mrs. B. said they'd been told that some rotten teenage boys in Florida had given him drugs, hallucinogens of some kind, when he was young, and now and again he still has effects. I've seen it. I've seen him standing in the middle of the master bedroom when he's emerged from under the bed, and all of a sudden his hazel eyes widen and his body tenses and he stares at the far wall, at something that I can't see. Sometimes, he dashes over to the wall or to a chair and stretches his body upward and bats at some imaginary enemy or prey. It lasts for a few minutes, and then he's okay.

He even has an issue with my cleaning his litter box. The first time I did that, I was a bit surprised when he meowed loudly and ran out of the room into the nearby den and hid behind a plant on a high table. Then he hissed at me when I came to see him. Maybe he somehow associates his litter box being scooped out with punishment. Who knows? "Don't be afraid, Harold," I told him soothingly. "Everything will be okay."

After a few days of that, I waited until just before I left to do his box. I later asked the Bergers about it, but they had no idea what Harold's problem was or what to do about it. I wish I could ask that weird Jackson Galaxy for his assessment. He'd observe Harold for a bit and figure out his psychology and know just what to do.

The Bergers—Arnie and Rose—did one thing that Jackson often suggests. They've built elevated skyways for Harold in the living and dining rooms—six-inch-wide white-painted boards on brackets—so he can be up high whenever he wants to and not feel threatened. They told me that he jumps up from the top of the piano and spends time on his walkways. I've not seen that yet, but hope to. Being up high probably helps control his anxiety.

"What do you think, Lucy? Would you want your very own skyway here in our apartment?" She looks at me from her toilet seat lid, but says nothing. She seems fine where she is. She's not anxious. She doesn't have issues, like Harold. She's been lucky in life—so far, anyway.

Arnie and Rose are good cat parents—good "guardians," as Jackson would say. They seem to love poor Harold and take good care of him. They seem to like each other, too, though who knows what the truth is? Maybe they secretly loathe each other, but put on a good face for the world. Maybe Arnie fantasizes about his wife falling into an elevator shaft and plunging twenty stories to her demise. Maybe she sometimes wants to pull down one of the white-painted boards and smash it over his head. Who knows? Rose chattered away when I met them, and her balding husband stood nearby with his brow furrowed and nodded a lot. She seems to be the force in the family. She stands very erect and is almost a head taller than Arnie—a big woman with a face like Eleanor Roosevelt and shoulders like Hulk Hogan, who wears her silver hair in a tight bun.

When I went to their house for our initial meeting, Rose went on and on about their two adult children, Doug and Evy. Doug's a rabbi in Morristown, New Jersey, and Evy's a nurse practitioner at a fertility clinic in Minneapolis. She should move to where her brother is. Most of the episodes of *A Baby Story* are filmed in New Jersey, so apparently there's a lot of boffing and baby-making there. No doubt a few folks have fertility issues. Maybe Evy could specialize in in-vitro fertilization for the wives of New Jersey Mob guys. "Listen," some hulking goombah wiseguy—probably a "made" man, maybe even a *capo*—would say. "Me and the old lady, we been screwin' our brains out tryin' ta make a bambino, but it ain't worked. What can ya do for us?" Evy would tell him that there are options, but it's expensive and time-consuming and there are no guarantees. "I don't worry about no expense, lady," the guy would say, his upper lip curled. "Our, uh, waste management business has been doin' real good, ya know what I mean?"

Before I cleaned his litter box, Harold and I sat in the bedroom and watched part of an episode of the first season of *Teen Mom*. It was an all-day marathon. Catelynn and Maci and Farrah were immersed in their usual dramas: fighting with sullen boyfriends and worried mothers, obsessing about money and child custody issues, complaining to their girlfriends, bemoaning their fates, and speculating about their uncertain futures. One of the segments with Amber and Gary made me want to cry. That cantankerous pair was having yet another of their numerous horrible arguments. Huge Gary, wearing a white undershirt and reclining on the sofa, his gut bulging and a few crumbs decorating his scruffy beard, was complaining that Amber was lazy. "You go to school six hours a week and take care of the baby and you can't find an *hour* a day to clean this house?" She comes back that he never picks up anything. "*You're* the laziest person I've ever met," she screams. "You're a poor excuse for a man. I'm DONE with you."

They're yelling at each other and wagging chubby fingers, and with each accusation the volume amps up. Then, at one point, the camera zooms in on pretty little blue-eyed Leah sitting on the floor, in her diaper, looking up in turn at each of her screaming parents' faces. That's when I wanted to cry. I couldn't get a handle on her facial expression. Scared? Certainly. But also: *Here we go again*. That poor child. That poor, sad little girl, having to endure those two bloated, self-centered, immature chuckleheads going at each other full throttle. How scary for her. What a way to start life. If their fight had been an isolated incident, that would have been one thing. But no.

This is a continuing saga for Leah. This is her life now. That episode was filmed a while back, but Amber and Gary are still on the show, now *Teen Mom 2*, still fighting and carrying on, still hurling a cacophony of insults and accusations. Maybe they'll be on for years to come, still screaming and fighting with each other, and the world will have the chance to see Leah's pretty face change over time, mature as she gets older and goes from baby to toddler to kindergartner to grade-schooler to middle-schooler to high-schooler, as the camera periodically zooms in on her yet again having to endure her nutso parents arguing. Lovely!

"Sometimes, Lucy, I think that if I could, I'd rescue Leah, adopt her. She could be with us. Would that be okay?" But Lucy's noncommittal. She has a kind heart, but I don't know if she's up for any significant changes in our life.

Well, maybe Leah will be okay. Amber, when she's not fussing with Gary, seems to be a good enough mother—tender and caring and kind. I've never seen her yell at the baby—so far, anyway. She talks to the kid nicely and takes very good care of her and clearly loves her a lot. You can see that. And Gary loves the baby, too, and seems tender enough in his own giganto way. So at least there's that. Maybe Leah'll be fine.

But perhaps a little intervention is in order. Maybe some of us in the Legion of Overweight Cat Avengers, deviating from our original mission, could kidnap and blindfold Gary and Amber and shove them into a locked room and sit their fat asses down on uncomfortable card chairs. There'd be a table at one end of the room piled high with an assortment of Dunkin' Donuts selections and cupcakes from Gigi's. "Okay," one of us would say, "here's the thing. You two have been behaving badly. *Very* badly. God knows how, but somehow the two of you've produced a lovely little girl, and she's wonderful, but you immature, self-centered, oversized knuckleheads keep screaming at each other in front of her. How do you think that makes your daughter feel, to have to witness her parents doing that all the time? Have either of you ever *thought* about that? Have you once thought about that? Well, HAVE you? No? I didn't think so. Well, some changes have to be made. Either the two of you shape up and stop this nonsense immediately, or there *will* be consequences. You want to fight, fine—just not in front of your beautiful little girl. See those doughnuts and cupcakes over there? Well, if you want any you'll both have to sign this agreement. If not, you can just sit there and drool and watch us indulge. The ball's in your court, folks."

Hopefully, they'd quickly sign the agreement to never fight in front of their daughter again. If so, we'd find a notary public somewhere to make it official. If they didn't agree to sign the document, we'd tie them to their chairs and all of us would stuff our faces with numerous cupcakes and doughnuts in front of them, licking the crumbs off our lips and moaning with pleasure, and wash it all down with Diet Pepsi, until Amber and Gary eventually relented.

After that, perhaps some or all of us in the Legion could take a little vacation trip to Florida, where we'd track down the nasty teenage twitheads who'd drugged Harold and exact some revenge. They'd probably say they were so *very* sorry and claim youthful indiscretion, but that wouldn't hold any sway with us. Maybe we'd shove some magic mushrooms down their gullets and haul them to some godforsaken swamp area in the Everglades, with quicksand and nasty alligators lurking, and wait until the mushrooms kicked in and leave them to their own devices. Or maybe we'd tattoo "I'M SORRY I WAS SUCH A JERK TO HAROLD" on their faces.

Afterward, we'd all put on our bikinis, some with side-ties, and sunbathe on the beach at Ft. Lauderdale. People would probably stare and scrunch up their faces and go, "Yuck! Who are these porkers? Have they no shame?" Some yo-yo would say, "Wouldn't you ladies be more comfortable in one-piece bathing suits?" We'd all glare at him, stern-faced. "Oh, no," one of us would answer. "Not at all. We're just *fine* in our itsy-bitsy teeny-weeny bikinis. Not that it's any of *your* business, bucko." Then we'd romp in the waves and enjoy the sunshine and the lovely salty Atlantic breeze, and after a while we'd have a few drinks—mai tais, piña coladas, banana daiquiris, and the like—and then have a lovely seafood feast of steamed shrimp, yellowfin tuna, clams, mahi mahi, red snapper, tilapia, and blue crab. We'd prepare a huge tub of jambalaya. There'd be big bowls of Macadamia nuts. It would all be good.

Well, if nothing else, maybe I could just get Amber and Gary to let me borrow Leah for a while—a few weeks each summer. It'd be a respite from her obnoxious parents. We could have fun. We'd go down the waterslides at Noah's Ark in Wisconsin Dells on hot July days. Maybe we'd go to the Dane Dances on the Monona Terrace rooftop on Friday evenings in August, and Leah'd get a kick from seeing me dance like Elaine, giggling if I imitated Elaine's backward thumb thrusts. We'd go to the Dane County Farmers' Market on the Capitol Square on Saturday mornings and buy some spicy cheese bread at the Stella's Bakery booth, and maybe we'd even get some triple-thick chocolate brownies from the Sugar River booth. We could even drive to Milwaukee and go to the State Fair, where we'd get a couple of those huge and disgusting, though delicious, cream puffs that you can barely hold in one hand, and maybe some chocolate-covered bacon on a stick.

She and Lucy and I could watch DVDs of Disney movies—*Dumbo, Snow White, The Lion King* and *The Little Mermaid.* Leah'd probably cry when Dumbo gets separated from his mommy. "It's okay, honey," I'd say soothingly, stroking the back of her head. "Just wait till you see how Dumbo gets back at those nasty clowns who tormented him. Sweet revenge, girly-girl!"

I hope Lucy'd be okay with Leah. "What do you think, Lucy-Goosey? Could the three of us have a good time?" That's something she'll have to consider, though. Lucy's not one to commit to anything without some serious thought first. I respect that. It's one of the things I love about her.

Having Leah for a little while might prepare me if Corinna ever came along—if I ever get to a place in my life, that is, where doing the deed and getting preggers is even a possibility. Hopefully, Lucy'd like Corinna and not resent her intrusion into our quiet life together. Maybe it *would* be fun to have a little girl of my own to hang around with, to do things with. I see moms and their little girls all the time out in the world. They seem to have fun together. The girls are cute and their mommies are so proud. They have little replicas of themselves, not yet corrupted or disappointing. But I don't want to go through Corinna's first year or two or three, when she's a baby and a toddler. If she'd just come along when she was four or five, maybe that'd be okay. That'd be better. They're easier then. Maybe Lucy'd be okay with that.

Well, I don't know. The thought of having a little girl is nice, I guess. It's a nice fantasy— something pleasant to imagine. But, really, I don't think I'm up for it. I'm too lazy. I don't want to work hard—not at a relationship, not at parenting. I just don't. I don't want the responsibility of a kid. I don't want to be tied down. I just want to do what I'm doing—tending my cats to make a few dollars, maybe doing my flower paintings sometime down the road, and hanging with Lucy in our little apartment and listening to Sinatra every night in the tub. I just like living alone.

Something must be wrong with me that I don't have more ambition, more drive, like most people. I must be deficient, somehow, that my sights in life are set so low, that I'm so damned lazy. I've often thought that. Something must be wrong with me that I don't drool at the prospect of motherhood. Well, hell, I guess it's just who I am. Like Sammy sings, "I've gotta be me." Even if "me" is pretty boring and will never make much of a splash in the world.

It is nice to live alone—for now, anyway. I'm used to it. It's nice to come home to my apartment and know that I don't have to please anyone, compromise with anyone, share with anyone. I can eat what I want, when I want, and I don't need to close the bathroom door when I poop.

I wonder if people in some of those primitive societies ever envy people like me. I imagine a lot of them never get to be alone much. They're with other people all the time. No privacy. They eat, sleep, go potty, and fornicate in public. That's not for me. Well, who knows? I don't imagine that some pygmy living in a hut in Africa with her parents and grandparents and eight brothers and sisters spends a lot of time saying to herself, "Damn! I sure wish I could just live in a small apartment with only my cat, like Maggie Mullen in Madison, Wisconsin."

The other thing, though, is that having kids is risky. Too many bad things can happen. You can't control the genes a kid gets. That's another major crapshoot. Even if a kid's parents are okay, not sick or crazy, the kid can inherit worrisome genes from further back—a grandfather, say, who was down in the dumps and practically catatonic one day and the next day was bouncing off the walls and talking a hundred miles an hour, not always making sense, and pissing away the family fortune on needless extravagances, like a Rolex GMT-Master or a half-dozen high-end Italian silk shirts of the same style, in six different colors.

A kid can be okay for a while, and then after a few years the bad genes kick in and she starts getting weird, maybe disturbed, and you're hauling her to doctors and kiddy shrinks. And maybe you have to live in fear of her, hoping that she doesn't murder the family in their sleep or do unspeakable things to the pets.

Or a child can get sick or injured. He can end up in the cancer ward at American Family Children's Hospital on the west end of the UW campus, his hair gone from the chemo, hoping that some burly Badger football player will come around and give him a signed ball or jersey and talk about his athletic exploits and how he has high hopes for the coming season, and tell the kid to hang in there.

Once Corinna started school, I'd be a wreck worrying about what could happen. Her school bus could stall on the train tracks, and a Wisconsin and Southern freight train could plow into it. Or she could be playing soccer on a rainy day, the grass still wet from a thunderstorm that had just passed through, and a stray bolt of lightning could incinerate her. Or maybe some twisted psychopath would kidnap her and demand a ransom of a hundred thousand dollars. "I'm so sorry," I'd say, "but I don't have that kind of money. Would you be willing to settle for this lovely strapless bridesmaid's dress, with ruching, and these amazing Lyric silver heels instead?"

Too many worries.

At the least, I'd always worry that Corinna wouldn't get along with Lucy, would maybe even torture her. Maybe the kid would pull her tail a lot or dress her in ridiculous outfits or slather her fur with strawberry jelly. Poor Lucy. She's used to a quiet, uneventful life with just me, and then here comes this noisy, hyperactive ragamuffin to disrupt our peaceful routine.

"What do you think, Lucy-Goosey? Do you worry about that?"

I'd have to put Corinna to bed before Lucy and I did our nightly bath routine. But suppose I was soaking in the tub, listening to Frank and fantasizing about him gazing at me with those eyes and singing just to me while he gently stroked my right cheek with the backs of his fingers. Maybe I'd be touching myself. Sleepy Lucy would be on the toilet seat lid next to me. Then we'd hear, "Mommy! I want a glass of water. Oh, *Mommy!* Where the hell *are* you?" I guess I'd have to get up and accommodate the kid. As I'd be standing in the tub toweling off and reaching for my green terrycloth robe, irritated and muttering to myself, Lucy'd look up at me as though to say, "See? I told you this sort of thing would happen. You should have left well enough alone."

Damn! The wedding rehearsal and then the rehearsal dinner at Claddagh are in two days. And then the wedding is the day after that.

I'm upset with Mindy about the rehearsal dinner, though. I told her a long time ago that I'd help with that. I'd picked up a copy of Claddagh's event menu and saw that we had to choose one of two entrées from each of the four main categories: chicken, beef, seafood and pasta. Everyone would get to choose what they wanted—chicken, beef, etc.—and then they'd get the selected entrée for that category. I only cared about the chicken entrées, since that's what I want. The options were Drunken Cherry Chicken and Gaelic Chicken, wherein the chicken breasts are pan-seared and lightly seasoned on a bed of mashed potatoes. Yum! The other chicken entrée sounded okay, too, except for the dried cherry sauce. But the Gaelic Chicken was clearly my number one pick. As for desserts, the options were Irish Car Bomb Cheesecake, Warm and Tipsy Bread Pudding, and Traditional Banoffee Pie. The latter has toffee, bananas, and fresh whipped cream in a graham cracker crust, topped with chocolate shavings. Oh, sweet Jesus! We had to choose one of those three options, and then everyone who wanted a dessert would get that. The Banoffee Pie was my clear favorite.

But when I told Mindy about my planned selections, she overruled me. "Oh, no," she said. "We'll go with the Drunken Cherry Chicken. That sounds lovely. And I definitely want the cheesecake. Oh, I adore cheesecake." We argued a bit, but the muckety-muck bride prevailed.

That's not the only headache. "I'm obsessing, Lucy, about the damned toast I have to give at the reception. What the hell am I going to say?"

Well, maybe I can base it on the cute song Frank's singing now.

Just what makes that little old ant
Think he'll move that rubber tree plant?
Anyone knows an ant can't
Move a rubber tree plant.

But he's got high hopes, he's got high hopes,
He's got high apple pie in the sky hopes.

"So, Mindy and Richard," I'll say, "as you two lovely people move forward together in your adventurous journey through life, just keep in mind that perpetual optimism is a good thing. Always have high hopes. If you ever have doubts that you can succeed in life, just remember that ant trying to move the rubber tree plant. And remember that ram who wanted to punch a hole in a dam. No one could make him scram …he kept butting that dam. And, finally, *voilá!* Yes, he did it—a big hole in the dam. Of course, then the dam burst and flooded the town and thousands drowned, but so what? The ram's high hopes paid off. He got what *he* wanted. And isn't that the point?" Hah!

I wonder if that old man that Sheila told me about has hopes, high ones or otherwise. I wonder if he knew his wife was going to die. Maybe they told him she would, but he refused to believe it. Maybe he hoped for a miracle. And now he's alone—no children, no grandchildren. There were no other visitors in the six days she was in the hospital. I hope he has a dog or a cat, or both, at home. A cat or two will keep him company. A cat will sense his sadness, his loneliness, and will rub against him in sympathy. A cat will sit on his chest as he lies alone in the bed he shared with his wife for almost sixty years, watching his revenge movies or whatever he likes.

Petting a cat will make him feel better—a little better, maybe. That always works for me. If he doesn't have a cat, maybe Kat Grammy and I could get him one—perhaps a nice domestic shorthair that the Avengers liberated from some nasty subhuman diddlehead—and we'd bring it to him personally and advise him as to what to feed her, and what kind of litter to get and how often to scoop it and change it, and the kinds of toys that cats like. We'd suggest good vets. We'd do what we could to make the old man feel better.

Tough days are ahead. I'll have good thoughts for him.

I wonder, too, if he and his wife were soulmates for all those years they were together. I hope so. Even though I have doubts about anyone being soulmates, I hope it was true for them. They just had each other, and were together for so long. Maybe that soulmates deal worked for them. I'm sure they had their arguments, though. They must have had *some* bad times. Hell, I can't imagine that you can live with someone for more than fifty years and not hate them once in a while. Well, I hope he has some nice pictures of her on his walls or hutch or dresser that he can look at and remember their time together.

Three days! My sister's wedding is in three days. *Yikes!*

At least I probably won't have my period at the wedding. I've started PMSing now, which is bad enough, but my period should hold off until after the blessed event. I've been worried about that. I don't want to worry about any mishaps, any red spots on that Capri-blue bridesmaid dress. I don't want to worry about whether I remembered to bring pads or tampons. If it's one of those damned heavy-flow days, I'll probably need both.

I suppose that if I had my period, I could ask Toni to add "holding onto Maggie's feminine hygiene supplies, plus a bottle of Midol" to the detailed list of personal attendant duties that she's prepared.

As I predicted, Toni's just *thrilled* to be a personal attendant.

The funny thing is that I'm not having my usual PMS craving for Brach's Circus Peanuts. Instead, I'm wanting potato chips and ice cream. Just before my bath, I ate a big dish of Ben and Jerry's Peanut Butter Fudge ice cream, doused with Hershey's Chocolate Syrup, and now I have a big bag of Ruffle's Sour Cream & Onion chips next to the tub, with a small plastic container of Bucky Badger Wisconsin French Onion Dip. I may have some Froot Loops with banana slices later, if I can't sleep.

Lucy looks at me askance as I pick a few potato chips from the bag and dip them and shove them in my mouth. I don't think she likes the crunchy sound as I chew. "Oh, stop being such as fussbudget, Goosey. Potato chips are one of God's tender mercies, you know."

I keep thinking about Larry's friend Jordan. I love those crinkly blue eyes. *Whew!* I wouldn't mind doing the deed with him sometime, if I ever have the opportunity do that again with anyone. I wonder if point guards like doing cowgirl. If so, and if it led to my getting off, he could get credit for an assist.

The Tender Trap

THE WEDDING rehearsal wasn't as horrible as I'd anticipated, even though I was in a bad mood beforehand, and the dinner at Claddagh turned out better than I thought it would, food-wise.

I wasn't in too bad a mood when the damned rehearsal started. I got to St. Bernard before anyone else and was sitting alone in one of the back pews, admiring the stained glass windows and thinking about earlier today when I went over to Ian's house to take care of Clarence and Murphy. I remembered how pissed off Murphy was when he saw Clarence through the kitchen window, romping in the backyard. I believe he was jealous. I believe that he's always jealous when Clarence gets to go outside and he doesn't. I think I know Murph's little moods very well.

Sitting in the back pew thinking about that furry pair made me smile. But then when Mindy and Richard waltzed into the church, my mood went south because my mind, for some reason, zoomed in on our disagreement about Claddagh, the one where Mindy overruled my choices as to the dessert and chicken entrée options. *Why*, I thought, *did she have to be such a little control freak about that? Why couldn't she just have left it to me?* "Oh, Maggie," she could have easily said. "I just don't care at *all* about the food selections at my rehearsal dinner. Use your judgment. I trust you completely, dear sister, when it comes to food issues. I know that's your forte." But no.

She looked good, I'll say that for Mindy. She wore a short light-green skirt and a cute yellow top that revealed her belly button, an innie. Her pretty hair was down. Her pretty face glowed. By the time she and Richard arrived, both sets of parents and the whole bridal party, plus Toni, were already there and gathered in the back of the church. When the happy little couple toodled in, everyone clapped and Katie raised both arms high and went, "Oh, YES. *Woo-hoo!*"

After a bit, Father Connor had everyone sit in the front pews and went over the proceedings. That guy has one of the pinkest heads I've ever seen, with thinning white hair arranged in a not-terribly-flattering comb-over. He's also the most pigeon-toed priest I've ever seen. He was standing on the steps to the sanctuary talking sugar: how he's known Mindy since she was a little girl getting ready for her First Communion; what a splendid young woman she's turned out to be; how, in their pre-marital counseling sessions, he's gotten to know and like Richard; what a *blessing* it is that Mindy and Richard have found each other and, with the Lord's blessing, are on the brink of a "glorious life adventure together"; how we all want everything to go perfectly smoothly and wonderfully tomorrow, with no glitches; and blah blah blah. During that whole speech, I couldn't help staring at his feet. The heels of his shiny black leather shoes were maybe six inches apart, but the toes were practically touching. I remember wondering if that was hard on his ankles, standing like that with his feet angled inward so much. I noticed that one of his black shoelaces was cloth, but the other was some kind of shiny plastic.

The rehearsal itself was tedious. We had to gather at the back of the church and then practice going down the aisle, in order. The other three bridal party couples sauntered down the aisle together, but I had to go by myself after them, since Mark had entered from the side and was standing at the front already with Richard. Father Connor had suggested that all the groomsmen, not just the best man, enter from the side with the groom, but Mindy said she preferred that the groomsmen and bridesmaids go down the aisle as couples, except, of course, for the maid of honor. And, of course, little Miss Priss prevailed. So I'll be alone going down that damned aisle tomorrow, with all the rubbernecks staring at me. Well, I knew I'd have to endure that particular indignity.

Then came Mindy and our jerkface old man. Mindy also had the choice of coming down with both parents or just Dad, and she chose the latter. I wonder how Mom feels about that. As I stood at the front with Julie and Katie and Diana and all of us were watching my father and Mindy coming down—she holding onto his arm and he standing so straight—I had ungenerous thoughts. I imagined it was tomorrow, and I was standing up there dressed in my silly Bill Levkoff strapless floor-length gown, grasping my bouquet to my tummy, nervous. I was watching Mindy and Dad start slowly down the aisle to the usual processional music—either "Jesu, Joy of Man's Desiring" or that Pachelbel thing they often do. All the guests were standing and smiling at lovely Mindy and her beautiful Allure Couture dress with the chapel-length train of delustered satin. As they were about halfway down the aisle, in my fantasy, Dad's belt suddenly loosened and his pants fell to his ankles and he tripped and pitched forward with a loud "*Argh!*" All the guests initially gasped but soon immediately commenced laughing uproariously, slapping their knees, and pointing toward my father sprawled facedown on the now-bunched-up white runner, his black tuxedo pants down around his calves and the back of his white boxer shorts on full display. Mindy was mortified, not at all happy that everyone was guffawing during her moment of glory. She turned to glance down the aisle at me, hoping for some sisterly support and solace, and was dismayed to see, instead, a smug, self-satisfied expression on my bloated face.

Back in reality, after the practice walk down the aisle, we had to rehearse the rest of the tedious ceremony: just where the bridesmaids and groomsmen were to stand, and which ways to face; how to hold our bouquets; the hymn; the readings; the psalms; the vows; the ring ceremony; the kiss; and the priest's blessing. We went over what the bride and groom were to do and when to do it: when to face each other, when to face the priest, lighting the unity candle, and on and on. Father Connor discussed the Communion. Then we practiced the recessional, with the grinning couple going up the aisle at a quicker pace than during the processional, followed by the bridal party and then the parents.

Father Connor ran the whole show, and not badly either. For all his pinkness and bad hair and pigeon-toedness, the guy has an air of competent authority. We had to run through the whole deal twice, the second time much more quickly than the first. Father Connor finished by reminding me, as maid of honor, to be sure that the bride drinks enough water tomorrow. I nodded and smiled sweetly at him and then looked over to Toni to see if she got the message. Keeping the stupid bride hydrated should be the personal attendant's job, not *mine*. I have enough damned worries, thank you very much. I have to worry about keeping my boobs from spilling out.

"Well, Goosey, I finally met the other three groomsmen dudes—Eric, Russell, and Josh. Josh is a doofus, but you might like Russell. He's quiet." I didn't hear him say a word the entire evening. He's skinny and maybe six-five and towered over Richard and Mark and Eric and Josh as the five of them stood in front after their part of the processional, watching the bride and her oh-so-proud daddy coming down the aisle. Russell has a nice head of dark, curly hair and sweet blue eyes, but a perpetual downturned-mouth scowl. Plus, the guy has one of those concave chests and no shoulders. Well, he has some shoulders, but not much. They're almost smaller than

Julie's, and it seems there's less of her every time I see her. Poor girl. She probably has to run around in the shower now to get wet. If she sat on a quarter, fifteen cents would show.

I worry about her. I wish I could help her, but don't know how. Well, maybe she's okay. Maybe she's fine—just one of those naturally thin women. Maybe I'm overreacting. It was funny, though, watching her and Josh walking down and then back up the aisle tonight. He's only a little taller than she is, but he's thick and muscular and broad-backed, with a barrel chest, and has a big brown mustache and a huge shaved head—a buffalo head. Mindy said he was a wrestler in high school. He struts when he walks—quite impressed with himself.

After Mark and I'd reached the end of the aisle during the recessional practice, I turned around to watch the other three couples, and had to stifle a laugh at the sight. First came Eric and Katie, a fairly blah and normal-looking pair, followed by way-too-thick Josh and way-too-thin Julie, looking for all the world like Mr. and Mrs. Jack Sprat. Finally came Russell and Diana, him towering over her by more than a foot and looking totally uninterested—like he'd rather be elsewhere. His elbow was too high for her to hold onto, so she had to grasp his forearm, close to the wrist. I noticed that at one point Diana craned her neck to look up at his face, her brow furrowed. I wondered what she was thinking.

Mark barely said a word to me during the whole rehearsal deal, or, for that matter, at the dinner at Claddagh afterward. He's not horrible-looking, I'll say that, what with being a bit taller than his brother and having nice hazel eyes and good, strong shoulders. But his parted-in-the-middle thin hair is very wrong, and that scruffy little goatee is a horror story. He has just the hint of a coming bald spot on the crown of his head. And I don't think he's all that bright. We were standing at the back of the church after the second recessional practice, with Katie and Mindy all bright-eyed and giggling about God-knows-what and Julie staring, expressionless, at poor, mostly naked Jesus wearing his crown of thorns, slumped on the huge cross on the front wall of the sanctuary. Richard and Josh and Eric were huddled together, scratching their behinds and talking about tomorrow's Packers exhibition game against Arizona. I asked Mark if he was looking forward to the dinner at Claddagh. He furrowed his brow and pursed his lips. "I dunno," he finally said. "What's that? Like a restaurant or somethin'?"

Earlier today, I'd told Clarence and Murphy how much I was looking forward to Claddagh. "Well, kiddos, I'm still pissed that I won't be getting the Gaelic Chicken, but I guess that other chicken deal, the Drunken Cherry, should be okay. The cheesecake will have to do, even though I wanted the Banoffee Pie, with the lovely banana. And a few drinks will make it all fine, right?"

Clarence had looked up at me with his tawny head cocked, and he may have nodded. "Well, that's just wonderful," he'd maybe have said if he could talk. "We're so glad for you. In the meantime, Murphy and I will get the same damned cat food that we always, *always* get. Same old blah Friskies Indoor Delights. Just like every day of our tedious lives, right? Oh, but, believe me, Aunt Maggie, Murph and I are just *thrilled* for your upcoming feast at Claddagh, even though we certainly feel your pain that the bill of fare isn't *precisely* what your dear little heart desired. Oh, poor you!"

I would have been well-rebuked.

I like old Clarence. Ian and his mostly-live-in girlfriend, Louise, have a weird deal going with their cats. Ian had Clarence first, and when he lived in Sun Prairie Clarence was pretty much an outside cat and came in only when he wanted to, via a little wooden cat door. Ian told me that Clarence liked to explore the city sewers and would often come home from his wanderings after being gone for a day or two, filthy and sometimes stinking and ready for a good meal and a comfortable indoor nap before his next excursion. When he moved to Madison two years ago, Ian didn't want Clarence to have to modify his wandering ways too much just because of their new location, so he let Clarence out in the fenced-in backyard a few hours a day. He can't wander the sewers, but at least it's something.

Then, when Louise more-or-less moved in with Ian shortly after he moved to Madison, she brought her cat, Murphy, to live there. A nice little blended family. But Louise didn't want Murphy to be an outside kitty. She thought he'd kill birds or other little creatures and would probably run away or get hurt. She thought he wasn't streetwise, like Clarence.

The instructions they gave me were to feed the cats as soon as I arrived for each visit and then let Clarence out until it was time for me to leave. Clarence knew the routine, and as soon as he'd gobbled down his kibbles this morning he zoomed to the back door and glared back at me, impatiently, as though saying, "Okay, c'mon, let's go here. Time's a-wasting. Let me out. Let's GO, lady. *Now*, huh?"

Murphy knew the routine, too, and wasn't at all happy about it. As soon as I'd opened the door to let Clarence out, Murph jumped onto one of the kitchen window ledges and tensed his little brown body and peered out into the backyard, a definite pissed-off look on his furry face. Murph watched Clarence intently as he sauntered across the yard and, at one point, stretched hugely and rolled on the grass. When Clarence moved to the far end of the yard, Murphy quickly jumped down and scurried over to another window to get a better view. After a few minutes, he turned to glare at me and meowed loudly, practically screaming, his yellow eyes wild. He even dashed over to the parakeet cage in the living room and screamed at little Ralphie. Poor Murph! He's outraged; he feels cheated, deprived, abused. Yet despite his distress, I couldn't help chuckling.

"What do you think, Lucy? Would you like to be an outside kitty now and again? Would you like to experience the great world outside this little apartment? Do you envy Clarence?" She's noncommittal on the issue. But I believe my Lucy's perfectly content with her quiet, cloistered life with me. But even if she wasn't, it wouldn't matter. She's not going outside. No way! Too many dangers there. Too many possible dire outcomes. I agree with Louise. Louise and I are better cat guardians than Ian in regard to that issue.

I always had the idea that when the Morrisons' cat, Jake, sat on his haunches and stared at me, he was trying to communicate that he dreamed of being able to go outside and see what was out there. I advised him to forego that little dream and be satisfied with his quiet, safe inside life. I don't know if my advice sank in. Probably not. But Jake's entitled to his dreams, his fantasies. So am I.

I wonder what Louise sees in Ian. But I think I know what he must see in her. Ian had mentioned her when I'd been to his house previously, but I hadn't actually met her until recently, when I came to get a new key. Ian's not a bad-looking dude: tall and thin, decent shoulders, long brown hair tied back in a ponytail, little brown mustache and goatee, and thin wire-rimmed glasses. He always wears blue jeans and dark solid-color T-shirts. He's some kind of a manager at Whole Foods on University Avenue. His big pride is his vegetable garden out back; the guy goes on and on about his beloved kohlrabi and squash and whatnot. Almost every time I've seen him, he's been slurping a blueberry-and-mango smoothie. He's okay, I guess, though not my cup of tea.

Ian's never once asked me anything about myself beyond "How are you today?" Louise, on the other hand, has. She's biracial, I believe, and has amazingly beautiful tea-colored skin, big almond-shaped light-brown eyes, and wavy short black hair. She usually wears thin cotton dresses, often brown or beige, sometimes showing pleasant cleavage. When I met her, she was sitting at the kitchen table eating a lunch from McDonald's: a Quarter-Pounder with Cheese and fries from a large red-and-yellow paper container and a big Coke. Ian was watering a small potted plant on the far corner of the counter. "Nice to meet you," she said in a low, husky voice, looking into my eyes and extending her hand. "Want some fries? I don't think they ever put enough salt on them, so I poured on more." Ian gave her a look when she said that, and she shrugged her shoulders and stuck out her tongue at him.

"Sure," I said, and took a few. "Thanks." *What a sweet face*, I thought. *What a lovely voice!* Whoa!

We ate our fries in silence for a minute or so, Louise dipping each of hers in both ketchup and mustard, and then she asked me to tell her about my cat-tending business. She wanted to know how I'd gotten into it, how many cats I took care of, which were my favorites, and what I did on my visits. I told her I'd started doing it four years ago, part-time, after I'd seen a flier at Sentry from someone advertising in-home pet care, and after a while my business grew to full-time. I'd never talked so much with anyone about what I do.

She listened politely, never losing eye contact, and nodded. "Sounds nice," she said. "It sounds like a good thing. I'm very sorry about poor Bella, though. I'll have a good thought for her."

Louise told me that she stays at Ian's most of the time, but has her own apartment on Few Street, on the near-east side. "I like my own space," she said. "I stay there at least two or three times a week, and more if that guy over there bores me or gets on my nerves." She said that Murphy mostly lives at Ian's. She likes it that Murphy and Clarence have each other for company, but now and again she brings Murph home with her to the apartment.

She met Ian when she worked at Whole Foods, but now she works as a cook at Dotty Dumpling's Dowry downtown. "Absolute *best* freakin' burgers in town, Maggie," she said. I told her that I was quite familiar with the place.

On my first visit to Ian's, I'd noticed some interesting paintings, in simple black metal frames, on the walls in the living room and the hallway outside the main bathroom. They were all close-ups of dark-skinned black women—many of them *big* women—looking out directly and unsmilingly. My favorite was of an imposing, solid-looking woman with a big Afro, prominent cheekbones, intense dark-brown eyes, and sensuous lips. She was wearing a low-cut purple silk blouse and had on big gold-colored hoop earrings. When I asked Ian about the pictures, he told me that Louise had done them. "She's been painting since she was in middle school," he said. "It's her passion. She spends a lot of time at it. Pretty good, huh? I'm jealous of her talent, I'll tell you that."

Sweet Louise. "Ian made a good choice in that one, Goose, that's for damned sure."

Ian's house is comfortable, though sparse. He doesn't have a TV downstairs, though there's a small, older Zenith in one corner of the main bedroom. I didn't see a DVD player. I never watch that TV. I'm not comfortable spending time in his bedroom. I don't know why not. He doesn't have a sofa, though there are four older-but-comfortable green-upholstered chairs in his living room. One has a big brown stain on the upper-right corner of the seat. He has two big potted plants downstairs and a smaller one upstairs, in the hallway just outside his bedroom. There're two blue wooden bookcases downstairs, each with four shelves, and another one in his bedroom. They're mostly filled with books and magazines about gardening and recycling and nutrition and yoga and assorted spiritual stuff—*The Alchemist, The Celestine Prophecy*, a few by someone named Deepak Chopra—though he does have a nice red-and-pink hardcover set of Jane Austen's novels. That's nice. I opened three of them, and had the impression that, except maybe for *Emma*, they'd never been read.

Deepak would be a good name for a cat. He could be Deep for short.

It's good to soak in my tub, here in my own bathroom, with my sweet Lucy nearby, as I sip my chardonnay. It's good to slowly run the big sea sponge that I got at Soap Opera for $12.95 over my thick legs. Tonight I slathered the sponge with Provence Sante Lavender Soap. This will be my only relaxation until after the damned wedding and reception tomorrow. Damn! I'm so nervous about having to do my toast at the reception that I could almost puke. As soon as that silliness is over with, I'm going to head straight for the open bar and get semi-plastered. If anyone's in line at the bar, I'll elbow them aside. "I'm the damned maid of honor!" I'll growl. "Get the *hell* out of the way! I have special privilege here."

Well, tomorrow will bring what it does, but at least the rehearsal and the dinner at Claddagh are behind me now. I just have to wash my hair to get it ready for the hairstyling tomorrow morning. Mindy'd told all of us bridesmaids to wash our hair the night before the wedding rather than in the morning because her stylist at ANiU had said that freshly washed hair doesn't hold a curl as well as dirtier hair. Who knew?

Claddagh Irish Pub and Restaurant. I'm glad that Mindy at least agreed with my suggestion to have her rehearsal dinner there. One thing I like about that place is that they have bowls of pretzels on the bar—and not cheap, chintzy ones either, but high-quality hard and twisty pretzels made from good dough and baked to a perfect golden-brown. They might even be hand-rolled. I love the soft pretzels I get at Auntie Anne's in West Towne, but those are a close second.

When we arrived at Claddagh, I went right to the bar and munched down some of those pretzels while waiting for the bartender, Jason, to get done talking to some long-haired, horsy-faced blonde with a little silver nose ring and a tattoo on her right upper arm that said "BLESSED." She was looking directly into his eyes and flashing a charming little feminine smile that showed her sparkling white teeth, while twisting the ends of her hair with her left hand, batting her false lashes at him, and taking sexy little sips from her margarita. The red-nailed pinky finger of her right hand was extended. I scarfed down most of a whole bowl of the pretzels while waiting. When Jason'd finished with the flirty little slut, I asked him where the ladies' room was. But I already knew the answer; I'd been to Claddagh before. My waiting at the bar was just a pretext to get at the lovely pretzels. "Oh, thank you so much, sir," I murmured, batting my own lashes a bit. "I really *appreciate* it."

The dinner in the Trinity Room at Claddagh was okay. Sitting there made me thirsty at first because the walls and ceiling were plastered with little triangular paper Budweiser banners, as well as two plastic signs indicating "GUINNESS SOLD HERE." I quickly ordered one of those and so did Diana, who was sitting beside me. The bridal party and Toni and the parents sat at a long table in the middle of the room, and others, including Aunt Grace and her blah sons, sat at booths along the walls.

Diana had the Claddagh New York Strip, cooked medium-well, with potato boxty, vegetables, and—*yum!*—a side of peppercorn cream sauce. She poured some of the sauce on her steak and poured the rest in a little pool at the edge of her plate. She dipped pieces of soda bread in the sauce and chewed each piece slowly and lovingly. "Damn!" she said. "This is heavenly. Peppercorn cream sauce and soda bread! I'm gonna have sexy dreams about *this*, I'll tell you that much."

As for me, the Drunken Cherry Chicken was, surprisingly, acceptable. The chicken fillets were simmered in a lovely red-wine-and-dried-cherry sauce. That was okay. The cherry flavor wasn't as bad as I'd thought it would be, but it didn't exactly make me orgasmic either. The mashed potatoes, though, were magnificent—way better than I'd anticipated. The rosemary-infused Irish whiskey sauce on the potatoes was perfectly lovely.

Claddagh's wonderful Irish Mac 'N Cheese might have been comforting, considering that I'm PMSing. But it wasn't a special events menu option. Oh, well. The mashed potatoes filled in nicely.

At one point, I saw that Diana was looking toward the far end of the table, where the groomsmen, except for Mark, were sitting together. Eric and Josh were talking and laughing while stuffing their faces, but Russell was just sitting there quietly, picking at his food, scowling and staring at the beer signs. "Man," Diana said, "that guy's spooky. He's always been spooky. And I've gotta *dance* with that stringbean tomorrow? Good Christ! My nose will be in his damned navel." She took a big swallow of her Guinness and burped. "What a pain in the ass!" she muttered.

At the far end of the table, Dad and Diana's parents were talking together. At one point, her father glanced toward us and made eye contact with Diana and winked. She winked back, and he blew her a little kiss. That was nice. I felt jealous. Dad was gesturing with both hands, probably letting Richard's parents know what an important and accomplished person he is. Mom was eating the last of her grilled salmon, delicately cutting off little bites, looking down, now and again dabbing at the corner of her mouth with her maroon cloth napkin, not talking to anyone. For a moment, I wanted to jump up and rush over to her and put my arms around her from behind and hug her. But I didn't. Now, sitting here in my tub, sipping my chardonnay, I wish I had.

Then Dad and Mr. Sanders stood up and tapped their glasses with spoons. *Oh, Christ*, I thought. Mr. S. went first and burbled on nicely about how happy he and his wife, Cynthia, were to have this opportunity to get together and bond with Mindy and her family, and how glad they were that their son had found a "gem" like Mindy, and how tomorrow would be such a proud and happy day for both families, blah blah. I guess it was okay. But I wasn't at all interested in what my father would have to say, assuming he'd go next. "Excuse me," I whispered to Diana and exited the Trinity Room. I headed to the bathroom and sat in the left-hand stall. I had to pee, but that aside it was nice to be alone for a while. I didn't want to hear my father blathering about any happy family crap.

"But I did think about *you*, my sweet Lucy. While I was sitting there on the potty, going number one, I thought about how much I looked forward to being with you tonight here in our bathroom. Just the two of us. And here we are, right? It's all good, little Goose."

Well, I also briefly imagined sitting there in the stall in the ladies' room at Claddagh, on the evening of my sister's wedding rehearsal dinner, and feeling like I needed to poop, and then straining and being surprised to instead push out a brat. I imagined pulling it out of the water and swaddling it in a bar towel and walking slowly back to the Trinity Room, holding my new child in my arms. Dad would be standing there doing his stupid toast, going on about how very *proud* he was of his sweet golden girl, his beloved Mindy, and what high hopes he had for her, and how glad he was that Richard would be part of our family. He'd stop mid-sentence when he saw me walking in. "Sorry for the interruption, folks," I'd murmur, with a demure little smile and a shrug. "Gosh, I didn't even *know* I was pregnant."

While finishing my Drunken Cherry Chicken a bit later, I noticed a nice oil painting on the wall above the fireplace. It was of a soldier dressed in a bright-green uniform and a green cap with a black visor. His arms were folded across his chest and he was looking to his right, with just the sourest of facial expressions. I supposed he was an Irish soldier, given the general theme of the joint and the hue of his clothing. Maybe his facial expression was a statement about the horror and futility of war. Maybe he missed his wife and children in County Cork and feared he'd die in a filthy trench in some lonely foreign land and never again know the joy of their warm embraces. Or maybe he just had a serious case of the runs and was bemoaning the lack of Porta-Potties in combat zones.

The Irish Car Bomb Cheesecake—a Guinness brownie topped with Bailey's Irish Cream, excellent cheesecake, and Jameson cream—was good. The Banoffee Pie, with the toffee and bananas and whipped cream in a graham cracker crust, topped with those chocolate shavings, would have been heavenly. *Yum!* But the cheesecake was okay. The cheesecake was fine. After Clarence's right-on scolding, I realize I need to work on not being petty. I need to be grateful for what I have. I'll try. I'll probably fail, but I should try.

While eating, I glanced across the table at the other bridesmaids and was surprised to see Julie enthusiastically scarfing down her dessert. She polished it off in four big bites, and washed it down with half a glass of White Zin. Then she leaned in toward Katie and whispered something in her ear. Katie nodded and pushed the plate with her half-eaten dessert toward Julie, who promptly polished that off as well. I'd watched Julie when the entrées came and had noticed that she'd barely touched her Galway Pasta, which had looked good—linguine pasta with garlic, diced tomatoes, sliced mushrooms and fresh basil, topped with parmesan shavings. She'd eaten part of one piece of soda bread, but not enthusiastically. Between bites of her dinner, she'd kept looking at her phone for messages. I remembered that she'd declined the Gigi's mini-cupcakes in the limo at the bachelorette party. So I was a little surprised when she gobbled down that Irish Car Bomb Cheesecake so voraciously.

"Well, Lucy, it just goes to show you. You just can't get into other people's heads. Am I right? Other people are mysteries, right, Goosey?"

But Lucy couldn't care less about that. She doesn't need to get into Julie's head. She's not worried about Julie or whatever issues that girl may have, nor is she at all perplexed by her. She gives Julie no thought. Her turquoise towel looked a bit dirty when I came home, so I threw it in the hamper and replaced it with a dark-gray one. She didn't mind. She didn't care. She just cleaned her forepaws, first the right and then the left, and then washed her face with her tongue-moistened right paw. Now her eyes are closed and she's happily listening to the song that Sinatra's singing now:

You see a pair of laughing eyes,
And suddenly you're sighing sighs.
You're thinking nothing's wrong,
You string along, boy, then snap!
Those eyes, those sighs: they're part of the tender trap.

I know just what you're saying, Frank. "Those eyes." Believe me, I can relate.

Some starry night, when her kisses make you tingle.
She'll hold you tight, and you'll hate yourself for being single.

And all at once, it seems so nice.
The folks are throwing shoes and rice.
You hurry to a spot that's just a dot on the map.

And then you wonder how it all came about.
It's too late now; there's no getting out.
You fell in love, and love ... is the tender trap.

The tender trap. That's what love is, huh? "All at once," the song says, "it seems so nice." She holds him tight and he does likewise, and their blood heats up, and pretty soon the cymbals commence clashing for both of them and keep clashing for a while, and before you know it people are throwing shoes and rice, and one or both of them wonders how it all came about. As the song says, "You're hooked; you're cooked. You're caught in the tender trap."

That's not how it was for Mindy, though. She doesn't wonder how it all came about. Hell, she *made* it all come about. She engineered the whole deal from first to now. She wiggled her little butt and competently set the bait and caught Richard and reeled him in perfectly, and tomorrow will be the culmination of her long-planned and well-thought-out tender trap. I don't know how Richard feels about it. I don't know if he feels hooked, cooked, trapped. I don't know if he scratches his head now and again and wonders how it all came about. Maybe he does, or maybe he's into the whole love-and-marriage-and-children deal the same as Mindy—the whole nice-little-nuclear-family deal. Maybe he's just fine with his journey from boyfriend to fiancé to groom and, tomorrow, to husband. And then, at some point, daddy.

"What's your thought, Lucy? Is Richard good with the whole scheme?" She just yawns.

I wonder if their chances for happiness, down the road, would be better or worse if Richard and Mindy had had an arranged marriage instead of all this bother. With so many poor slobs getting divorced and so many others staying together but miserable, I have to think that arranged marriages couldn't do much worse than people meeting the usual way or on-line. As Tevye in *Fiddler* sang to Golde, "The first time I met you was on our wedding day ..." He was scared; she was shy. They were both nervous. But they ended up having five daughters and staying together and making a life. Sure, she henpecked him horribly; and yes, he wished he were a rich man instead of a poor struggling milkman; and they certainly had their troubles, what with headstrong daughters defying tradition and those nasty pogroms. But they seemed okay. So maybe arranged marriages aren't that horrible

Maybe instead of the wedding rehearsal silliness and the rehearsal dinner tonight, there could just have been a little introduction ceremony before the wedding tomorrow, perhaps like Golde and Tevye had. Father Connor could have presided. "Richard," he'd say. "I'd like you to meet your new bride, Mindy. Mindy, this is your soon-to-be husband, Richard. Today, you two will start a glorious life adventure together. I'm aware that you don't know each other at all, and may or may not like each other once you *do* get to know each other. In fact, you may even feel *repulsed* by each other. There's no way of knowing if you're physically attracted to each other, and, of course, we have no idea if you'll be at all sexually compatible. The odds are probably against this whole thing working out, now that I think about it. But let's face it: Your odds of being happy weren't great in any case, so what the hell's the difference? Let's just see what happens. Okay, kids? Now let's get this ceremony going."

But maybe that would be too harsh. Maybe he could just say, "Listen, kids, this deal won't be easy, but remember that when Tevye married Golde, his father and his mother said they'd learn to love each other. After twenty-five years together and five kids, he finally got around to asking Golde if she *did* love him, and we remember her answer: 'I suppose I do.' His reply: 'And I suppose I love you too.' So there you have it. *Maybe* this'll turn out okay. Maybe. So, Richard, do you take this complete stranger—uh, I mean, this *woman*—to be your lawfully wedded ..."

Tevye. He can be my father any day. A milkman probably couldn't afford to pay for Mindy's hoity-toity wedding, and Mindy would no doubt be ashamed to have a lowly milkman for her old man. But I'd be fine with it. It's not important. I just want a caring father like Tevye who'd sit beside me at the railroad station, waiting on a bench outside for the train to take me to Siberia to be with my beloved. "Why did they arrest him, this barber of yours, and send him to that frozen wasteland?" he'd ask." I'd smile up at him, grasping his strong arm tenderly with both of my cold little hands. "Oh, Larry got sent away for cutting off the ears of one of his customers, Papa. But it wasn't his fault. Aunt Grace made him crazy with her sarcastic passive-aggressive remarks about what he does for a living." We'd then sit silently for a time while we thought about how very much we'd miss each other. "Oh, Papa," I'd cry out as I was about to board the train. "God alone knows when we shall see each other again!" He'd nod slowly and furrow his strong brow and purse his lips and look heavenward toward the gray sky. A small tear would appear in one eye. "Well, my beloved daughter," he'd intone in his deep, manly bass, "we will leave it in His hands."

In the unlikely event that I ever decide that I want to partner up with someone with a view toward getting hitched, maybe I'll try to find a matchmaker to "find me a find, catch me a catch." I'd find a local version of Yente and tell her my qualifications, my expectations. He doesn't have to be an Adonis and doesn't have to have a fat wallet or be a muckety-muck of any kind. A barber or a carpenter or a bricklayer will do. An artist is more than fine. He just needs to be nice and considerate, not full of himself or mean or rude or disrespectful, like some. I won't put up with that. Do you hear me, Dad?

He should know how to listen. He should care about my opinions, my feelings. I'll do likewise. He should put down his damned phone now and again and actually look at me and make eye contact. He should be willing to talk about things, like whether or not Pete Rose should be in the Hall of Fame. He should laugh at my jokes once in a while, even if he doesn't actually find them funny. I'll do likewise. He should be okay with lying together in bed on a cold winter night and watching *Pride and Prejudice* or *Sense and Sensibility* with me, and not mock me if I get all misty. Little considerations are important. Someone who thinks to bring me a chocolate-glazed cake doughnut or a blueberry scone when I'm sad or PMSing would be great. He needs to be a decent kisser, a soft kisser, not one of those oil drillers. He should be a good lover, if possible. He doesn't have to have a huge thingie, but it shouldn't be one of those "golf pencil dealies," as a drunken Diana might have said, either. He should be willing to be imaginative in bed, willing to do cowgirl or reverse cowgirl or even any of those contorted tub and shower positions in the book I gave Mindy at her bachelorette party, that *Kama Sutra* one with the perfect little cartoon lovers. He should be good, giving, and game. I'll try to be likewise. He needs to not be jealous of my three-speed, four-pulse vibrator. It's no threat to him. I don't think it is, anyway.

Maybe my Yente could check around and see if there's a reincarnation of Ol' Blue Eyes somewhere out there—someone with Frank's eyes and face, who'd sing his songs to me gently every night when I take my bath, and brush my earlobes and cheeks and the sides of my neck with his warm lips. If so, I'll take him.

Of course, he—or anyone—would have to love my Lucy. If not, then the deal's off. That's my condition, and it's non-negotiable. I don't care who it is—Sinatra, Paul Newman, Alex, Larry, Charles Bronson, Jackson Galaxy, Matt Damon, or whoever. If you don't love my cat, goodbye and good luck. "Don't worry, Goosey. There's no wiggle room there. None at all. *You're* number one."

If Yente recommends a she—a Louise, say—I wouldn't necessarily say no. I'd take that recommendation under serious advisement.

Louise and Ian are on vacation in Jamaica. I'm sure she looks good in a bathing suit. I imagine she'll find some wonderful models for her paintings down there—large, serious Jamaican women with strong faces and big hair. If Ian turns bad or ditches her or even tips over, Louise can call me and I'll rush down to console her, to be with her. Ian did call yesterday, but only to say that they'd be delayed in returning for a day because of some event they want to attend—maybe a ganja festival. Before I left today, I told Clarence and Murphy that their guardians would be back later than expected. Clarence took the news in his stride, but Murphy got upset. He meowed loudly and his ears and tail went down and he turned and started to slink out of the living room. Poor guy. I tried to ease his disappointment with a little joke. "Hey, guys, what happened when the leper's mother died?" Murph turned around and looked up at my face, still unhappy. "He fell apart. Get it?"

The Way You Look Tonight

WELL, AT least my damned period held off. I feel like it'll start tomorrow, or maybe Monday, but at least I got through the tedious wedding today. Tomorrow will be okay. All I have to do is go to the silly gift-opening and then—*thank* you, merciful God!—it's all over with.

I am *so* tired. I don't know when I've been this exhausted. What a day. I've been up since six this morning, and now it's way past midnight—almost one o'clock. "But at least I'm here with you now, my sweet Lucy. Finally, it's just we two. You and me and Sinatra and chardonnay and maybe a little weed. It's all good, Goose."

My poor little Lucy. She was alone all day and all evening with just her harp music for company. "I'm sorry, kiddo. If I could've gotten out of it, I would've. I'll make it up to you. I don't know how, but I will."

I need to be careful tonight with the wine, though. I had a lot to drink at the reception. Probably too much. The vodka and tonics were my well-deserved reward to myself. So I should take it easy now. I'd hate to pass out here in the tub and drown. I imagine that would dampen Mindy's joy, to say nothing of Lucy's.

At least we didn't have to go to Macy's or Boston Store or anywhere to get our makeup done. Except for Mindy, we did makeup at the church ourselves. We did have to get our hair done, of course. We had an early appointment at ANiU Salon on Deming Way. Toni was there too. I learned that Mindy'd been going there for months already, getting a haircut every six weeks and manicures and pedicures and cuticle treatments and customized facials and I don't know what else. For six months now, she's been doing some kind of bi-weekly deep conditioning home hair treatment they'd recommended, with some high-priced, hoity-toity product she bought there—something about "preserving shine and brilliance." She'd even been working with someone there to reshape her eyebrows. They apparently have people at ANiU who specialize in different services. Plus, she'd gone there last month to get a trial up-hairdo.

They styled the five of us competently, with the usual wedding day up-do's, curling and spraying and pinning up our hair. The chairs were comfortable enough, but there was a huge mirror—maybe eight feet high—in front of each of us. I didn't mind looking at myself in that damned mirror for a few minutes, but the better part of an hour was way too much. I should have closed my eyes and taken a nap. But I was too intrigued by my neighbor. The woman in the chair next to mine was telling her stylist, Laurie, about her affair with one of her work colleagues. She wasn't loud, but I heard her anyway. She didn't call it an "affair." She said they'd started having drinks now and again after work, and that progressed to the occasional dinner, and then one night, when they'd both had a few drinks—more than a few—they'd kissed and shortly thereafter tumbled into bed at a Holiday Inn Express. After that first inebriated porking, they did it again. And again and again. She felt guilty about sleeping with another man, she said, but eventually thought that it helped her marriage, rather than hurt it. "To tell you the truth," she said, "I was thinking of leaving my husband before this started. Charlie's a good man, and we both love our kids, but for the last few years I've been bored as hell and restless. After a few good tumbles with Norton, now I'm happier. Now I can go home to Charlie and put up better with him and the kids and work and every damned thing else. Things are better. And Charlie's noticed I'm happier, though he doesn't know why. Neither of us wants to break up our families, so this has been good."

Laurie, combing out the woman's hair, asked her what she'd do if she fell in love with Norton. The woman paused. "Well," she said, "I sort of love him now. I guess I do. He's funny, he's cute, and he's good in bed. But I don't think I'm in love with him. I don't know what I'd do if I was."

I was surprised that she was so open about her infidelity. Maybe it's easier to be open with someone who knows the color of your roots.

Norton. She's porking a guy named Norton. "Oh, Norton, Norton. Oh, that feels so good, Norton! Oh, *thank* you, Norton."

After our stylings, we had to hang around ANiU for another hour while Mindy got her damned makeup done. That was tedious. At least we got to drink mimosas that Toni'd prepared—one-third orange juice and two-thirds champagne, with a splash of orange liqueur and garnished with a curl of orange peel. *Yum*! I'd brought an assortment of bagels with butter and various flavors of Philadelphia Cream Cheese in little containers—mostly my favorite, Chives and Onion; a few of the plain flavor; and even fewer Garden Vegetable or Strawberry flavors. The eating and drinking were good, but I had to listen to Mindy go on and on to the chick with purple hair who worked on her face about how she and Richard met, his romantic proposal, how much she'd had to drink at the rehearsal dinner, and details of the day ahead. I noticed that there weren't a lot of we or us references. It was "*my* rehearsal dinner" this and "*my* wedding" that. "I can't wait to go on *my* honeymoon to Mexico," she said.

At the church, we got dressed in a meeting room off of one of the corridors. The walls had a few Jesus pictures and a poster with a nice Scripture quote from the *Book of Matthew*—"Come unto me, all ye that labour and are heavily laden, and I will give you rest"—and three intriguing framed woodcuts of crowns of thorns. There was also a large woodcut, apparently by the same artist, that looked abstract at first but on closer examination was of a crucified Jesus. It had the same thorns motif as the other pieces.

I'll remember that Scripture quote if I ever get pregso and am heavily laden, with my belly out to here, and about to go into labor. It should be comforting.

Toni was a princess of efficiency while we were getting ready. She'd brought a box of assorted Subway sandwiches and a cooler with bottled water and sodas. I had a Sweet Onion Chicken and Teriyaki. Toni had Mindy's gown and veil hanging securely in a corner, covered in plastic. And she'd prepared an emergency kit with extra pins for the guys' boutonnieres and bobby pins for the veil, and even Static Guard spray if the dress fabric got sticky from being hauled around. She even did her job of urging the bride to drink enough water, per Father Connor's directive, though she was a nag about it: "*C'mon,* Mindy, that's enough Mountain Dew. You need to have some *water!*"

Toni even flitted back and forth between all of us as we did our makeup, happily helping with eyebrow pencil or lip gloss or mascara. I needed the most help, I admit. When it came to doing faces, I was clearly the least competent woman in the room. I'd had the least practice, and probably cared less about it than any of the rest. So I appreciated Toni's help. She must have learned about doing war paint from Aunt Grace, who needs a lot of that to hide her essential ugliness, though all the Clinique or Chanel or Estēe Lauder in the world couldn't mask the ugliness of her soul.

Toni started with foundation, applying it with her finger in a circular motion. "Concealer is huge," she said. "Particularly if you have a blemish. We need to conceal our blemishes from the world, right? But we can't rub it; we just pat it and set it with this powder." Then, after helping me add a bit of blush to my cheeks, she helped with my eyes. She applied dark chocolate-brown eyeliner on top and the bottom, "to make your beautiful eyes look whiter," and black mascara. She said that we had to do darker eyebrows than usual for a wedding so that they looked good in the photos. "We want the tail to be as long as the eye, to enhance the arch," she said. That sounded okay, I guess. Finally, she guided me in doing my lips—pale pink lipstick almost to the edges of my lips, then lip liner to "define the shape and seal it all in," and then a little more color. I started to smash my lips together, as I'd always done. "*Hey!*" Toni yelled. "Don't *do* that, Maggie. You're gonna ruin it all."

I looked around at Katie and Julie and Diana, competently putting on their makeup. They all knew what they were doing. Julie, in particular, was quite the little expert. Her big eyes looked even bigger, and the whites seemed whiter when she was done. Huge dark lashes. Her taut skin was perfect, if too pale, though she maybe put a bit too much color on her cheeks. Mindy's face, too, looked perfect. Of course.

Toni'd said that we have to conceal our blemishes. Hell, what with all the time and effort and money that we spend on hair and makeup and nails and clothes and shoes and jewelry and blah blah, we broads must have a *lot* of blemishes. We must think we're very flawed, very imperfect. Or *someone* thinks we are.

I imagined that Richard and the groomsmen, getting ready in some other classroom or meeting room, with more Jesus images and Scripture quotes and maybe crown-of-thorns woodcuts, had it easier. They probably just casually scraped their faces with razors and splashed on some aftershave and rolled on a little deodorant, and maybe rubbed a little gel in their hair and ran a comb through it, and threw on their tuxedos, and called it a day and got back to analyzing the Packers and Cardinals. They don't think they're blemished. They don't worry about that. And none of them have to worry about their damned periods coming, or be sure they have pads or tampons. Plus, I'm sure they can just throw on any old pair of briefs or boxers. They don't need special nude-color panties from Victoria's Secret that cost $11.50. Toni told me that, based on her experience at other weddings, the groom and groomsmen are so blasé that most of them have no idea which side of their chests their boutonnieres are supposed to get pinned on or precisely where to pin them. They've given it no thought until that moment, and then they just go with the flow. They just do whatever the florists or someone like Toni say to do. Oh, well.

"Don't worry, sweet Lucy-Goosey. *You* don't have any blemishes. You're quite perfect just as you are."

I sort of liked the fashion jewelry we all wore: an Anne Klein glass crystal collar necklace and matching bracelet. Mindy'd given those to us bridesmaids at the rehearsal dinner last night. The funny thing was that I'd given zero thought to jewelry before Mindy handed each of us the Anne Klein stuff, in little white boxes wrapped in light-blue paper with pink ribbon, sitting in pretty blue paper bags with handles. I guess I'd figured that on Saturday morning, I'd just look through my very scant jewelry collection that I keep in a Converse shoe box in my top dresser drawer and see what I had. Katie'd squealed when Mindy handed her the bag.

Happily, there were also five silver-foil-wrapped Hershey's Kisses in each blue bag. "Those chocolates were good, Lucy. I ate four and saved one for later. Aren't you proud of Mommy's self-control?"

The only irritating thing about getting dressed was that Darcy, Mindy's mousy little photographer, flitted around the room taking pictures—candids of Mindy and her attendants getting ready for the blessed event, along with some posed pictures. I don't like having my picture taken; photos make me look bigger than I already am. Plus, I hate smiling for pictures and usually look silly when I do. So when Darcy snapped one picture of me putting on my makeup, with Toni's help, I gave her a hard-faced look that hopefully communicated my thought: *No more!* It must have worked because she stopped at that one. But I noticed that she took several of Diana and at least five apiece of pretty Katie and pretty Julie.

The big photo event was Mindy getting into her gown, with the help of her bridesmaids, and then putting on her veil. That was followed by posed pictures of Mindy, in her dress and veil, and Mom in front of a tall mirror, with Mom standing behind the bride and adjusting her veil. My mother had a tear in her eye. Darcy took the picture from an angle behind Mom and Mindy so that it showed their body and facial profiles and their frontal reflections in the mirror. Mom touched Mindy's shoulder gently with her left hand while adjusting the veil with her right. It was nice, I admit. All the bridesmaids watched and Katie said, "Oh...My...GOD! How sweet."

When we all finally had our dresses and shoes and accessories on, I wanted, for a moment, to sink through the floor. But then I looked over at Diana and saw her bare arms in that silly strapless dress and again noticed her tattoos—the butterfly on her left arm and the Japanese or Chinese character on the right. Some of the blue on the butterfly perfectly matched the

Capri blue of the dress. I wondered if Diana had other tattoos. I suspected she did. I remember thinking that she probably had a creative tat of some kind on her butt. That would be like her. She was standing near one of the crown of thorns woodcuts with her left arm raised high, rolling on deodorant. She noticed me staring and lowered her arm and stuck out her tongue and crinkled her nose and made a face. She extended to her full height, such as that was, and stuck out her chest and fluttered her eyebrows. I laughed. Just then I didn't care how I looked. If I looked like a hippo waddling down the damned aisle, so the hell what? What do I care what anyone thinks?

While we were dressing, I'd noticed Julie stuffing something into her Victoria's Secret bra. So good for her.

Toni competently folded Mindy's clothes and put them in a red plastic bag and carted them out to the car. I looked at one of the Jesus pictures and said a little prayer of thanks that my sister'd agreed to have Toni be her personal attendant. I added a quick thank you to the nameless consultant at Vera's who'd given me the idea. "Some things work out, right, Goose?"

We had to do photos in the sanctuary before the ceremony: first, the lovely bride; then the bride and me, her proud maid of honor; then the bride and all of her sweet little bridesmaids; and finally, the bride and her personal attendant. Toni's main job during this was to be sure that Richard didn't wander in, because the blessed couple was doing one of those deals wherein the groom doesn't see his blushing bride on the wedding day until she comes toodling down the aisle, at which point, upon observing her great blemish-free beauty, he's supposed to be in awe and have a lump in his throat and a tear in his eye. *Here comes my prize*, is the idea. *What a truly lovely woman I'm blessed to be calling my wife*, we suppose he's thinking.

More likely, he's saying to himself, "Hot damn! Yes, indeed! Tonight's the *night*, baby! Tonight I get to officially bang that luscious broad. Sure, we've done it lots of times before, and, yes, I know that little body quite well by now, but still. Look at her coming down the aisle in that beautiful dress with the train and that lacy veil. Look how *proud* her daddy is. My sweet, blushing little bride. Hah! I've seen her so drunk she can't find her way to the bathroom to pee. Well, we'll see how much she blushes tonight when she's all liquored up and naked as a jaybird and bouncing up and down on it."

As we posed on the steps of the sanctuary in different groupings with hyper-smiling Mindy usually in the center, and holding our bouquets against our bellies, Darcy kept saying, "Okay, I'm going to count to three.

On three, nice smiles and no blinks." Katie couldn't keep from blinking even then, so Darcy had to tell her to close her eyes and only open them on "three." The sixth time she gave that directive, Diana leaned toward me and cupped her hand to her mouth. "If she says that one more time," she whispered, "I'm gonna shove that telephoto lens up her ass." I nodded. *This is going to be a long damned day*, I thought to myself.

It was. By the time we'd all gathered outside the nave, waiting for the processional to start, I felt exhausted. I closed my eyes and popped a butterscotch hard candy into my mouth and asked God to let me make it down the aisle without falling over because of the stupid Lyric shoes, modest as the heels were, or without my boobs spilling out.

Standing at the back, I had to stifle a chuckle when I watched the bridal party go down the aisle to "Jesu, Joy of Man's Desiring." Josh took up at least two-thirds of the space made up of him and Julie walking down side-by-side. That gown looked good on her, I'll say that. Strapless gowns are okay for chicks like her, with thin arms and shoulders. It makes them look feminine, unless they have stick arms, whereas for heifers like me, with big arms and shoulders, it makes us look more gargantuan. I remember wondering, though, how Julie's dress stayed up, considering that she has no boobs to speak of anymore—no anchors for the dress, as it were. But then I recalled that she'd addressed that problem, at least a little.

Seeing Russell and Diana was even funnier. With Diana wearing the heels, he didn't tower over her quite as much as in the rehearsal, but the difference between then and now wasn't much. She turned her head now and again and did her phony little smile that I'd seen before and made eye contact with people in the audience, but he had on his usual downturned-mouth scowl and stared straight ahead and showed zero emotion. His blue eyes were good, though who knows what was going on in his head behind those nice eyes as he walked down the aisle? Maybe he was wishing he were somewhere else, perhaps alone in a boat out in the middle of a quiet lake in northern Wisconsin, maybe near Minocqua or Eagle River, fishing for bass or crappies and listening for the loons to do their strange call. Maybe he was wishing that he could be at the State Fair in Milwaukee and about to enter that long red brick building where they sell the cream puffs. With his size, I imagine he could hold a State Fair cream puff in just one hand, unlike the rest of us mortals. Or maybe he was speculating on the possibility of scoring later on with Diana or one of the other bridesmaids. I briefly imagined him and Diana in bed together. It would be like that huge, hypersexed Wilt Chamberlain boffing little Rhea Perlman. If they lay there face-to-face in their afterglow, she could scratch his itching kneecap with her big toe. Or maybe Russell is one of those guys who prefers big girls, like me, and that's what he was thinking. Well, if it came to that, I'd have to at least consider the possibility. I like his eyes.

"Well, Goose, I made it down just fine, and didn't even give a hoot in hell about all those rubbernecks staring at me and pointing their damned phones and cameras."

What I concentrated on was looking at the audience to see if Larry'd made it. And there he was, sitting about halfway back on the left side and wearing a navy sport jacket, gray slacks, and a dark-red tie. His beard was nicely trimmed. He'd recently had a haircut. He looked good. I gave him a little smile as I passed and he smiled back. I felt glad he'd come. I resolved to make sure, later, to bring him to the cupcake table at the reception. We'd chow down some delicious cupcakes, just we two, and talk about what Chester and Festus and Miss Kitty have been up to. *Just get through this silliness*, I thought, *and those cupcakes and the open bar will be your earthly reward.*

Mindy'd chosen not to have a flower girl. I'm not sure why. But if she had gone that route, I briefly imagined my Corinna in the role. I'd watch her from the front of the nave, by the sanctuary, feeling proud as she shyly walked down the aisle just after I did and before the bride entered. She'd be dressed in a pretty white tea-length dress with a blue satin bow, and there'd be a garland of little white flowers on her sweet head. She'd cutely scatter rose petals along the bridal path. If a tragedy happened—dropping her basket, say—her eyes would puddle up and her chin would tremble and she'd look at me. "Oh, Mommy," she'd squeal. "I screwed up big-time. I ruined Aunt Mindy's wedding!" I'd rush over and kiss her forehead and help her pick up the basket and the spilled rose petals. "Don't worry, kid," I'd say gently. "We all screw up from time to time. Just turn your little butt around and keep on keeping on."

That nice thought faded when the organ music volume amped up and the audience stood, and Dad and Mindy started down the aisle. Here was her long-anticipated moment of glory—Melinda Mullen, lovely bride, center of attention. Princess Mindy, in her beautiful gown, sashaying down the aisle on her precious wedding day with scores of people staring at her and smiling. And she *was* beautiful, no one can naysay that. I felt happy for my sister. This was what she'd wanted and worked her ass off for, so good for her.

But there was our father in his tux and boutonniere, short salt-and-pepper hair, and perfectly shined black shoes. He stood ramrod-straight, looking so proud, so self-satisfied. I had to look at the floor. I don't know. I have a poor attitude, I admit. I should have a more generous outlook. I should take the high road. I really should. Easier said than done, though.

I looked over at Mom sitting quietly in the second wooden pew to the left of the aisle. She looked nice in her simple blue dress and pearl necklace.

I sort of spaced out during parts of the ceremony. I like Catholic wedding ceremonies—the solemnity and all—other than that they're so damned long. The ritual is nice, comforting. Father Connor's voice was comforting, too, as he led the gathering in prayer, introduced the hymn, did his homily, and so on. His voice is sort of like George Kennedy's, that big guy who was in *Cool Hand Luke* with Paul Newman. George's character was named Dragline. That would be a good name for a cat. "Not a prissy little girl like you, Lucy, but a tough tomcat-type guy. Maybe someone like Clarence, who's wandered the sewers and probably fought with other rough cats and stray dogs and raccoons and the like."

I paid attention to the doings the best I could, even to Toni's Old Testament reading from the Book of Sirach about the qualities of a good wife. My favorite line was, "Choicest of blessings is a modest wife, priceless her chaste soul." Mindy modest? Mindy with a chaste soul? Hah! I remembered her studying the *Kama Sutra* book at the bachelorette party, wanting to try some of the sex-in-a-tub positions—Camel's Hump, Climbing the Tree, and so on. I remembered Mindy on the dance floor at Plan B, inebriated and bent forward as Katie ground her pelvis against my sister's butt.

But now and again, my thoughts wandered. My mind turned to my cats. For some reason, I found myself thinking of Maria. I thought of her and Carlos snuggled up together at the end of the Barretts' king-sized bed on a frigid winter night, the wind howling, and then Maria alone there after Carlos died. I thought about poor Bella, thin and sick, her end likely nearing. Hopefully, Mr. Randall was home with her and taking care of her. Numbnuts Mr. R. likely wouldn't be stroking her and singing to her, like he should be, but at least she wouldn't be alone. I thought of poor Harold, with his many issues. I thought of Miss Kitty sitting queenlike on her thick white pad on the stuffed chair in Larry's living room, oblivious to Festus ambushing Chester. I even thought about Bosco, the cat that I'd just started taking care of on Thursday. Claire had told me that Bosco's most annoying habit is knocking things off her dresser at six o'clock each morning, while she's still asleep, because he thinks it's high time she gets up to feed him. I'll see Bosco tomorrow. Today, Sheila's taking care of him and my other charges. I chuckled as I thought of Murphy, outraged, staring out of Ian's kitchen window at Clarence roaming free in the backyard. *No fair!* he might be thinking. And I thought of the many abused felines that the members of the Legion of Overweight Cat Avengers and I would rescue and seek vengeance for. Ah, sweet vengeance!

Maybe tomorrow night, when I'm not so damned tired, Lucy and I'll watch one of our revenge movies—*Kill Bill*, perhaps, or *The Limey*, or even *The Brave One*. That's a good one. "Should we watch that, Goose? We like Jodie Foster very much, right? Her character's a bit of a head case, but we like to see her blow away the three nasty jerkheads who beat her up and killed her fiancé and stole her German shepherd, Curtis." Well, I do. Lucy, I'm sure, disapproves of such violence. I remember that the first time Goose and I saw that movie, I felt just incredibly joyful at the end when Jodie's character, Erica, did in the lowlife bastards who did what they did. My favorite part is when she locates the dirtbags at 90 Clayton Avenue in New York City and one, holding Curtis on a leash, notices her and approaches. "Want somethin'?" he sneers. "I want my DOG back!" she snarls and shoots him through the eye.

As to the Avengers, while standing up there at the start of the ceremony with Julie and Katie and Diana—all three relatively thin and mostly pretty—I recalled my fantasy of all the bridesmaids being porkers like myself so that I wouldn't stand out. I closed my eyes for a few moments and happily conjured that image, and it was good. When I opened my eyes and looked around to face reality, and then looked over to see Richard and my sister—Mindy looking so beautiful, blue-gray eyes sparkling—I sighed. I glanced at Katie and Julie and Diana, holding their bouquets against their bellies that didn't stick out, and sighed again. But then I scanned the audience and saw Larry halfway back and noticed that his eyes were shutting for a moment or two. He was either very moved by the ceremony or taking a little catnap. Either way, it made me feel glad.

Thank God, we—the groomsmen and bridesmaids—didn't have to stand up during the whole deal. We had to stand for part of it, forming an inverted V on the steps of the sanctuary with me at the top of the bridesmaids' half of the V. But then, following the opening prayer, we got to sit in the front pew on the left side of the aisle. That was good. At least no one in the audience could eyeball me for a while.

Richard's Uncle Lester, his godfather, did a reading from the New Testament—one of Saint Paul's Letters to the Corinthians. I'd learned at the rehearsal dinner that Lester is Russell's father. He's almost as tall as his low -key son. I was surprised at how reedy and high-pitched his voice was, considering his size—at least his height. He never changed his wooden facial expression and read in a dread monotone. If I ever have insomnia, I'll be sure to call Lester and have a pleasant conversation with him about the weather. That should do it. I'll be snoring in no time.

As to his selection, I'd heard it before. It was the one about how love is patient and kind, not jealous or pompous, not inflated or rude, doesn't seek its own interests, isn't quick-tempered, doesn't brood over injuries, and doesn't rejoice over wrongdoings. Love "bears all things, believes all things, hopes all things, endures all things." Love, it says, "never fails." *Whew!* That's a damned tall order. If all that's the standard for love, I think I'm doomed to failure if I'm ever the person who's supposed to be doing the loving—if not on all those counts, then at least on most. I might be okay on the "not pompous" and "not inflated" parts, but the rest might be a stretch, especially that deal about love believing all things and enduring all things. I don't think I'm down with that. There're some things I'm not willing to endure—nastiness and rudeness, for two.

Father Connor's homily was better. His soothing George Kennedy voice was easier to listen to than Uncle Lester's. A lot of what he said had to do, again, with love. No surprise there, I guess. Love, love, love. Blah, blah, blah. He said we were "witnessing the forming of a covenant, a bond of love," and then some stuff tying together God's love and Mindy's and Richard's love for each other. "Your love makes the reality of God's love more real," he said. "Your love is the measure of God's love for all of us. Your love becomes a public manifestation of God's love for us." I don't know about all that. It sounds pretty lofty for a couple of ordinary, flawed mortals like my sister and Richard.

But I did like something he said a bit later. "Many people here today are aware of the ups and downs of being married," he intoned, looking out knowingly toward the audience. I wished that he would have asked for a show of hands about that—not about the ups, but the downs. "Now how many of you out there," he'd ask, "have ever been so desperately unhappy with your spouse that you wanted to jump off a bridge? How many of you ladies have ever woken up one morning and glanced over at your husband asleep and snoring and thought about plunging an icepick into his eye? How many of you gents have had it up to here with the nagging, the nattering, the henpecking, the bickering, the crying—all that crap? How many of you sometimes sit in a darkened living room late at night with a scotch and soda in one hand and regret you'd ever said 'I do'?" That would have been more interesting, to me, than anything about God's love for us. Much more.

All this wedding blather about love. It's irritating. A little goes a very long way. "What's that all about, Lucy? What's the idea here? Why can't they talk about something else for a change, something you can actually get a handle on? Something real. Maybe butterscotch pudding with Nestle's Morsels mixed in. Or a peanut-butter-and-banana sandwich on oat bran bread. Or even a run-of-the-mill roast beef sandwich on light rye with Thousand Island dressing. Or Oreos. Or even Thin Mints. Those are good. Those are *tangible*. Or maybe even one of Mom's nice framed pond paintings. Am I right, Goose?" I think she agrees, but she'd add catnip to the list. "Don't worry, kid. I love you lots and lots, and always will. I can say that much about love."

Mindy didn't blather, during their vows, about Richard being her soulmate or about how he completed her. They didn't do their own vows. Instead, it was a canned deal in which they each promised to be true in good times and in bad, in sickness and in health, and to love and honor each other all the days of their lives. That was nice enough, I guess. Then there was a blessing and the ring exchange with the usual stuff from each of them about taking the ring as a sign of love and fidelity.

The love part I can see—sort of, anyway—but I don't know about the fidelity. If fidelity means not shtupping anyone other than your spouse for as long as you live together, maybe that's overrated. What about Laurie's customer at ANiU, the one who was boffing Norton? She said her marriage was *better* because of it, that she could cope better with all the tedious stuff in her life—her boring husband, her kids, her job. If she'd vowed to be faithful and had held to that vow no matter what, she maybe would have been more unhappy. Maybe she and Charlie would have split up, and their kids would have had to shuffle back and forth between households and would have been with one parent on Christmas Eve and the other on Christmas.

I don't know. Vowing fidelity is maybe one of those things that sounds good when you say it in church on your wedding day, dressed pretty and standing there in front of the priest and your parents and relatives and friends and others who came to share your special day. But I'm not sure how practical it is, given real life. If I ever get hitched, I won't vow that. I'd rather not vow anything. But if I have to say something, it might be, "Listen, my friend, I promise nothing. I'll try, I'll say that much. I'll try to be a good friend to you, and I'll try to be polite and respectful and considerate. I'll try to be interested in what you're interested in. I'll try not to take it out on you if I'm having a bad day, or if I'm moody because I'm PMSing. I'll try to remember that little things mean a lot. I'll try to be good, giving, and game in bed. But, damn it, I'm only human, so I'm gonna fall short sometimes—maybe a lot of the time. And I know you're only human, too, so my expectations are humble. As far as love and fidelity go, I love you now. I feel love for you. I have affection for you. Okay? But I can't say for sure that I'm *in* love with you, whatever the hell that means, and I sure can't promise that I'll *keep* loving you. Lots of things can change, right? Sorry. We'll see. But I'll *try*, okay? That's the most I can say for now." I'd pause. "And as for the fidelity, let's table that discussion for now and revisit it later." That'll have to do.

I think I did a decent enough job of fulfilling my maid-of-honor duties in regard to straightening out the bride's silly train and holding her bouquet while she was otherwise occupied and then handing it back to her following the kiss. I was glad we'd done the rehearsal so I knew what I was doing. Mindy's chapel-length train wasn't too hard to straighten out. It wasn't ridiculous, like the one that poor Princess Di wore when she married that sourpuss, weak-chinned Charles. Di's train was still barely through the door of St. Paul's Cathedral by the time she was halfway down the aisle. It was almost as long as the distance from the pitcher's mound to home plate. At least Mindy didn't get one of those. It would have taken me a year and every ounce of my energy to straighten it.

The ceremony, including the Communion, went on for what seemed like a long time, and I felt a bit woozy when Father Connor at last led us in the Lord's Prayer just before the deal was finally over. So I was happy to be able to hold on to Mark's arm on our little journey up the aisle. I forgot, though, that we were supposed to walk faster during the recessional than the processional. Toni'd told us to smile when going up the aisle because Darcy would be taking pictures, but I didn't feel much like doing that. I was too worried about falling on my fat butt due to having to wear those stupid heeled Lyric sandals by Touch Ups. But I made it.

"The receiving line, Goose …now that was a pain in the ass. Oh …my …GOD!, as Katie would say."

It was just as I'd imagined: a long line of people—many of whom I didn't know, or had maybe met but couldn't remember who the hell they were—congratulating Mindy and Richard and the groomsmen and bridesmaids and both sets of parents. Some were women I'd seen at the shower at Aunt Grace's house, including that snooty strawberry-blonde vampire with the witch face. People shook my hand and said who they were—"Oh, hi, I'm Richard's great aunt from Fargo …"—and I smiled and nodded and tried to say something fascinating in reply. "Oh, Fargo. It's very cold there, I hear."

Sure enough, several women commented on my dress, though they were at least polite enough not to mention how ridiculous the ruching looked. I had to bite my tongue to keep from making some bitter remark about how I'd had to order a size twenty even though I'm a size sixteen. "Oh, you're the sister," one broad said. "Well, let's hope it's *your* turn next."

Well, if I ever do get married—which right now seems doubtful—I guarantee it won't be a spectacle like Mindy's. Maybe we'll do a destination wedding to Las Vegas without telling anyone and get hitched by an Elvis impersonator at one of those little storefront wedding chapels. I'll wear my best blue denim jumper. The whole event will take ten minutes at most. No receiving line. No reception. If I get misty and shed a little tear, the Elvis officiant might break out in a poignant verse of "Crying in the Chapel." I imagine you can get a decent wedding in one of those places for a hundred dollars or less. Hopefully, that includes a witness. If not, we'll have to duck into the nearest casino and hire one of those blue-haired old ladies who smoke and cough and hack constantly while playing the slot machines. "I'll be right with you, dear," she'd say in a deep, throaty, smoke-ruined voice. "Just let me finish this roll of quarters and I'll grab my oxygen tank and we'll be on our way."

"You can be my maid of honor if I do that, Lucy-Goosey. We'll get you a little Capri-blue ribbon to wear."

When Aunt Grace came through the receiving line, her bored and expressionless sons trailing like ducklings, I braced myself for one of her smart-ass remarks about my weight. But all she said was, "You look good today, Maggie." I just smiled and said, "Oh, *thank* you!" But now I'm wondering: Was the bitch sincere or sarcastic? Maybe I should have just assumed the worst and tried to zing her back. "Oh, Aunt Grace," I could have said, "your face is so lovely today. That Botox is great stuff, huh?" Or maybe worse. "So tell me, Aunt Grace. Did all that work you had done on your labia help you get a man? Has anyone come sniffing around since Uncle Edgar ditched you? No? Oh, I'm *so* sorry. I can't say I'm surprised, though, given your givens."

Well, that's probably too snarky. Maybe she was sincere. "What do you think, Goose?" As usual, she's neutral on the subject.

By the time the receiving line deal was over, I was exhausted from all the standing we'd had to do during part of the tedious ceremony and then the receiving line, to say nothing of all the damned smiling and small talk. And then we had to go back and do the stupid formal photos on the steps of the sanctuary, with that huge crucified Jesus in the background. I gritted my teeth and took the high road when it was time for our little family picture. I was glad that Darcy positioned Dad to Mindy's right and Mom to her left and then me to Mom's left, so I was close to my mother and far away from my father. At least *that* worked out.

I was happy and relieved when we, the bridal party, finally left the church and piled into the white stretch limo. Katie poured champagne and we toasted the happy little couple as they sipped and kissed, with Darcy snapping away. I took advantage of the occasion to eat three butterscotch hard candies and two Tootsie Roll Midgees. The driver was the same guy we'd had for the bachelorette party, Nick, with the nice curly hair. I'm sure he was relieved to see that Kiersten wasn't part of the group, so he wouldn't have to worry about her puking all over his clean, shiny limousine. Maybe he was sad, though, that Brooke wasn't there to drool over him and offer him something sweet—perhaps herself.

I'd noticed Kiersten and Jessa and Lauren sitting together in the audience during the ceremony. Kimmy was in the pew behind them, and I wondered how things had worked out for her with the dildo. Apparently, she was still able to walk.

Our first stop was the State Capitol downtown, where we did bridal party photos on the high steps of the south entrance. That was okay, and I admired Darcy's work in positioning us on the steps and against the stone railings on the upper level. But I felt like smooshing my bouquet into her pale little face when she had us descend to the lawn and said we were going to do a picture with all of us jumping into the air, arms raised, at her cue. Pretty much everyone was into it, and Russell at least went along, though he never changed his wooden expression. But I hated it. Darcy counted to three and we all jumped "as high as you can." For me, that was maybe two inches.

And that wasn't the only humiliation. After the photos at the Capitol, we walked across Main Street to Brocach—yet another Irish tavern—for a few drinks, and Darcy's idea was that Mindy and her bridesmaids would sit on the bar and hold our bouquets and lift our dresses above our knees to show our legs—each right leg crossed over each left—and lean forward a bit to show off our cleavage, while smiling like fools. For a moment, I wanted to reach over and put my hands around Darcy's little neck and squeeze until her hazel eyes bulged and her tongue turned black. "Hey!" I wanted to hiss. "Are you *serious?* You want me to somehow hoist my fat ass onto that damned bar and bare my big legs and show my boobs for a picture? No! Enough is enough already. Now put that damned camera down and let's all have some pretzels and a beer. Or two or ten."

But I gritted my teeth again and went along with it. Diana, to my surprise, was enthusiastic. She was the first to jump up onto the bar and immediately pulled her dress above her knees—practically to mid-thigh—and stuck her chest out and vamped. I noticed that she had nice little calves, shapely and muscular. I hadn't paid much attention to her legs before. She had a small tattoo of a sunflower just above her left ankle, on the outside of the calf. So I'd been right about her having more tattoos. If I ever get around to doing watercolors, I'll start with a nice sunflower and have it framed at Catura's Gallery and Framing, where Mom gets her paintings framed, and give it to Diana. I think she'd like that.

Richard helped Mindy onto the bar, which was a bit of an ordeal because of her dress. Then Katie and Julie hopped up effortlessly. I had to drag a chair over from one of the nearby tables. Eric held the chair steady and Josh held my elbow and helped me onto the chair. Once there, I cautiously eased my bulk around and slid my butt onto the bar, next to my sister. We did one shot with all of us smiling and looking into the camera, and then another with only Mindy looking into the camera and the rest of us grinning and gazing adoringly at the bride's smiling face.

Finally, we jumped down and got to watch as that damned Darcy did shots of the groomsmen holding up a horizontal and hugely grinning Mindy in front of them, grasping her bouquet in one hand and a brown bottle of Boddingtons Pub Ale in the other. Josh flexed his big upper body and stuck out his muscular chest during this, but didn't smile at all. Katie pumped her fist and went "*Woo!*" and I downed my Heineken in four big gulps.

When we finally got to the reception at the Concourse Hotel, Darcy had us pose for yet more damned pictures, this time on the wide, curved carpeted staircase that led from the lobby to the second floor. The bridesmaids were on one side of the couple, standing at different stair levels, and the groomsmen were on the other side, similarly situated. Then we had to do another picture with the bridesmaids and groomsmen standing together as couples, again at different levels, flanking the bride and groom. The whole thing was a pain in the ass. Diana smiled nicely through all of it, but I think that, given the chance, she would have strangled Darcy with the black coiled cord that connected her camera to the flash. I know I would have.

When we'd finished with the pictures, I noticed that there was a quintet of large, round clocks on one wall in the hotel lobby, just behind the registration desk, indicating the times in different places in the world in addition to Madison: Tokyo, London, Paris, and New York. Wiping perspiration off my brow and trying to get a full breath, I wondered who the hell would care what time it was in Tokyo. Well, I suppose people in Japan do. Maybe I should broaden my horizons and care too.

When we finally got upstairs, the cocktail hour was going strong. I headed straight for the bar in a far corner of the Capitol Ballroom to get a vodka and tonic. Three men were ahead of me in line to order, and I briefly considered shoving them aside with extreme prejudice and exerting my maid of honor privilege. But I thought better of it. While standing in line, I spotted Larry across the room talking to some long-haired chick in a cranberry-colored dress with just one shoulder strap. *I'll see about her later*, I thought.

The drink was good. I'd noticed they'd used Fleischmann's vodka, which is always lovely. I can't afford vodkas like Fleischmann's or Smirnoff, and instead always get the cheapest vodka I can—Nikolai or Burnett's, usually. Once, I bought a bottle of Death's Door Vodka, which is made here in Wisconsin, because I like that name. It makes you think.

I sipped my drink slowly because I didn't want to be in tough shape when I gave my toast. My damned toast. That stupid toast. Oh, lordy! I'd been anxious about that since I opened my eyes at six this morning. Well, I remember thinking, *I'll have to do the toast in a while and get that silliness over with, and then I can chow down a nice meal. Then I'll come back to the bar and really down a few. If anyone's in my way, that's when I'll exert the extreme prejudice.*

Mindy'd ordered both chilled and hot hors d'oeuvres. The only chilled selection that appealed to me was the poached shrimp, but the hot options were better. I took some pork pot stickers and a few lovely pieces of chicken tempura. It had sesame on it. *Yum!* I even tried a bacon-wrapped quail leg. It was okay, but not something I'd go out of my way to seek out unless I was starving.

Before we did the wedding party introduction, Mindy had to go potty. Katie and I went with her to the ladies' room down the corridor from the ballroom. We went into the stall with her and each of us stood to one side of Mindy and held up a side of her dress as she carefully pulled down her underwear and slowly eased herself onto the seat. We stood there holding up the dress as she peed—a strong stream that went on for a long time, emptying her bladder of the mimosa she'd had at ANiU and the Mountain Dews she'd had while getting ready at the church and all the water that Toni'd made her drink, plus the two Boddingtons Ales she'd downed at Brocach. Katie had to hand her a few squares of toilet paper when she was done. It would have been a tight fit in that damned stall with three normal-sized women, much less a porker like me and then Mindy wearing her poufy ivory-colored Allure Couture strapless gown with the symmetrical ruching. At least the bride didn't have to go number two.

Russell surprised me during the wedding party introduction. The bridal party was gathered outside the entrance to the ballroom. The idea was that we'd enter by couples as the DJ, Marv, announced us. We were all supposed to do something cute—dancing in, toodling around, waving our arms, whatever. Diana and Russell were the first to be introduced, after both sets of parents. Diana had a sexy little facial expression, and she threw her shoulders back and stuck out her chest and did an almost-ribald little dance, swiveling her hips, as she entered. Russell, with the same wooden facial expression as ever, just raised his arms and swayed his long body a bit. But after they'd gone about eight steps into the ballroom, music blaring, he stopped and raised his arms and stood perfectly still and took off and executed a picture-perfect cartwheel. At the end of it, he stood tall and threw back his head and raised both arms high in the air, grinning hugely and showing his teeth. The man actually smiled! Everyone applauded, and many stood and cheered.

Standing in the doorway of the ballroom, watching, I was stunned. It was as if Miss Kitty had suddenly jumped down from her white oval pad on the stuffed chair in Larry's living room, stood tall on her hind legs, and danced a jig. It's one thing when you see those munchkin gymnasts do cartwheels or tumbles during their floor routines, or when cheerleaders do that, but it's quite another when a six-five concave-chested doofus who's never previously shown an ounce of energy or emotion or fun does it.

Diana, I saw, was doubled over with laughter. She must not have known that was coming. She was laughing so hard, tears streaming down her cheeks, that I was afraid she might wet her pants.

None of the other couples could top Russell, though Mark tried. We had a plan. When it was our turn, just before the happy little newlyweds were introduced, Mark and I, holding hands, strolled out. He held my hand high as I twirled around once. I was glad that I didn't have to watch myself doing it. Then, after a few moments, Mark fell to the floor and lay on his back and pulled his knees to his chest with both arms and spun himself around to his right three times. There was a little applause.

Before we ate, it was time for the cake-cutting. Mindy'd ordered a four -tiered cake, with each tier a different flavor: White Midnight Magic, Red Velvet, Peanut Butter Cup, and White Chocolate Raspberry. She and Richard cut pieces from the lower tier and fed them to each other sweetly. I briefly imagined that he'd suddenly decide he'd had it with Mindy, and, instead of nicely feeding her a sliver of cake, he'd pick up a grapefruit-sized hunk and smoosh it into her face, like James Cagney did to Mae Clark in *The Public Enemy*. Mindy would stumble backwards with a surprised look on her pretty face. Some cake would spill into her cleavage. "Oh, Richard," she'd cry out, her chin trembling and blue-gray eyes puddling up as she wiped cake off of her bodice. "*Why?*"

When we'd all marched to the head table and were seated—the ladies to Mindy's left and the guys to Richard's right—I was famished. *Thank God the bridal party gets served first*, I thought. But before that, Father Connor did his blessing, and then Dad stood up to do his father-of-the-bride toast. Mr. Sanders followed him. *Christ!* I remember thinking when Dad stood up and clinked his glass. *Here we go again.*

Both toasts were variations of what they'd said at the rehearsal dinner: how happy they were that their wonderful children had found each other, what lovely people they'd turned out to be, blah blah. Dad went on and on about his memories of Mindy as a sweet little blond-haired girl on the swing set in the back yard. I noticed that he didn't mention Mom or me. Richard's father, on the other hand, gave nice shout-outs to his wife, Cynthia, and to Mark and Diana. During all that, my mind, for some reason, drifted back to the ceremony this morning, and I thought that even though I'd liked "Jesu, Joy of Man's Desiring" well enough, I wished that they'd done that Pachelbel piece, "Canon in D Major," instead during the processional. I like it better. It sort of soars.

Pachelbel would be a great name for a cat, except it's a bit long. It's a mouthful, with those three syllables. Maybe the cat could be nicknamed Pach, and he could just be called that most of the time. Then, if his guardian was pissed at him for something—knocking things off the dresser, say—she could use his whole name. "Alright, *Pachelbel*, cut the crap! It's six in the damned morning. I'll be up in a while. So just cool it and go look out the window, for Chrissake."

The Grilled Angus Fillet that I'd ordered was okay—not great but not horrible—and the grilled zucchini was more than acceptable. But the wheat rolls were surprisingly magnificent—a bit crusty on the outside and soft and warm on the inside. I scarfed down three of them almost immediately, each slathered with butter and dipped in what there was of the meat gravy. The absolute loveliness of those rolls almost made me momentarily forget that I'd have to do my damned toast soon. I was reminded when Mark stood up and clinked his spoon against his wine glass. The audience quieted. It was the usual tedious stuff: that he and Richard were great buddies growing up; that they played T-ball and football and hoops and that he, Mark, was always the superior athlete; that he remembered how they fought in the back seat during family vacations; how Richard got into trouble once in ninth grade for mouthing off to his algebra teacher; and that Mark remembered when Richard came home and said that he'd met this "really cool girl" named Mindy and that she was "totally cute." And then, of course, he went on about how he'd gotten to know and love Mindy and was so happy that she and his brother had gotten together, even though he wasn't sure that Richard deserved "a classy chick" like her. Blah, blah.

Mindy and Richard looked up at Mark's face during all of it, grinning and now and again chuckling. When Mark raised his glass and said, "To Mindy and Richard—many years of health and happiness," everyone raised their glasses and toasted.

Then it was my turn. The moment I'd dreaded had arrived. I'd thought about what I wanted to say, but when the time came I wussed out and took the safe option, the Mark route. The high road. I can't remember exactly what I said, but it was something blah to the effect of how incredibly happy I was to see my little sister so joyful, enjoying her special day, so honored by everyone here, and how happy I was that she and Richard had found each other out of all the people in the whole wide world. I mentioned how very close Mindy and I were growing up and how having a sister is *so* special and how I just *love* her new husband, and what a wonderful couple she and Richard are—*soulmates*, as anyone could tell—and how very happy I just *know* they'll be, and how glad I am that he's now part of our close and loving family. I said it looked to me that they were made for each other and completed each other and loved each other *all* the way. Hah!

I tried to think of some cute memories to mention from when we were younger, but that was a strain. The only thing I could think of was that once, when Mindy was in fifth grade and her soccer team had lost an important game, I'd made some offhanded and unsympathetic remark, and she'd thrown a tantrum and flushed my goldfish, Dickie, down the toilet. No one in the audience laughed or gasped or otherwise reacted. I didn't mention that after Mindy had dispatched poor Dickie, I'd furiously twisted the head off of one of her Barbies and tossed it in the garbage. Mindy hadn't noticed that the stupid doll was headless until after garbage day.

I said I was sorry that Grandma Liz couldn't be here for Mindy's special day. At least *that* was sort of sincere. Mom, seated at the parents' table nearby, smiled when I said that. I finished by hoisting my fat arm and saying, "So, everyone, let's all raise our glasses to love, *sweet* love!"

Following each of the long-winded toasts, it was nice, I guess, to see the happy little couple, with their arms intertwined, holding the set of toasting flutes I'd given them: the ones with crystal-and-silver hearts and their names and today's date engraved—the deal that cost me $118! They were smiling as they toasted after my ridiculous speech, and Mindy had the start of her blubbery-faced look, with the quivering lower lip and the misty blue-gray eyes and the rapid blinking.

I felt like a damned fool. Plus, the insides of my boobs were itching the whole time I was standing there. I couldn't do anything about it until Mindy stood and hugged me after my toast. While we hugged, I quickly stuck my right hand in there and scratched and hoped that nobody noticed.

Now, sitting here relaxing and sipping chardonnay in my bathtub with my sweet Lucy nearby, I'm trying to decide if I should light up a joint. I'm also thinking about what I wish I *would* have said: "Let me tell you something, people. This whole ordeal has been a *major* pain in the ass for me. All this damned wedding stuff has taken up *tons* of my time and irritated the crap out of me, and my bank account is down to almost nothing. I'm going to be living on Ramen chicken noodle soup for the next year, I'm telling you. Not that Ramen chicken soup is bad. I like it. The beef and pork and shrimp are good, too, but the chicken is best. I find that you have to use not just a spoon but also a fork to eat it, since those thin noodles are packed together so tightly and are so damned long. They're tasty, but long. Anyway, I'm glad for Mindy and Richard, and I wish them the best, blah blah. But to be honest with you, I get depressed when I think of what might be ahead for them. Marriage ain't for the faint of heart, folks. It's a *lot* of damned work, from what I can see. It's a grueling, sweaty marathon. There's likely going to be a lot of rotten moments for this pair, a lot of heartache. Love is okay, I guess, but it only goes so far. Let's hope these two aren't fools rushing in. My advice to both of you is to lower your expectations. Don't think you have to be *everything* to each other—great lover, best friend, therapist, paragon of virtue, whatever. Just relax, for God's sake, and have some wine—*lots* of wine— and maybe some weed, and listen to Sinatra and Dean and Sammy now and again. Rip that stupid "To Do" list off the refrigerator door and just lie down on the grass together once in a while to watch the clouds floating by. You don't even have to talk. What's there to say, anyway? If no one's around, you can shtup. Just be sure you don't do it near any poison ivy. And, dear Mindy, if things go to hell, if your new husband gets seriously on your nerves, which he certainly will, I'm always here for you. Okay? So I'll definitely have high, though modest, hopes for you guys."

I'd pause. "Anyway, the best thing about this whole deal is that I have a new, wonderful friend, and I'm just mad about her. Diana, stand up. Stand up, Diana. Oh, you say you *are* standing? Ha ha!"

I'd pause again and turn to the couple. "Richard," I'd say, "try not to be too big a doofus. Just be patient and considerate and remember to rub your bride's feet when she's tired or stressed or during the *ten* damned minutes each month that she has PMS. Don't get too bummed out by her yeast infections. When you order a pizza, don't be a controlling jerk about it. Compromise with her as to the ingredients. As I hope you know by now, Mindy likes sausage, but not pepperoni. She's okay with mushrooms and onions, but not crazy about them. She likes deep-dish, not thin crust. Hand-tossed is okay. And remember this, buddy boy: If you *don't* treat my sister well, some of my hefty cat-loving friends and I will be looking you up. We know where you live, bucko…So, everyone, here's to Mindy and Richard. Let's hope and pray that it doesn't all go to hell too quickly."

Yes, I hope that.

"Well, Lucy, I'd rather have sat with Larry than with Mindy and Richard and everyone at the head table. Except Diana."

That would have been nice. I'd looked over to where Larry was sitting, at one of the round tables toward the back, on the left side of the ballroom. I needed to know if that flirty bitch in the cranberry-colored dress with the single shoulder strap was at his table. She wasn't. I noticed that Larry was looking across the table and nodding while listening to some large bald guy with a white walrus mustache, who was gesturing with a tomahawk chop with his right hand while talking. Maybe the guy was a fellow barber and they were discussing how to handle difficult customers who piss and moan that you've cut their hair too short. Or maybe they were comparing state-of-the-art techniques for shaving heads.

I noticed, too, that Larry scarfed down two buttered rolls, one right after the other. My kind of guy.

The DJ played nice, soothing music during the dinner—"Our Love is Here to Stay" and "I'm in the Mood for Love" and "I Wish You Love" and the like. Marv even played a few Sinatras, including "Embraceable You" and "The Very Thought of You" and "It Was a Very Good Year." Diana sang along softly to "Sentimental Reasons" by Nat King Cole, her eyes closed.

I think of you every morning.
Dream of you every night.
Darling, I'm never lonely
Whenever you are in sight.

That was nice. Part of me wanted to put my arm around her shoulder and sing along with her. I wish I would have.

"Darling, I'm never lonely." That must be nice, too. "Are you ever lonely, little Lucy? Were you lonely today when Mommy was gone to the wedding? I'm sorry. Tomorrow night we'll have a special time, just the two of us. We'll take our bath early and then go to bed and have a nice Papa John's pizza and watch *The Brave One*. I promise, Goosey. If Manuel delivers it, we'll give him a big tip."

Well, hopefully Lucy was comforted by the story I'd told her just before I left this morning. "Little Lucy had a very special friend named Sissy, and whenever Lucy's mommy had to be gone for longer than usual, Sissy would come over and spend time with Lucy. The two would chase each other around the apartment and have just so much fun. Then they'd take a nap on the bed, with the sun coming in through the window and warming their furry bodies. Sissy would love hearing the soothing harp music on Lucy's favorite CD set, *The Most Relaxing Harp Album in the World—Ever!* When it was time for Sissy to go home, Lucy would feel a bit sad, but she'd be happy that she had such a nice friend to keep her from feeling lonely." I hope that got my cat through the day.

Then it was time for the couple's first dance. Marv announced it and started their song, the great "We've Only Just Begun" by The Carpenters. That poor Karen Carpenter, dying young from anorexia. She was skin and bones at the end. Her mother found her dead in their home, in her childhood bedroom. *That* was a sad deal. What an amazing voice, though—so warm and soothing. Maybe life was hard for that girl, maybe it was tortuous. But, sweet Jesus, her voice! It lives on.

A crowd gathered around three sides of the dance floor to watch Mindy and Richard. Katie and her husband, Scott, had their arms around each other and were swaying to the music. Julie was standing near them, staring into the distance on the other side of the dance floor, clutching her phone in her hand. Poor Julie. I believe Mindy said she has a boyfriend, so where the hell was he? I'd noticed that, during the dinner, Julie had eaten only about a third of her Poached Lake Superior White Fish, and a few bites of her smoked pearl onions, but had entirely avoided the spinach spaetzle. I can't fault her for that. Spinach. Yuck!

I thought, just then, that later I'd try to get Julie to eat a few Gigi's cupcakes. She seems to be okay with desserts, at least sometimes.

A half-dozen kids were seated or kneeling along the front edge of the dance floor, watching Mindy and Richard. Some of their mouths were hanging open. They were cute. I don't know if it was the dancing or the strobe lights that most fascinated them. I briefly imagined that Corinna was one of them, watching Aunt Mindy and Uncle Richard as she sat there quietly, her chin in her hands, wearing her pretty white flower girl dress, her brown hair in twin ponytails. I'd look over at her proudly. My sweet little girl. Maybe Grandma Lillian would hold her up to see the dancing better.

When the DJ said it was time for the father-daughter dance, I drifted over to the bar to get another vodka and tonic. I didn't want to watch. I loved the song Mindy'd chosen—those great lyrics:

Someday, when I'm awfully low
When the world is cold,
I will feel a glow just thinking of you
And the way you look tonight.

But I didn't like that she'd chosen it for that dance—not for *that* dance. I got back when the song was about half over and stood with the other bridesmaids. I looked up briefly to watch Mindy and Dad dancing, and then quickly lowered my eyes. I looked over at Mom standing quietly by herself a few feet away.

I turned to Diana, standing beside me, and, on impulse, asked her what the tattoo on her right arm meant. She looked up at me and giggled. "It's Chinese," she whispered. "It means 'moo shu pork.' I thought of it once when Adam took me to Imperial Garden for my birthday. It's my favorite on their menu, and you get these nice little mandarin pancakes with it. He'd been pestering me to get another tattoo, something symbolizing our great love, yadda yadda, so I did this and told him it meant 'forever.' He was very moved." She giggled again and kissed her fingertips and touched her three middle fingers to her Chinese tattoo. I remembered what she'd said previously about that guy, and asked what he wanted her to do besides wearing short skirts. She gave me a look. "He wanted me to get nipple piercings," she whispered. "He said that excited him. I told him no, and he pouted. He said that if I loved him, I'd do it. That was on New Year's Eve. We had a big fight about it. Adios, Mister Adam."

I was about to ask her if she had any other tats, including any on her butt, but just then the dance ended and everyone applauded. I looked up and saw my father hugging Mindy and kissing her cheek. I took a big swallow of my Fleischmann's and tonic.

"If I ever get married and have a wedding, Lucy, I'm going to see if it's okay to do a mother-daughter dance instead of the usual. I'd like that. What do you think?" She looks at me sweetly from her gray towel with those beautiful green eyes, and I take it to mean that she thinks it's an excellent idea.

I'd choose a slow, nice Sinatra song, but different from the one Mindy chose. That's for sure. Maybe "Someone to Watch Over Me."

Mindy'd decided to have a separate dance just for the bridal party, rather than the option of the groomsmen and bridesmaids shuffling onto the dance floor toward the end of the couple's dance. She'd selected "Unforgettable" for the bridal party dance. That was fine. Mark, it turned out, was a pretty good dancer—surprisingly good, though it would have been nice if he were a bit taller. I felt comfortable enough with him. He actually asked if I was having a good time at the reception and if I'd liked the dinner. That was sweet. I was surprised. I guess you never know. Still, I couldn't stand to look at his horrible goatee. For a moment, I closed my eyes and fantasized that it was Frank I was dancing with, his warm arms around me and singing that song to me. Just to me. "I'm so happy to be here with you, my sweet Maggie," he'd whisper in my ear, our cheeks touching. "None of these skinny broads can hold a candle to you, I'm telling ya."

I glanced over to watch Diana and Russell dancing. Her nose wasn't quite at the level of his navel, as she'd predicted, but near—somewhere between his belly button and breastbone. At first, his right arm was around her shoulder instead of her waist because her waist was too far down to get to without his bending over. He held her right hand with his left, but it was ridiculous because she had to raise that right arm to the level of the top of her head. Finally, they abandoned all that and he just put both arms on top of her shoulders and she slid both of hers around his waist. Even then, she had to elevate her arms a bit. If she'd kept them parallel to the ground, she would have been clutching his bony ass cheeks. That might have been interesting.

After that, it was time for the slide show. The sound track started with "Sunny Day" from *Sesame Street.* That was cute to hear as the big screen flashed image after image of Mindy as a baby and then a toddler and then a cute little blond-haired girl—and Richard's childhood journey likewise. Then came images of them both as older kids, playing and smiling and mugging for the camera, doing soccer and softball, and, of course, at lots of happy little family events—birthdays, picnics, vacations, First Communions, and the like. Mom was so young and pretty then. Even I was cute, at least in some of the pictures.

I remembered Mindy sitting on our living room floor smiling and giggling and waving her little arms as she watched Bert and Ernie and the

Count and Cookie Monster and, of course, that magnificent sweet-faced Maria. Well, I thought Maria was magnificent. I don't know if Mindy did.

In the slideshow, by the time Mindy and Richard looked to be middle-schoolers, the music changed, as I'd feared, to that horrible medley of "Somewhere Over the Rainbow/What a Wonderful World" by Israel Something-or-Other—"Bruddah Iz," as he was known, that morbidly obese and now-deceased Hawaiian guy. Everyone seems to like that montage, but not me. Not to speak ill of the dead, but there's something incredibly annoying about Iz's hyper-sincere voice. I don't so much mind the "Over the Rainbow" part, but that other, the "Wonderful World" part, is *majorly* irritating. All that crap about seeing skies of blue and trees of green and "the colors of the rainbow, so pretty in the sky" and friends shaking hands who're really saying "I love you." Argh!

And then, of course, there were dozens of pictures of Mindy and Richard together, happy little couple that they were and are. At least there were no photos of them porking in a tub.

When the slide show ended, I thought to myself that it would be a good time to take a little nap. I sat down and closed my eyes. I must have slept for just a moment, and in that short moment I had a mini-dream about cupcakes—mounds and mounds of them. Thankfully, Mindy'd let me deal with the cupcake table details, and I'd ordered 115 regulars and 220 of the minis. I'd carefully selected the flavors and made sure they included my favorites: Kentucky Bourbon Pie, Orange Dreamsicle, Lemon Dream Supreme, Triple Chocolate Torte, Chocolate Salted Caramel, and Merry Margarita. Yum! I'd told them to just throw in an assortment of the minis. *Soon!* I thought to myself when I opened my eyes. *They'll be setting up the cupcake table soon.*

Larry came over and sat next to me. "Hey," he said, "how's it going?" I was glad to see him. I asked if he was having a good time, and he thought for a moment and then nodded. He said he enjoyed talking to the big bald guy with the walrus mustache at his table. "He's a professor at UW, European history. He knows your dad." Then he excused himself to go to the men's room.

I glanced over to the dance floor. Marv had started playing music, and it was, at first, mostly kids and a few mothers out there, plus Katie and two of the fluffheads, Lauren and Sammi. One little dark-haired boy, maybe five years old, was zooming from one corner of the floor to another and now and again stopping to do a slide across the wooden floor. At one point, he flipped onto his back and pulled his knees to his chest and did a cute spin—a miniature Mark. Two little girls in pretty dresses and one of their moms were holding hands and dancing in a tight little circle. When the DJ played "Let's Twist Again," that trio and another mom got into it. Lauren and Sammi and Katie did too. It was cute to watch them facing each other, twisting the night away. Katie grasped the sides of her dress and swished them as she moved her little body.

Watching the little girls and their moms, I again imagined Corinna was there. I fantasized that she and I were out there dancing to Chubby Checker:

C'mon, let's twist again, like we did last summer.
Yeaaah, let's twist again, like we did last year.
Do you remember when
Things were really hummin'? ...

Corinna would giggle while pistoning her little arms and swiveling her hips, and her ponytails would sway. I'd grasp the sides of my Bill Levkoff bridesmaid dress, like Katie, and shimmy them backward and forward. Corinna'd giggle again to see me dance. Maybe at one point we'd face each other and hold hands while twisting. When Chubby sang, "Who's that, flyin' up there? Is it a bird?" we'd both raise our arms and yell, "*No-o-o-o!*" When he sang, "Is it a plane?" we'd yell, "*No-o-o-o!*" And when he went, "Is it the twister?" we'd yell, "*YEA-A-A-A-H-H!*" Lauren and Sammi would look over toward us and grin. Perhaps Mom, and maybe even Mindy, would join us. It would be nice.

When Marv played "The Hokey Pokey," at least two dozen kids and adults hurried to the dance floor and formed a big circle. Mindy dashed out, and Katie and Julie immediately joined her and flanked her. Diana joined them. I reluctantly did as well, not so much because I wanted to do the Hokey Pokey but because I didn't want to be the weird, antisocial bridesmaid. Larry joined in, too. Marv got out on the floor, in the middle of the circle, and competently led us in doing all the moves. All of us mouthed the words as we followed Marv and the song cues—putting our right hands in and then putting them out, then in again, and shaking them all about, turning ourselves around, putting our left hands and then right feet and left feet and heads in and out, and again turning ourselves around. When, on cue, I stuck my big backside in and then out and vigorously shook it all about, Diana laughed hugely yet again and, again, I feared she'd wet her pants.

Corinna would like doing "The Hokey Pokey" too. It'd be cute, watching her doing the moves on cue alongside the other children. Maybe we'd sing together: "You put your whole self in, you put your whole self out ..."

The dance floor grew crowded. Marv played a few songs that Mindy'd selected in advance: "Don't Stop Believin'" and "Just Dance" by Lady Gaga, and Bruno Mars doing "Just the Way You Are." Mindy and Richard danced one or two, and then she and Katie and Julie and some of the bachelorette party girls did others together.

I noticed that Mindy's dress had been bustled, the train folded up under the back of the dress. I don't know when that happened. Most likely, Toni'd helped with the bustling, maybe with Katie's and Julie's help. No one had asked me to assist. "Some maid of honor, huh, Goose?"

When Marv played "Sweet Caroline," Larry came over and pulled me out onto the floor. He was a decent dancer, and was enthusiastic when we all raised our arms and yelled "So good! So good!" on cue. It felt good to be out there dancing, just like I'd felt at Plan B. It felt good to move my big body to the loud music. And the good thing was that my boobs didn't fall out of my dress as I danced, as I'd feared. The two-sided tape I'd bought at Vera's worked. They sloshed around a fair amount, but didn't embarrass me by venturing forth from their safe zone.

And it felt okay when the DJ did a slow song, Elvis's "Can't Help Falling in Love," and Larry held my hand and led me to a corner of the floor. It wasn't an obligatory dance, like the one I'd done with Mark earlier, but it was nice. It felt nice to dance with a tall guy. We didn't talk at all, which was fine. That gave me another chance to fantasize about being with Frank, dancing with him and being held in his warm arms. He'd sing along softly, his lips close to my ear: "Like a river flows surely to the sea, darling, so it goes. Some things *are* meant to be." Oh, yes, Frank. Some things are.

But that spell was short-lived because, about halfway through the song, I looked to my left and saw my parents dancing together. It shouldn't have been startling, but it was—a little bit, anyway—because I couldn't recall the last time I'd seen them dance together. They weren't talking, or even looking at each other. While I was gazing in their direction, Mom looked up and our eyes met. She smiled a little. I smiled back. Dad didn't notice. He was probably fantasizing that he was dancing with some frizzy-haired, tight-assed little graduate student, or maybe with some attractive, young, sweet-smelling American history assistant professor from Baylor or Temple whom he'd met at a conference and had drinks with and was hoping to do nasties with. Maybe they'd whisper breathlessly about Antietam or Shiloh or the surrender at Appomattox while ripping off each other's clothes. "Oh, Warren," she'd pant. "Ravish me like Sherman marching through Georgia. Oh, *please!*" I looked away.

When the DJ announced that it was time for the bouquet toss, I decided to go hide out in the ladies' room. I was heading that way when I noticed the chick in the cranberry-colored dress who'd flirted with my Larry. Well, not *my* Larry—just Larry. She grinned and clapped her hands and almost forcefully positioned herself in the very middle of the crowd of twenty or thirty single women hoping to catch the bouquet so that they'd be next to stroll down the aisle. I marched over to stand beside her. My idea was that if Mindy threw the bouquet her way, I'd elbow the slut out of the way as forcefully as necessary to keep her from catching it. That'd teach her. If necessary, I'd even accidentally—*hah!*—slip a finger under her single shoulder strap and pull it down. The top of her dress would slip to her waist and she'd gasp and her face would turn red and she'd hunch over and protectively cross her arms over her breasts, further minimizing any chances of her catching the bouquet.

But that ended up not being necessary because Mindy, her back turned to the crowd, tossed the bouquet over her head to the left side of the group, and Lauren leaped in the air and caught it. She jumped up and down with glee. Kiersten and Sammi came over and hugged her. Miss Single Shoulder Strap looked disappointed. Her lips were pursed, her brow was furrowed, and she just stood there for a moment and looked at the floor. "Better luck next time, bitch," I murmured under my breath.

The cupcake table, when finally set up and ready to go, was magnificent—a thing of beauty. There were five tiers of cupcakes, crammed with regulars and minis of the lovely flavors of cupcakes. Standing beside it with Larry, I just stared. *It's almost a sin*, I thought, *to disturb it*. But that thought passed and I was, happily, the first to indulge. I got a Kentucky Bourbon Pie and Larry took, I believe, a Chocolate Salted Caramel. I closed my eyes while chewing slowly. Oh, sweet Jesus! That bourbon cake with pecans and chocolate chips, and that wonderful cream cheese frosting. The caramel and ganache! Oh, yes.

"Here's to Sister Agnella," I said, raising my cupcake. Larry smiled and nodded in agreement, raising his own arm with the Chocolate Salted Caramel grasped firmly in his large hand.

Larry was a neat eater. He actually held a paper napkin in his left hand to catch any crumbs from the cupcake he was holding in his right hand. He looked handsome tonight. He told me that two nights ago, Chester'd finally got fed up with Festus ambushing him and had chased his brother and "backed him into a corner and worked him over pretty good." I asked him how Miss Kitty had reacted. He shook his head and pursed his lips. "Slept right through it," he said. "Couldn't care less."

After I'd scarfed down my cupcake, I wanted another but didn't want Larry to think I was a pig. I briefly considered my options. I looked up at Larry as he was finishing the last bite of his cupcake, and smiled sweetly. I reached over to grab a Lemon Dream Supreme from the table and broke off a piece and reached up to feed it to him. He opened his mouth wide and accepted it, like a baby bird being fed by his mother. I smiled up coyly at him as he chewed, my head tilted just a bit to one side and eyes opened wide. I considered opening my own mouth as a signal for him to feed me a piece of his cupcake, but thought better of it.

"Too obvious, right, Goose?"

Larry soon got into a conversation with some sawed-off yo-yo with a pathetic mullet who recognized him from his West High basketball glory days and rudely interrupted us. I got another vodka and tonic and another cupcake—Triple Chocolate Torte—and sat down next to my mother at a round table not far from the dance floor. She was sitting quietly alone, sipping from a glass of merlot. God knows where her husband was. Before eating my cupcake, I unwrapped a butterscotch candy and was about to pop it into my mouth when I noticed Mom looking at it longingly. I handed it to her, and she smiled. "Yum!" she said. I unwrapped another and we both sucked on our candies in silence.

I looked over to the crowded dance floor. Diana and Julie and Sammi were dancing happily together to "Love Shack." Katie and Scott were dancing too. Hopefully, his mother had eased up on her controlling behavior. At the far end of the floor, I saw the back of the head of a short woman with bright-red hair. For a moment I thought it was Kat Grammy, and felt happy but surprised that she was at the reception. But the woman turned around, and it wasn't she. I was disappointed, but it made me think how nice it would be if Kat Grammy were there and sitting at the round table with Mom and me. And not just her but others, too—Sheila, Louise, maybe Annie and Giselle, even Jackson Galaxy. Larry and Diana would certainly come over and sit with us. Maybe Larry's point guard friend, Jordan, with those eyes, would be there. That'd be fine. I wouldn't be upset if Alex was there. I think maybe I'd like that. It would be nice to see him. It would. But, then again, would I want to see him while I'm with Larry?

We'd all drink alcohol and scarf down cupcakes, regulars and minis, and wedding cake if any was still left. Maybe there could be a huge bowl of those wonderful hard, twisty pretzels from Claddagh. We'd talk and laugh. We'd tell cat stories. Kat Grammy would tell anecdotes about the cats she tended, and I'd do the same. I'd talk about Groucho and Bupkis, and how proud Groucho is of his jumping ability. I'd tell about Princess and the shrimp. Louise could talk about Clarence and Murphy, and how upset Murph gets when Clarence ventures outside. I'd happily stare at Louise's face—that sweet, *sweet* face. Jackson, with his bald head and green-framed glasses and weird whiskers and heavily tattooed arms, could talk about the psychology of cats and how they need to use up their predatory energy. He could tell about his successes in helping people with difficult cats on *My Cat from Hell*. If he brought his guitar case, he could show us some of the cat toys he favors. Annie and Giselle would tell how they got Meepers. Maybe they'd bring out a stash and we'd all light up. Diana would, I'm sure, gladly indulge and she'd laugh at everyone's stories. Hopefully, she wouldn't laugh so hard that she'd wet her pants. She'd love Kat Grammy, no doubt about that. I'd introduce my mom to everyone, and they'd all say how nice it is to meet her. "Very nice to meet you folks, too," Mom would say softly. "I'm glad my Maggie has such friends." She'd sit quietly and listen to all the stories, enjoying herself.

"Anyway, don't worry, Goosey. I'd definitely say wonderful things about you, too. I'll tell how you like to take your nightly nap right there on the toilet seat lid and how you like to watch me shave my legs and what a very conscientious groomer you are." Kat Grammy and Jackson Galaxy would get a kick out of that.

And I even thought that it would be nice if that poor old man whose wife died of bone cancer had been invited to the wedding and reception and was sitting with us. It would be good for him to get out, to be with people. He wouldn't have to say anything. I'd bring him a nice cup of coffee and a piece of wedding cake or a cupcake. "Do you take anything in your coffee?" I'd ask. If he was hard of hearing, I'd maybe have to ask more loudly. "SIR, DO YOU WANT ANYTHING IN YOUR COFFEE? …No, not *toffee*, COFFEE …CREAM AND TWO SUGARS? Sure." Maybe I'd even raise my Fleischmann's and tonic and toast the memory of his wife, the almost sixty years they'd had together. But maybe that would be too hard for him. I don't know.

Well, I thought, *it would be great, too, if some or all of the Legion of Overweight Cat Avengers were there at our table.* Oh, that would be so awesome. After the cat stories, maybe one of them would tell about some numbnuts who had five cats and fed them only when he felt like it and neglected to give them water and kicked them whenever he'd had a snootful. "What should we do with him?" one of the Avengers would ask. "Let's do a waterboard deal on him," another would suggest. "Let's wrap his head in a burlap sack and slowly pour water on his face until he repents and agrees to change his ways. And, of course, we'll liberate the five cats." We'd all nod. "Water, *hell!*" another would insist. "Let's use vinegar." Diana would giggle and Larry would probably stare wide-eyed at the group of hefty women. "What kind of people *are* these?" he'd whisper in my ear.

Kat Grammy would maybe furrow her brow and take exception. "I admire your concern for abused felines, ladies," she'd say. "But I don't approve of your methods. How about trying to *talk* to the gentleman first? Try to get him to see and appreciate the error of his ways. If that doesn't work, you can always escalate to the next step. Am I right? Manners count for *something*, ladies."

Jackson might add his two cents. "I agree with the Avengers," he might say. "Some people are beyond redemption. Cats aren't, but people are."

Everyone would look toward Mom. "What do you think, Mrs. Mullen?" someone would ask. She'd look thoughtful and would take a delicate sip of her merlot. After a bit, she'd put her arm around my fat shoulder and say, "I support whatever my daughter says is right. I stand by my Maggie." Everyone would nod and the lesbians would clap their hands.

"Well, hell," one of the Avengers would say. "No point arguing. Let's eat." I'd signal one of the hotel staff, and she and three or four of her colleagues would haul platters of assorted sandwiches to our table, plus trays of cheese and sausage and huge bowls of Ruffles potato chips with various dips, including that lovely Bucky Badger Wisconsin French Onion Dip, buttered popcorn, and dishes of mint-chocolate-chip ice cream with sides of both chocolate and butterscotch sauce. There'd be a splendid assortment of miniature candy bars: Snickers, 3 Musketeers, Baby Ruths, Butterfingers, Kit Kats, Milky Ways, Almond Joys, and more. Perhaps there'd be some Little Debbie Mini Frosted Donuts. There'd be Dove dark chocolates and, certainly, Oreos. Maybe there'd be dried banana chips and an assortment of Girl Scout cookies, minimally including Thin Mints and Lemonades. We'd all happily indulge, and everyone would be joyous on the occasion of Mindy Mullen's wedding reception. "Here's to my pretty, thin sister!" I'd say, raising my glass high. "And here's to all my dear friends, not all of whom are similarly pretty and thin! And so the *hell* what?"

But it was just Mom and me at the table. I asked how her painting was going. She said she was doing a pond with three frogs and cattails in the background. She said she was having difficulty getting just the right shade of brown for the cattails. I told her that I hoped to start doing watercolors soon, and planned to do a sunflower for Diana. She nodded and said that sounded nice. "I like Diana," she said. "She's cute."

I glanced over to the dance floor, where Mindy and all of her other bridesmaids and most of the fluffheads were enthusiastically moving their lithe bodies to "We Are Family" by Sister Sledge and mouthing the words: "We are family! …I've got all my sisters and me …" Toni was there too. I'd noticed that she'd helped the hotel staff load up the gifts a little while ago, to haul them up to one of the hotel rooms or maybe out to a car. There'd been a ton of those presents, all beautifully wrapped and piled on a long table in one corner of the ballroom. I had the brief thought that I should, in my maid of honor capacity, have helped Toni in her efforts. Even though she'd agreed to be Mindy's personal attendant, she shouldn't have to do *everything*. I should have pitched in. But I shrugged and quickly dismissed the thought and took a big swallow of my vodka and tonic.

Later, I'll have to endure the present-opening at our parents' house. "Oh, gee," I'll maybe get to say. "A bagel slicer! Now who had the great idea to give you *that*?"

At one point, Julie walked by our table on her way to the restroom, holding her phone in her left hand. I jumped up and led her by the right hand to the cupcake table. "Have you had any of these yet?" I asked. She shook her head. "How about this?" I asked, selecting and handing her an Orange Dreamsicle cupcake. She took a small bite and chewed slowly. After she'd swallowed, she looked at my face and nodded just a bit. She ate two more little bites and was going to put the rest in the trash, but I told her it would be a sin to waste it and that my sister and I would be very disappointed in her.

"Oh, okay," she sighed and finished it off. I hugged her and patted her hard, thin back and returned to Mom.

While Julie and I were talking, I noticed Dad sitting at a far table with his bald mustachioed colleague, the European history dude. *Maybe*, I thought, *Dad can introduce that guy, if he's single, to Aunt Grace*. Dad could do a little matchmaking. If they then became a couple, I'd say a little prayer for the guy's soul. Maybe I'd get Father Connor to put in a good word for him as well. He'll need all the help he can get, poor man.

When Marv blasted "I Will Survive," Diana dashed over to our table and grabbed my wrist with her right hand and pulled me up from my chair. She took Mom's hand in her left, more gently, and pulled her up as well. She led us to the dance floor, where by now Julie and Katie and some of the fluffheads had encircled dancing Mindy, and a few were holding hands. Mom and I joined the circle. Soon, we were all singing along with Gloria Gaynor. Kiersten, it turned out, knew all the lyrics and everyone eyeballed her and followed her lead, including her gestures. She put on a serious mock-scowl, eyes blazing and brow furrowed, and extended her right arm and shook her index finger menacingly at some imaginary lover who'd done her wrong, as she sang:

Go on now. Walk out the door. Just turn around now,
'Cause you're not welcome anymore.
Weren't you the one who tried to hurt me with goodbye?
Did you think I'd crumble? Did you think I'd lay down and die?

Kiersten did a dramatic backward thumb thrust and jerked her head sideways in the direction of that thrust at "Walk out the door." I liked that. Then we all, including Mom, wagged our fingers and nodded our heads and sang along:

Oh, no, not I. I will survive.
Oh, as long as I know how to love, I know I'll stay alive.
I've got all my life to live, I've got all my love to give,
And I'll survive. I will survive ...

Damn, I'm exhausted. I don't know when I've been this tired, physically and emotionally. The reception was better than I'd anticipated, at least in some ways, but still. I feel like I could fall asleep here in the tub. I've had a lot to drink tonight. I'd probably better not smoke any weed, what with all the alcohol. But at the same time, I'm a little juiced. I'd like to stop thinking about this day, and just let my mind go mellow and enjoy being here in my steamy bathroom with my sweet cat.

I don't know if Mindy's upset with me because I chose to come home instead of staying at the Concourse, like the rest of the bridal party. I'd told her that I didn't want to stay overnight. At least I was honest about that, and didn't lie to Mindy again.

Right now, though, I don't care how she feels. I'm just so happy this wedding thing is behind me—*at last!* I'll have to think how to reward us—me for all I've gone through, and Lucy for my being gone lately more than I should have and leaving her alone. But at least we're here now, just we two, listening to Sinatra's sweet voice. He's doing one of our all-time favorites, and listening to it for the second time tonight is...well, bittersweet.

Yes, you're lovely, with your smile so warm,
And your cheeks so soft.
There is nothing for me but to love you,
Just the way you look tonight.

I remembered the father-daughter dance from earlier tonight, and Dad and Mindy clutched together, swaying to that song. I recalled how irritated I'd felt. Mindy's eyes had been closed and she'd looked so content as Dad led her competently around the dance floor. Darcy'd kept circling around them like a little vulture, snapping pictures. She took several close-ups of Mindy's face, the bride's eyes closed some of the time and a darling little daddy's-girl smile on her pretty face. Of all the songs in all the wedding receptions in all the world, my sister had to choose *that* one for that dance! I wish she would have consulted me first. It just pisses me off.

Oh, well. "It's behind us now, right Goosey? Nothing but blue skies ahead, right?" Lucy looks up at me from her folded towel, her left eye half-closed. She looks directly at me with her right eye and holds her stare. "Sure, Mommy," she seems to be saying. "It's all good."

One for My Baby (And One More for the Road)

BELLA DIED this morning. Mr. Randall called me on my cell while I was at Claire's house, taking care of Bosco. He was returning my call. Last night, for some reason, I thought of Bella. I hadn't thought about her much for the last week or so since the wedding. Then, when I was making macaroni and cheese last night, for some reason she came into my mind. I called Mr. R. and left a message asking how she was. He got back to me just before noon. He said she'd been failing—had stopped eating and wasn't drinking much, didn't move around a lot—and looked bad. He called his vet early this morning and brought Bella in, and the vet said it was time. They put her down. He was sniffling a bit when he told me. Maybe he isn't as horrible as I'd thought.

Poor little Bella. My baby. I hope she wasn't suffering too much. She couldn't have felt well. At least she had a peaceful death and wasn't alone. But I'm ashamed of myself. I'd thought about her a bit at the wedding, but not since. I should have. I should have stayed in touch with Mr. R. all along. But no. I'm too damned self-centered, I guess.

"Well, Lucy-Goosey, I guess our idea to have Bella be with us for her last days didn't work out. Are you sad about it?" She raises herself from her toilet seat and looks directly into my eyes. I washed her turquoise towel last Monday and replaced the gray one with it. I think she likes the turquoise towel best of all. Her brown fur always looks good against that color, and she knows it.

I told Bosco about Bella, just after I'd fed him. I believe he was sad to hear the news, even though he didn't know Bella—sympathy for one of his one.

Bosco's a good guy. I like him. He's an orange-and-white longhair with an unusually fluffy tail. He loves to play with a shoelace and my mouse-on-a-wire and also with the laser pointer. I think he's frustrated that he can't catch that elusive red dot. He's a major cuddlebug, too. He loves to curl up on my lap when I sit on Claire's tan sofa after I've done my chores. We like to watch TV together.

Today we watched an episode of *A Baby Story*. The show was about a young couple, Tim and Megan, from—of course—New Jersey. They have a nine-month-old girl, Bridget. The parents are both heavy. Megan got pregnant again within a month after Bridget was born and they're overjoyed about it, bubbling that their kids will be "Irish twins." Their little red-haired boy, Peter, is born on Bridget's ten-month birthday via C-section, as was the first brat. Well, I shouldn't say that.

Tim and Megan smile non-stop and are thrilled. Their hopes for their children are that they'll be happy, grow up to enjoy and appreciate family life, and pursue their dreams and ambitions. Both sets of grandparents are similarly joyful. It's a huge extended family, and Bridget and Peter have twelve or fifteen smiling little cousins who, with their parents, come to Tim and Megan's house for a big celebration. There's a boatload of food, including huge platters of chicken and four big bowls of potato salad. The kids play happily on slides and swings in the backyard. Many of the cousins, mostly the girls, hold and cuddle Peter. Megan's Irish mom, Nancy, looking out contentedly at her tribe of grandchildren at the end of the episode, says, "If not for family, what else is there?"

That's the question, huh?

Claire doesn't have kids. She was married for eight years and then stayed in the house after the divorce two years ago. It's a nice little place, with older and fairly simple furniture. She doesn't have a dishwasher. Only one side of the toaster works. She has an old-fashioned Formica-topped kitchen table with four metal chairs with yellow-orange vinyl-covered seats. The hardwood floors are a bit worn and scuffed, and covered with throw rugs that are noticeably frayed at the edges. Those rugs have seen better days.

The bookcase in her living room is filled with some hardcovers and many paperbacks, almost all fiction. Some books are flush to the edges of the shelves, but others are pushed in. Some are piled up behind the front rows. It's quite cluttered. There's a lot by authors such as Fitzgerald, Hemingway, Sinclair Lewis, Bellow, Updike, and Philip Roth and a few by Doris Lessing. I've never read her, but I like the name *Doris* for a cat. I'd definitely name a cat that. One of her five Roth paperbacks is *The Human Stain*. I recall that the Morrisons had that on their coffee table. Most of her books have clearly been read. The spines of the paperbacks are creased, and she's bent over the corners of many pages, maybe as bookmarks. I opened a few books and saw that Claire had written notes—in green ink, in small and very neat handwriting—in many of the margins. On the last page of Updike's *Rabbit at Rest*, she'd written, "Yes, dear Harry. Enough is enough." I wonder what's that all about?

In her bedroom, she has a pink Princess phone on her nightstand and I noticed that the coiled cord has dozens of little bite marks on it. I wondered about that, too. And then today when I plopped down on the bed and tried to get Bosco to lie on my chest and nap with me, I had my answer. He didn't want to lie on my chest, but he did spread his little body next to mine and closed his eyes for a few minutes. Then he opened them and saw the phone cord and immediately jumped up and began chewing away on it for a while. I don't know what pleasure or gain he gets out of it, but it must be something.

Claire has three framed photos hanging on the wall of her living room opposite the bookcase. Two are of her and her ex in happier times. In one, they're both wearing blue bathing suits and standing together on the dock of a lake somewhere, his arm around her shoulder and hers around his waist, both grinning and showing bright white teeth. She has a nice little body, I'll say that. Good thighs. He's not bad, either, with washboard abs, though his legs are unusually skinny. In another picture, they're dancing together at a wedding. The bride's dancing in the background, her arms raised, still wearing her veil. Claire looks nice, in a pretty yellow dress. The third photo is a black-and-white close-up just of her, looking directly into the camera but not smiling. She looks very serious, maybe even annoyed. The background is blurred, so you're not sure just what it is. I like that picture.

Claire intrigues me a bit. I don't know her very well—she's not much of a talker—but I'm curious. I'd love to snoop and read her journal or whatever. I'd like to go through her drawers, her files. I probably won't, but I'd like to. I'd like to know what goes on inside that quiet woman's head.

Her ex-husband, in that photo in her living room, looks a little like Larry—tall, little mustache and beard, nice smile. "I haven't seen Larry since Mindy's wedding, Lucy. But it was nice to see him then." I'll be going to his condo to take care of his cats at the beginning of October when he goes to visit his grandmother in St. Louis for a few days. I don't know if I'll actually see him. I hope so, but I doubt it. But I miss him. We had fun together at the wedding. It was good to dance with him and to eat cupcakes together. I can't say that I felt any cymbals clashing, but I like Larry. I'm glad that Sheila spoke up at Mickie's and got him to be my date at the wedding. That worked out okay. I just hope he's not seeing that slut in the cranberry-colored dress. But I don't know if Larry's a boyfriend prospect. Maybe someday, if I'm inclined to have a boyfriend, but I'm not panting about it either way. I have no idea how he feels about me—no indication one way or another, on his part.

I'm going to get one of those furry toilet lid covers, like Larry has in his condo. I've been thinking about that for a while. They probably sell those covers at Target or Walmart. Hopefully, they have them in turquoise. "Would you like that, Goose? I think you'd be very comfortable."

Sheila and I should go to Mickie's soon. Maybe Diana could go with us. And Louise too. We'd sit at one of the tables or booths rather than at the counter, so we could see other and talk. That would be nice, the four of us. Sheila'd like Diana and Louise. Sheila could point out the old '50s menu, and she'd tell about the virtues of the various malts and shakes. I'd put in a good word for the butterscotch. Maybe we'd all share a big order of yank fries with gravy. Louise could tell about her trip to Jamaica with Ian. "Who's Ian?" Diana would ask. Louise would smile mysteriously and glance at me. "Oh, just some guy I'm seeing. We sort of live together, as long as he doesn't bore or annoy me too much."

Well, I don't know. Lunch with that trio, now that I think about it, might not be a good idea. Sheila and Diana aren't dense. I have to think that they'd pick up on my vibes. Maybe Sheila would call me later. "Hey, Maggie," she'd say, "what's up with you and Miss Louise? Are you, uh, thinking of crossing that bridge?"

I was hoping I'd see Louise yesterday. Kat Grammy and I finally got together for lunch at Dotty Dumpling's Dowry, which, she said, was her favorite place to eat after Hubbard Avenue Diner. But Louise wasn't working. I was disappointed. I'd really wanted to see her. I'd hoped to hear that lovely low, husky voice again. Oh, well. Kat Grammy's hair was even brighter red than the last time I'd seen her, and she was wearing a purple top and tight green pants and red tennis shoes with yellow laces. We both ordered cheeseburgers and fries. When we got our orders, she scarfed down half of her fries before she took a bite of her cheeseburger, dipping each into mayonnaise. She also spread mayo on her burger.

I asked Grammy if she'd ever seen Jackson Galaxy's show. She shook her head. "I don't watch much TV, honey" she said. "Most of it bores the hell out of me. Now and again I watch old movies on TCM—Bette Davis, Lauren Bacall, Ingrid Bergman. Bogie. I love those. I've seen *Casablanca* and *The Maltese Falcon* probably thirty times. Plus, I go to take care of my cats a lot in the evenings." But she said she'd check out *My Cat from Hell* some time.

She told me that she sometimes spends nights at clients' homes so that the cats will have company. I should have done that with Bella. I wish I'd done that. I hate to be away from Lucy in the evenings, but I would have done that now and again for sweet Bella.

Grammy—her name is Catherine, but she's prefers just *Grammy*—said that she talks a lot to her cats, practically non-stop. "Hi, kiddos," she says when she comes. "Grammy's here." She asks each of them how their day is going. She praises them and tells them not just how beautiful they are but also how talented and nice. She reads to her cats a lot, excerpts from *Cat Fancier* and *Modern Cat* and other magazines, or whatever else she happens to be reading at the time. She said she mostly reads mysteries and crime stuff. Dashiell Hammett and Raymond Chandler are her favorites. She likes the Harry Potter books. She thinks that her cats like the word "Dumbledore." She's even read to her cats from the Little House books now and again. How lovely! Most of the cats, she claimed, listen and like being read to.

If their behavior is unacceptable, she tells her cats that she's disappointed and expects better and sets forth specific expectations for improved behavior. But she's generous with praise as well. She thinks that cats can understand more than a hundred words.

She's seventy-two years old. I asked her how long she thinks she'll keep tending cats. "As long as I can, dear. As long as this old body and mind hold out. I hope for a lot more years, but who the hell knows? I'll take what I can get. But retire? Never. What would I do?" She paused and ate five more fries, slathering each with mayo. "Besides," she went on, "my cats need me."

Grammy said she'd been married once, not long after high school, and it lasted nine years. She's been alone since and has always lived by herself, along with her own cats over the years—all rescues. "It's good," she said. "I'm fine with my own company. I like what I do. I don't want to ever have to worry about pleasing anyone else. The hell with that, huh?"

She was an elementary school teacher before she became a cat tender. She said that many of her clients over the years have become her friends. She spends a lot of time talking with them when she goes to their homes. "Maybe some think I'm strange," she said. "Well, hell, Maggie, I probably am, compared to most. So ask me if I care."

When we were done eating, Grammy asked me about myself. I was surprised. I don't know why. It seemed natural, but I was still surprised. It felt easy to talk to her. I told her that I hoped to paint watercolors of flowers, though I didn't tell her that my flowers would maybe look like vaginas.

"I told Grammy all about you, Goosey. I told her about our bathtime routine. I told her how we like to watch our movies in bed. I told her how much you like "The Candy Man" and "The Unicorn Song" and your harp CDs. She nodded and was interested."

I even got some cat tending ideas from Grammy. She does daily logs on each of her cats: what they did, if they ate well, any problems or concerns—even anything she noticed in their litter boxes, such as dime-sized clumps that could indicate urinary problems. She leaves the logs for her clients. She brings cat brushes with her, and spends a lot of time brushing her cats with a slicker brush to get the hair off their undercoats. I need to do that more. She even has softer brushes for kittens and older cats. She has her clients leave some of their clothes around so that the cats can see and smell them. And every year she sends a personalized Valentine to each of her cats.

I think I'm going to do the logs and the Valentines, too. "What do you think, Lucy? Should we also send Christmas cards? That's a thought, huh?"

I think I even gave her some ideas. Like me, she tries to leave a radio on for her cats when she's not there, but she didn't know that cats are especially partial to harp music. She said she might try that with her own cats, Helen and Miriam. She also liked my idea of needing to know where fuse boxes or circuit breakers are in each house. "Damned good idea," she said. "You never know when things might go to hell."

I wanted to ask Catherine if she was afraid of dying alone. Maybe I will sometime. I wonder what she'd say.

It'd be nice to have photos of Kat Grammy and Jackson Galaxy in my bedroom. I'd like to be able to look at them when I'm feeling low or if I'm in a crappy mood or PMSing.

Now that the wedding nonsense is over, I don't know when I'll see Diana again. I hope I don't have to wait for some lame family event, Thanksgiving or whatever. Well, maybe we'll have lunch. Or maybe she and I will go to Johnny's for a drink or even dinner on December 12th. We'll see that eccentric old lady who's there for dinner with her well-dressed son and goes around to every table to remind them that it's the birthday of Ol' Blue Eyes. That would be good. Maybe I could ask the old lady what her favorite Sinatra songs are.

It'll be good to see Diana again, whenever that happens. I need to think of some things to say to get her to laugh. I still want to know what she thinks of Mark. I'll have to remember to ask her if she has a tat on her butt. If she has one, maybe I'll get one too. She and I could have twin tattoos on our behinds.

If Diana ever has a kid and I have Corinna, we could have fun once they stopped being babies. We'd take them to Vilas Park Zoo and let them ride on the carousel. Maybe we'd go the Children's Museum on the Square and take them through that old log cabin and let them play in the Funkyard. We could take them to the Easter egg hunt at Wingra Park. In the summer, we'd go to the Union and have ice cream on the Terrace and listen to a bluegrass band. I wonder what Corinna's favorite ice cream flavor would be.

Well, I don't know. It's always nice to think of having fun with my cute little girl. My baby. But am I mommy material? I really don't know.

Poor little Bella. My baby. I loved her. I'm going to miss seeing her, miss lying on the couch with her sleeping quietly on my chest, and miss stroking her sweet neck and back. I'm going to miss singing to her. Well, at least her suffering's over. She's crossed that Rainbow Bridge and is healthy and strong again. Maybe she's ascended to the Heaviside Layer and has been reborn into a new life. Next time I see a brown kitten with yellow-green eyes, I'll wonder if it's reborn Bella. If I do see that cat and she needs a home, I'll take her. Lucy will have to be okay with that. "You will be, won't you, Goose?"

Lucy and I love the song that's playing now:

It's quarter to three
There's no one in the place 'cept you and me.
So set 'em up, Joe.
I got a little story I think you oughta know.
We're drinking, my friend,
To the end of a brief episode.
So make it one for my baby
And one more for the road.

Well, maybe I'd be in the place too. It'd be just Frank and Joe and me. I'd be sitting at the far end of the bar, alone, with my vodka and tonic. Maybe after Frank told his little story, Joe would go into the back room to check his liquor supply for the next day. Frank would glance over and grin. I'd smile back. He'd arch his eyebrows and raise his glass in a friendly little greeting, and I'd do the same. After a moment, he'd wave me over. After a modest pause, I'd shrug and lift my big butt off of the stool and go over to sit next to him. We'd clink glasses. "So what brings you here so late?" he'd ask.

I'd tell him that my sister got married and I was the maid of honor and the whole deal was a pain in the ass, though some of it was fun, and I wanted to have a little nightcap before I went home from the reception to my lonely apartment, where it's just me and my cat. "I see," he'd say. "Well, Maggie, I know all about being lonely, I can tell ya that much. In fact, I just came to the end of a brief episode. Would you like to hear about it?" I'd nod and look into those amazing blue eyes as he told me his sad story. "I hope you didn't mind my bending your ear," he'd say when he was done.

"Of course, not," I'd answer. "You can tell me anything, Frank. I hope you know that. I hope you know that I'm *always* here for you."

His eyes would moisten and he'd nod and take one of my hands in both of his and squeeze just a bit. "I know, Maggie," he'd say. "Oh, *believe* me, I know that." We'd clink glasses again and take big gulps. Maybe he'd take two Tootsie Roll Midgees from his jacket pocket and offer me one. I'd graciously accept, and we'd both unwrap our Midgees and chew. We'd be silent then for a moment. After a bit, he'd look into my eyes. "Miss Maggie," he'd murmur quietly, "would it be okay if…if I gave you a hug?" I'd smile sweetly and nod again.

Just then, Joe would return from the back room. …

I raise my glass of chardonnay and look at my sleepy cat on her closed toilet seat lid. "Well, here's one for my baby." I take a swallow and then another. "And one more for the road."

About the Author

The Cat Tender is Martin Drapkin's third work of fiction, following *Now and at the Hour* and *Ten Nobodies (and their somebodies). Poor Tom* is his latest work of fiction. He's also a photographer, specializing in black-and-white street photographs and portraits of mothers and daughters. He still uses film. He and his wife, Erica, live in rural Cross Plains, Wisconsin, with several mildly neurotic rescue dogs.

For more information, please visit www.drapkinbooks.com.